Dear Reader,

This book is especially dear to me—I love to write stories that involve family, especially blended families. As the world about us shifts and evolves, becoming blended itself, I find comfort in those we hold closest. And then, there's the incomparable love of my home state.

Being a Texas girl, this story brings me back to my roots—to my first love, and later to my best. Love moved me across the country to the foothills of the Rockies, and yet lets me keep part of my heart in the Lone Star State.

I hope you'll share this sense of homecoming and adventure—and that the joy of your own special family surrounds you.

Warmest wishes,

P.S. This one's for Jean Baker. You can take the girl out of Texas. But you can't *ever* take Texas out of the girl.

GREATEST TEXAS LOVE STORIES OF ALL TIME

GREATEST
TEXAS LOVE STORIES
OF ALL TIME

HIS-AND-HERS
FAMILY
Bonnie K. Winn

TEXAS TYCOONS

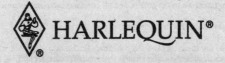

HARLEQUIN®

TORONTO • NEW YORK • LONDON
AMSTERDAM • PARIS • SYDNEY • HAMBURG
STOCKHOLM • ATHENS • TOKYO • MILAN • MADRID
PRAGUE • WARSAW • BUDAPEST • AUCKLAND

HARLEQUIN BOOKS
225 Duncan Mill Road, Don Mills,
Ontario, Canada M3B 3K9

ISBN 0-373-65238-0

HIS-AND-HERS FAMILY

Copyright © 1998 by Bonnie K. Winn

This edition published by arrangement with Harlequin Books S.A.

® and TM are trademarks of the publisher. Trademarks indicated with ® are registered in the United States Patent and Trademark Office, the Canadian Trade Marks Office and in other countries.

Visit us at www.eHarlequin.com

Printed in U.S.A.

BONNIE K. WINN

Being a hopeless romantic and having written incessantly since the third grade, it seemed only natural that Bonnie K. Winn turned to romance writing. A seasoned author of historical and contemporary romance, her bestselling books have won numerous awards. *Affaire de Coeur* chose her as one of the Top Ten Romance Writers in America.

Bonnie loves writing contemporary romance because she can set her stories in the modern cities close to her heart and explore the endlessly fascinating strengths of today's woman.

Living in the foothills of the Rockies gives her plenty of inspiration and a touch of whimsy, as well. She shares her life with her husband, son and a spunky Westie terrier who lends his characteristics to many pets in her stories. Bonnie's keeping mum about anyone else's characteristics she may have borrowed.

Books by Bonnie K. Winn

Harlequin American Romance

The Newlywed Game #624
When a Man Loves a Woman #646
The Daddy Factor #680
His-and-Hers Family #720
The Accidental Mrs. Mackenzie #775
The Mommy Makeover #812

Harlequin Superromance

The Wrong Brother #898
Family Found #964

Steeple Hill Love Inspired

A Family All Her Own #158
Family Ties #186

Silhoutte Intimate Moments

The Hijacked Wife #954

Dedicated to my editors: Bonnie Crisalli,
who shared the inspiration, and Huntley Fitzpatrick,
who completed the vision. I'm grateful to you both
for your unfailing generosity and support.

And to my agent, Jane Jordan Browne,
who guides me through it all.

Every writer should have it so good.

Prologue

Twin Corners, Texas

Blake Matthews slammed the door of his rental car in frustration. Arriving that day in the small Texas oil town to close a business deal, he'd expected no problem finding a hotel room. Despite the concerns of his competent secretary in Los Angeles, he'd brushed aside her offers to make a reservation, preferring to get the lay of the land himself.

He hadn't counted on Rodeo Days. The century-old celebration lasted for weeks and brought in visitors from surrounding areas and tourists from around the country. The limited number of hotels in town were full, and would be for the duration of his stay. And there wasn't one thing his wealth or his influence—or his level of frustration—could do about the situation.

Blake glanced at the paper in his hand, directions to a boardinghouse that a sympathetic desk clerk had offered him. Since he'd now run out of both hotels and choices, Blake realized, it was a question of bunking down in either some quaint throwback boardinghouse or his car. And he didn't relish the thought of cramping his six-foot-two frame into the back seat of a compact.

Resigned, Blake started the car. It didn't take long to find the street or the boardinghouse in the small town. Minuscule town, he corrected himself. Blake critically examined the house as he got out of the car, noting that the white wooden exterior could definitely use a coat of paint.

The old Victorian house, larger than he'd expected, sprawled across a lot shaded by huge oak trees that he guessed were as old as the house. Steps led to a wrap-around porch that ran the length of the house. Decorated with white wicker lounge chairs, an old-fashioned swing and a multitude of flowering plants, the place looked as though it had somehow missed the passing of the past one hundred years.

Sighing, Blake rang the bell. This ought to be some visit, staying in an archaic house that probably lacked not only comfort, but practical modern necessities such as a fax center and modem connections, as well. He wondered whether the owner was as archaic as the house.

The door swung open suddenly. A much younger-looking woman than he'd expected stared at him for a moment before easing her generous mouth into a smile. "Can I help you?"

"I'm looking for Cassandra Hawkins."

"You've found her."

Blake's gaze skipped over her rapidly. Though she was not the gingham-aproned senior citizen he expected, she was certainly countrified in other ways. Dowdy, out-of-style clothing covered by a well-used apron, a fresh-scrubbed face without a shred of makeup, and hair that obviously had not seen a qualified stylist. They all screamed *frumpy*. She was no L.A. socialite, that was certain. Yet he was satisfied that she looked clean and respectable. Glancing beyond her, Blake saw that the house looked equally tidy.

"I understand you rent rooms, Ms. Hawkins."

"Cassie," she corrected him, in what Blake suspected was an automatic gesture. "I do rent rooms, Mr...."

"Matthews."

"As I said, I do rent rooms, however, the house is full right now."

The day's frustrations whipped up Blake's impatience. The steel he used in business negotiations flared in both his eyes and his voice. "Not to me, Ms. Hawkins."

Chapter One

Cassie stared at the stranger on her front stoop while absently wiping soapy hands on her apron. Had she heard him correctly? Although the darkly handsome man exuded both success and arrogance, she doubted he intended to force his way inside. "Excuse me?"

"Ms. Hawkins, I am in Twin Corners to complete a vital business deal. As you probably know, all the hotels are full. I cannot expect to work at my optimum level if I'm forced to sleep in my car."

Her gaze darted out to the rental car parked at the curb, then back to the stranger. Cassie's conscience pricked her, along with the insistent training she'd received from her mother. Southerners, especially Texans, always extended a welcome, whether it was convenient or not. And in a community where neighbor still helped neighbor, the thought of leaving someone to sleep in his car was unthinkable.

Nibbling on her lip, Cassie felt her all-too-often easily swayed firmness start turning to mush. She could make room for him on the sofa, she supposed. She suppressed a sigh, and eased the door open a bit wider. "Come on in. Have a seat in the parlor. I'll get some iced tea, and then we'll figure out what we can come up with."

Blake watched her tall, slim figure disappear as she pushed open a swinging door that led from the dining room into what he guessed was a kitchen. *Parlor?* Did anybody talk like that anymore?

Shaking his head, Blake stared at the furnishings. Although the highly polished wooden floor would be appreciated by contemporary standards, everything else seemed to come from another era.

He moved through the hall and into the room she'd indicated. It was even more unusually decorated. If he wasn't mistaken, the stiff-backed sofa was upholstered in horsehair. He didn't know pieces like these existed outside museums. Ornately carved handles and legs drew his eye, along with the red velvet of the massive chair angled close by. While the rugs were threadbare and the drapes just this side of shabby, the antique grace of the furniture was overwhelming. As were the seemingly genuine Tiffany lamps and the player piano.

He wondered why a young woman would choose to live in a home that was better suited to her great-grandparents. Looking around the unusual room, Blake sensed that telling anyone about the anachronistic boardinghouse would make him sound like the front page of a tabloid: Businessman Abducted By Out-Of-Step Aliens.

She returned with a tray that held large glasses, a pitcher, and an assortment of intriguing-looking cookies. Homemade, if he didn't miss his guess.

After placing the tray on the claw-footed coffee table, she took a seat on the sofa, indicating that he join her. "Lemon or sugar?"

Blake sat down. "Both."

To his amazement, she stirred in the sugar, instead of offering it to him, then added lemon. It reminded him of the old-fashioned teas his grandmother had served. Of course, those had been complete with sterling silver and Dresden china, but the manners were the same. When Cassie finished stirring, she offered him the glass of tea.

Then she extended the plate of cookies, tilting her head a bit, her face open and animated as she spoke. "Oatmeal raisin, that's Jimmy Ray's favorite. Peanut butter is David John's, and the chocolate chip is Katherine Ann's. I'm partial to the fruit-filled ones, myself.''

He looked at her blankly as she finished the monologue.

"They're my children," she explained. "I always say I'm only going to bake one kind of cookie at a time, but then I can't decide whose favorite to make, so I wind up making them all." She stared at him expectantly, then held the plate a bit closer. "Cookie?"

Wondering whether she always talked this much, he took one.

"Oatmeal raisin. Good choice. Won't spoil your appetite. The fare's plain, but it's filling. Fried chicken tonight. And, of course, mashed potatoes and gravy. Matter of fact, I need to be starting the biscuits soon, and that oatmeal praline pie won't bake itself. I got behind doing laundry and scrubbing floors." Self-consciously she raised one hand to the scruffy knot of hair piled haphazardly on her head. "But then, I guess that shows."

Blake cleared his throat, not yet having tasted his forgotten cookie. "We haven't discussed the room arrangements. The rest isn't necessary—I'll eat my meals out."

She waved a surprisingly delicate hand. "No need. The price includes meals, as well. No point wasting money when there's a home-cooked meal." She frowned suddenly, her gaze moving over him thoughtfully. "I imagine you're used to fancy food. Fried chicken probably doesn't sound like much." Cassie smiled, a burst of white teeth and sunshine. Then she leaned toward him in a confidential manner. "'Course, the restaurant in town won't have the kind of food you're used to either. In fact, one meal there and you'll be wishing you'd had the fried chicken.''

Feeling that he'd totally lost both control and the thread of their conversation, Blake put his glass of tea on the table and tried to organize thoughts that she'd managed to scatter in a thousand directions. "Ms. Hawkins, we need to discuss the room."

"That *Ms.* thing is a big-city expression, isn't it? Nobody around here uses it. You're either single or married, no in between and no hiding it.'' She waved her hands again. ''And trust me, there are plenty who wouldn't mind hiding it.''

His thoughts took flight again. She'd be an effective weapon in battle—she'd distract the enemy into defeat.

The door opened, and he heard a clatter of shoes at the front door, along with happy, young male voices.

''Jimmy Ray, David John, come into the parlor.''

''Yes, ma'am,'' they chorused together.

Ma'am? Did kids still address their elders like that? If his children ever did, he'd probably drop dead of shock.

In seconds the boys were in the room, more subdued, yet at ease. The older, taller one was a male version of Cassie, right down to the easy smile. Blake guessed he was about fifteen, a surprise, since the Hawkins woman didn't look over thirty. If that. The other one looked about five years younger, a freckle-faced towhead.

''Mr. Matthews, these are my sons, Jimmy Ray and David John. Boys, this is Mr. Matthews.''

Jimmy Ray stuck out his hand. Surprised, Blake rose, accepting the firm handshake.

''Nice to meet you, sir.''

As Blake managed a response, he shook hands with the younger boy.

''Nice to meet you, sir,'' David John echoed.

Although the boys were both polite and grown-up, their grins were pure teenage mischief. Struck by their respect and manners, Blake took another look at their mother. Must be some sort of sense beneath all that babble.

''Mr. Matthews needs a place to stay. The house is full, but we're trying to work something out.''

''You can have my room, sir,'' Jimmy Ray offered. ''I'll bunk on the sleeping porch.'' Apparently he saw the confusion in Blake's gaze, as he went on to explain, ''That's the back porch that's screened in—keeps the mosquitoes out.''

Even though he needed a room, Blake didn't want to take the boy's. ''That's not necessary. I'll take the porch.''

Jimmy Ray grinned. ''I like sleeping out there. Do my best thinking outside.''

Blake wondered briefly what the boy thought about.

"You could have my room, but it's in the attic," David John added. "You gotta be kinda short to stand up in there."

"I'm the oldest. It's up to me," Jimmy Ray insisted, turning to his mother. "We can use another boarder." The boy looked suddenly serious, older than his years.

"True. And that's a very generous offer." Cassie smiled fondly at her son, her eyes softening. "Get your things together, and then I'll show Mr. Matthews the room."

"Yes, Mama." Jimmy Ray turned to Blake. "Won't take me long, sir."

Cassie glanced between her sons. "And, boys, don't fill up on cookies before supper."

Their grins were impish, even though they sang out together, "No, ma'am."

She refilled Blake's glass as she muttered, "They're going to eat too many cookies."

As her children left, Blake turned to Cassie. "Jimmy Ray's very responsible, isn't he?"

Cassie watched her oldest son walk up the stairs, and when she spoke, her voice was as soft as her eyes had been. "He had to grow up in a hurry after his daddy left. Thinks he has to be the man of the house."

So, she was a single parent, too.

"He wears the responsibility well. I don't know when I've seen such well-mannered children."

She nodded, seemingly not surprised by the compliment. Apparently she was accustomed to their good behavior. "They've been brought up right."

His gaze met a sudden challenging flare of fire in her eyes, and he wondered whether he'd judged her too quickly. Beneath her easygoing country ways, he guessed, there might be more than he'd originally suspected. Apparently his comment had put her on the defensive—one of the side effects of single parenthood. "I'd say that's obvious. I wish my own children had some of their sense of responsibility."

Her smile was back, the challenge replaced with understanding. "I hear it's hard raising kids in the big city. Lot more temptation and distractions, that's for sure."

"How do you know I live in a big city?"

She surveyed him with a frank gaze. "You didn't get that suit in a place like Twin Corners."

Maybe she *had* been exposed to some things in this century, Blake decided. "You're right. But I'm not sure I can blame my kids' behavior on L.A."

Cassie's delicately arched brows lifted. "My, that *is* a big city." Then she hesitated, seeming to choose her words with care. "But from what I read, when both parents have careers, it's hard to find enough time to spend with their children."

"That's not the problem," he replied quietly. "My wife passed away three years ago."

Her expression was at once both contrite and understanding. Impulsively, she reached out to cover his hand with her own. "I'm sorry. Sometimes words just fall out of my mouth like they're being pushed off the edge of a cliff. And I don't any more know what's tumbling off that edge until I've said it." The flood of words slowed as she met his gaze. "I didn't mean to poke an old wound." That unusual smile simmered, filled with warmth and softness. "I've had enough of my own not to be wanting to cause anyone else pain."

Despite the frustrations of the day, the night in a teenager's room to come, Blake felt the stirrings of humor. Cassandra Hawkins was an oddity, but she was an amusing one.

"It's all right. As I said, it was a long time ago."

Her voice became brisk. "Fine, then. Jimmy Ray should be finished in two shakes. More tea? Or would you like something to tide you over till supper? I could make a sandwich, some cheese and crackers, or—"

"I'm fine. Isn't it time you started cooking that famous fried chicken?"

Cassie nibbled on her lip, and he suspected she was torn. "It is about time, but it won't matter if supper's a few minutes late."

"I appreciate the hospitality, but I'm fine on my own until Jimmy Ray's ready to show me his room."

She glanced toward the kitchen, still hesitating. "I should get things started, I suppose."

"If you stay here entertaining me instead, I'll be forced to eat at the restaurant in town. Wouldn't want that on your conscience, would you?"

That seemed to decide her. "All right, then. But if you need anything, just holler." She flushed, as though just remembering her guest wasn't one of the locals. "I mean, I'll just be in the kitchen."

He nodded, watching her retreating figure. Swallowing a sip of the tea, he reached for a cookie. After one bite, he was glad he'd reconsidered the coming dinner. If the fried chicken was half as good, he'd be a fool to eat in a restaurant.

As sunshine streaming through the parted lace curtains warmed him, Blake tried each kind of cookie, then opted for seconds. He hadn't had time for lunch, and it had clearly been too many hours since his early-morning breakfast.

For the moment, he was content to unwind in the bizarre room, listening to the quiet noises of the house along with the distinctive clanks from the kitchen that told him dinner was under way. The lace curtains rippled in the breeze, and the chirping music of the birds in the huge oak trees added to the comfortable sounds.

Blake took a deep breath of the sweet-smelling air that mingled with the distinctive aromas in the room. They were triggering some forgotten memory.... Blake realized suddenly what he'd been smelling. Lemon and beeswax. Everything about the Hawkins house was an anachronism, like a page torn from another time.

Then the door was pulled open again. This time the footsteps were quieter, gentler. Glancing up, he met a face as inquisitive as his own must be. A young girl, probably thirteen or fourteen years old, stared at him. Apparently, the missing link between the two boys. Then she took a few steps into the room.

"Hello," she ventured.

Blake stood, inclining his head in her direction. "Hello." Then he saw her tremble, a touch of fear in her eyes. He wondered if he'd caused it. Perhaps she was afraid of strangers.

"Are you here to see Mama?"

"In a way. I'm here to rent a room."

Relief flashed across her pretty young face. "Oh, good! I mean, it's nice to meet you, sir."

This one, too, had manners. But he wondered what had caused first the fear, then the relief. Knowing how seriously the Hawkins children took their manners, Blake solemnly offered his hand. "I'm Blake Matthews."

"And I'm Katherine Ann Hawkins."

"Nice to meet you, too. Tell me, Katherine Ann, why do people here go by both their first and middle names?"

The question didn't seem to surprise her. "I know in books and on TV most people don't, but it's a custom that's part of our culture. I don't know how it originated, but it's a common practice here and in Oklahoma."

Blake pushed a hand through his carefully styled hair. The girl talked as though she had swallowed an entire college syllabus. He'd only asked the question to put her at ease. "I see." Not having any daughters of his own, he wasn't certain how to talk to a young girl. He didn't think they were much like the adult variety.

But Katherine Ann rescued him. "If you'll excuse me, I need to help my mother with supper."

She turned away quickly, a thin slip of a girl, but one who already moved with grace and agility.

As she left, Jimmy Ray ran down the stairs, then skidded to a quieter pace before entering the living room. Blake hid a grin. At least the boy had *some* teenage behavior in him.

"If you're ready, sir, I'll show you to your room."

"Only temporarily. It's still yours. How 'bout dropping the *sir?* Blake or even Mr. Matthews would suit me better."

"Yes, s—Mr. Matthews."

Blake glanced at the boy curiously. "I didn't see you come downstairs with anything. You sure you're ready?"

"I used the back stairs. It's closer to the sleeping porch."

"Makes sense. I still don't like putting you out of your room. You'll miss watching TV and listening to your stereo."

For once, Jimmy Ray looked stumped. "The TV's in the

back parlor.'' Then he shrugged—an even more typically teen-age gesture. ''And we don't have a stereo. Closest thing to music is Mama's portable radio, and we have to make sure we don't run down the batteries, in case there's a storm.''

Blake thought about his own boys. Their professionally decorated rooms were all equipped with televisions, VCRs, stereos and telephones. And they still complained of boredom. ''I'm glad I'm not putting you out of TV, too.''

Jimmy Ray shrugged again. ''I have too much studying, anyway.''

''Your teacher really poured on the homework?''

''No, s—Mr. Matthews. I finished that right after school. Mama won't let us play baseball till we're done. But I want to put in some time on my SAT prep.''

Blake raised his brow. ''Aren't you kind of young to worry about your college entrance exams?''

''The first PSAT, the preliminary one, is next year. To get a scholarship my scores have to be the best.''

Blake considered this unusual teenager. His own fourteen-year-old felt mistreated because he had to attend his classes. Homework was another battle. Perhaps they *were* all aliens, after all.

Jimmy Ray kept up a steady stream of chatter until they reached his room. Simply furnished in heavy, oldish oak, it didn't resemble the teen rooms he was used to, but Blake could see himself as a kid being happy in a room like this. While the room didn't have designer bedding, the latest electronics or expensive furniture, its spaciousness more than made up for that. Blake tried to view the room through his own kids' eyes, but couldn't. He was pretty sure they would be appalled by its old-fashioned simplicity.

For a moment, Blake envied this simpler lifestyle. No faxes, no CD players... Then reality struck. He knew he'd be stark raving mad inside of a month. ''This is a great room, Jimmy Ray.''

A touch of pride lined the boy's face. ''I get it because I'm the oldest.''

''Makes sense to me.''

Jimmy Ray reverted to his role as man of the house. "Do you want me to get your luggage?"

Withdrawing his keys from his pocket, Blake tossed them to Jimmy Ray who caught them easily. "Sure. They're in the trunk. I'll need my briefcase and computer, too."

"Yes, s—Mr. Matthews."

Blake heard him bound down the stairs, then moved to the window. A glance outside confirmed what he already knew. A sleepy neighborhood of old homes, rich with greenery that thrived on the high humidity. He wondered what it would be like to grow up here. Deciding it suited Beaver Cleaver more than him, Blake watched as Jimmy Ray seriously went about the task of retrieving the luggage.

It didn't take long for the boy to return. Jimmy carefully placed the suitcase in front of the closet, then put the computer and briefcase on the desk.

Withdrawing his money clip, Blake peeled off two bills. Knowing he was overtipping, but deciding the Hawkinses needed the money, Blake held out two ten-dollar bills.

But Jimmy Ray didn't reach for the money. Instead, he stared at it, puzzled. "What's that for, Mr. Matthews?"

"For bringing up my luggage."

Although Jimmy Ray's eyes widened, he shook his head. "We don't charge for that."

Blake chuckled. "No, this is a tip. For extra service."

Jimmy Ray looked tempted, but he still didn't reach for the money. His serious blue eyes scarcely wavered. "I don't think Mama would like me taking money for something I'm supposed to do anyway. I'd better head downstairs. I need to help with supper."

"I think Katherine Ann's helping your mother."

"We all have our jobs. With the house full, it's too much work for Mama." He hesitated for a moment. "Unless you need something."

"No. I can get some work done while dinner's cooking."

Jimmy nodded, then slipped out of the room. In seconds, Blake heard him pounding down the wide, curving staircase.

Ignoring his suitcase in favor of his computer, Blake took

the laptop from its case and looked for the nearest outlet. Then he sighed. It didn't take an electrical engineer to determine that the ancient wiring in the house wouldn't accommodate a three-pronged plug.

Cursing under his breath, Blake wondered where the nearest office supply store was, and whether they had a dozen battery packs in stock. Blake shoved a hand through his hair, once again disturbing the carefully cut strands. How had he managed to maroon himself in this time warp? Abandoning the computer, he reached for his briefcase.

Later, absorbed in his contracts, it took him awhile to realize that someone was knocking on his door. "Come in," he called out, still distracted.

"Supper's ready, Mr. Matthews."

Blake tore his eyes from the papers. It was the youngest Hawkins this time. Judging from his expression, which was just short of impish, this one was no doubt the most mischievous of the children. "I'll be down soon."

David John drew white-blond brows together as his face scrunched into a frown. "Mama doesn't tolerate anybody being late to supper."

Blake was tempted to tell the boy that he had paid for a room, not for Cassandra Hawkins's house rules. A second look at David John's face changed his mind. It wouldn't be wise to tell the boy that he planned to ignore Cassie's rules. No sense inciting insubordination. "Then I guess we'd better go downstairs."

The cloud lifted from the boy's face. "Wait'll you see what's for dessert."

Blake's lips curled. "Don't you think we'd better eat dinner first?"

David John shrugged. "Sure. Mama's fried chicken is the best. Won blue ribbons the last three years in a row at the county fair. And we're having buttermilk biscuits and gravy."

His mouth watering, Blake forgot all about cholesterol as he walked downstairs with David John. Entering the dining room, he quickly assessed the other guests. Most appeared to be tourists. He wondered which ones were the regulars. But after another quick study, they all still looked like tourists.

Since Cassie's chair was at the head of the table and his own was at the opposite end, he wondered if he'd been given a special honor. She glanced around at the guests, smiling, putting them at ease. Blake watched her, thinking this was like visiting with a favorite relative. Ridiculously, it brought to mind the word *cozy*.

Then Cassie folded her hands together. "As most of y'all already know, we begin our supper each evening with a word of prayer, something we like to share with you." Her smile rested again on the circle of faces sharing her table. Then it zeroed in, focusing on Blake. "And we like to ask our newest guest to lead that prayer. Mr. Matthews, would you do us the honor?"

Chapter Two

Feeling like a student caught without his homework, Blake squirmed as he searched his mind for a remnant of a prayer. This shouldn't be that difficult. They used to say grace in his home.

Or he could simply refuse. For the price of a room, he wasn't required to say grace. Still, he mumbled out a few words.

As soon as the amen was voiced, chattering voices dispelled Blake's uncharacteristic moment of self-consciousness. The sound also interrupted his reverie as the food was eagerly passed around the table.

Although the Hawkins's children dug in enthusiastically, he noted, their table manners were impeccable. And, as the babble of voices rose, competing with the clanking of utensils against dinnerware, Cassie presided serenely. It was almost as though she enjoyed the bustle and controlled chaos. She had a seamless quality to her hosting, efficiently providing newly filled platters and bowls before an item could be missed, yet not missing a beat of the energized conversation.

The shrill of the telephone could be heard over the noise. Cassie and Katherine Ann rose at the same time. After a look from Cassie, the girl sat back down. It was the first time Blake had seen that particular expression on Cassie's face. Glancing down the table, he saw that Jimmy Ray's troubled expression matched his sister's. Curious now, Blake toyed with a buttermilk biscuit, watching rather than eating.

It didn't take long for Cassie to return. Her face was a shade paler than before, her eyes were troubled, and a pinched tightness circled her mouth. Still, she smiled at her guests as she took her chair. Blake suspected he was the only one who noticed the faint trembling of her hands before they disappeared beneath the napkin.

So everything in the Hawkins house wasn't a "Leave It to Beaver" rerun. There were troubles here in paradise, after all.

Cassie reached for the nearly empty biscuit plate. Looking concerned, Jimmy Ray jumped up, picking up the plate before she could. "Let me get it, Mama."

She squeezed his hand, then nodded her head.

Something was definitely going on here.

It wasn't any of his business, but the intuitiveness that had propelled him to success in the corporate world had already kicked in. And it was focusing on Cassie Hawkins.

EVENING SETTLED over the countryside, the Texas sky reaching endlessly, the stars shining brilliantly. It was Cassie's favorite time of the day, a time to reflect, to gather her defenses. Cicadas and crickets provided a comforting accompaniment to the creaking of the porch swing. Dew settled on the grass, glistening beneath the moonlight. And the familiar scents of honeysuckle and magnolia sweetened the air.

Still, she wasn't feeling any peace. This was the town of her birth, and she knew it as well as she knew herself. Each nuance of gossip, each store that lined Main Street, each house that filled her neighborhood.

Much like her own home.

It was the only tangible thing she'd gotten from her ill-fated marriage. The house and its furnishings had been in the Hawkins family for generations. Cassie took the responsibility of preserving that heritage very seriously.

None of it had mattered to her ex-husband, Chuck. He itched to travel beyond the confines of Twin Corners. They'd married so young, too young. The responsibility of a wife and family had terrified Chuck, made that itch grow out of control, until he left.

Despite the burden he'd dumped on her, both financial and emotional, Cassie wasn't bitter. They had simply wanted different things. In his own way, Chuck had loved her. At least, he once had. And he'd cared for the children, as well, but not enough to stay and be a father to them. It had been a long time since they heard from him. *Child support* and *alimony* were foreign words to him. Despite his grand dreams, he could scarcely take care of himself, much less anyone else.

But still Cassie felt strongly about the house. In some ways, it no longer seemed to be Chuck's heritage, but her own. Gently rocking the porch swing, she breathed in the sweet, humid air, watched as the Carstairs, an elderly couple from the neighborhood, strolled down the street. Still hand in hand, she noted with a bittersweet smile. What must it feel like to share a love so enduring?

Restlessly she shifted in the swing, lifting her face to the moonlight. What had brought on such unfamiliar musings? The full moon? Or the handsome stranger now occupying her son's room? Not that a fancy man like that would ever take a second glance at her. And not that she could return that look. Her life was her children. There was no room for anyone else.

She reached down to pat Gulliver's head, and he thumped his tail contentedly against the planked wooden floor. The dog had been her companion these past years, the one to whom she confided worries that she couldn't burden her children with. "Must be too much full moon, Gulliver. Messes with my good sense."

"Not so it shows."

Cassie whirled toward the sound, nearly tipping herself out of the swing. "Mr. Matthews. You startled me."

"Blake."

Cassie hoped she hadn't conjured him up with her restless thoughts. "Running a boardinghouse isn't always easy. Hard to think of it as business when it's all in your home. It helps if I can address my guests like they do in regular hotels. Then it seems like a real job."

Blake shrugged in the near darkness before moving closer,

allowing the moonlight to chase some of the shadows away. "Whatever suits you, Ms. Hawkins."

At the moment, she wasn't sure what that was, and she took refuge in the familiar. "Is the room all right? I know it's not what you expected. It's not one fixed up for guests. It's Jimmy Ray's room, through and through. And I know it's not what you're used to. I imagine you usually stay in big-city hotels with room service and swimming pools. 'Course, I could take your breakfast up on a tray, if it'd suit you. But my cooking's pretty plain. No eggs Benedict...but I can whip up some pretty fluffy French toast. As for swimming, the closest thing we've got to a pool is the pond down the end of the lane. It's not really ours, but Mr. Jenks doesn't care that we swim there. He's too old to go swimming anymore, and—"

Blake's low chuckle stopped the flow of words.

"Did I say something funny?" she asked, all too conscious that she didn't know how to act with someone this sophisticated.

"No, I just never heard anybody talk that long without taking a breath."

Cassie clasped her hands together, knowing her chatter was a habit that increased with nerves. She was glad of the darkness that hid the sudden warmth in her cheeks. He must think she was a fool. "I'm sure you haven't."

"I didn't mean that unkindly. No guarding each carefully chosen word, or gauging its effect. It's refreshing." He propped one long leg against the railing, pulling the material of his fine slacks taut. Apparently, there was muscle beneath that smooth exterior. Plenty of muscle.

Cassie tore her eyes away, then searched his expression suspiciously, but saw only relaxed amusement, no cynicism. "No offense taken. I do speak my mind." She gestured to indicate the wide, quiet street, the soft glow of lights in neighboring homes. "Not much point trying to hide anything. Here everybody knows your secrets. Pretending they don't exist wouldn't last the blink of a firefly."

"Firefly? Are there still fireflies? I thought they'd disappeared after civilization crowded them out."

"Not here. Guess there's not that much civilization."

"Or too many people, you mean. Like in L.A."

"I wouldn't know about that. I've never been to California."

"You mean you're one of the few people in America who never had California fever?"

She shrugged. "Nope. But I *have* got fireflies."

They shared an unexpected smile.

Too aware of the shared moment, the slash of white teeth against his sensual lips, Cassie glanced away, turning to the refuge of darkness to hide the unexpected flutter she felt. Considering how long it had been since she even acknowledged that there was another sex in the species, she was surprised to recognize the quick flare of attraction. Must be the moon, the night air, enhancing the mystery of the sophisticated stranger whose long, lean body stretched against her railing.

At that moment, two fireflies sparked in front of them, lighting the darkness briefly before they flew away.

"I can't believe it," Blake murmured. "This whole place is like stepping back in time."

Cassie heard the change in his voice. It had stayed authoritative and brisk until now. She liked the change, found it easier to be herself when he didn't sound so intimidating. "When I was a kid, we caught fireflies in jelly jars. We'd punch airholes in the lid so they wouldn't croak. Then they'd light up like a lantern when the jar was full." She smiled, unable to resist teasing him. "Could be why there's a shortage of fireflies where you live. Lots more kids in the big city—and maybe they forgot about the airholes."

He chuckled again, his voice scraping beads of awareness over her skin. "Could be. More likely the fireflies got tired of the smog." He looked down the quiet street. "This seems like a great place to grow up."

Cassie felt a familiar pang, then forced it away. "It was. I like knowing my children are safe, happy."

"You never thought about going anywhere else?"

The pang deepened, and she purposely shifted the questioning away from herself. "How about you, Mr. Matthews? Did you ever want to live someplace besides the big city?"

"Almost everybody in L.A. thinks about retreating to the middle of nowhere. But I know I'd enjoy it for a few days and then I'd go nuts."

Cassie laughed softly. "Then Twin Corners will probably send you around the bend."

"I won't be around long enough to let it. Once the deal closes, I'll be gone."

Of course he would. And he could take his disturbing effect along with him. She shook her head to clear it, pushing her heavy hair back. "That's good. Then you won't have to be away from your children too long."

"That's the truth. The housekeeper threatened to quit on my last trip. She doesn't like having to corral the kids. Said it's not part of the job, but I can't keep a full-time sitter. Most of them prefer younger children. But the kids are tough, they don't need someone hovering over them all the time."

Cassie flinched at the thought of someone caring for children who felt it was strictly an inconvenience, and also at Blake's callous-sounding view of nurturing. But she decided his lack of parental concern wasn't her business. "Then, an even better reason to get back to civilization."

"Yes, even though there aren't any fireflies."

Feeling a smile tugging at her lips, Cassie met his gaze briefly. She'd noticed earlier that his eyes were a deep blue, and in the diminished light they seemed even darker, even more provocative. She suspected those eyes had sent more than one female heart running for cover. And even though she'd steel-belted her own susceptibility to men, it was escaping through that locked door.

She purposely tamped down the unfamiliar spurt of attraction, surprised she could still feel such a thing. But then, Blake Matthews was hardly the average man. Tall, leanly muscled, his dark hair an intriguing contrast to those incredibly blue eyes, he was a mouthwatering man, made-to-order for her fantasies. Not to mention that he had a face that could belong to a Hollywood star rather than a businessman.

At least he wouldn't be around long enough to be a worry. Even though he'd awakened a long-buried feeling, she would stash it firmly back in place. Her time for being attracted to men was past. And it certainly wasn't in her future. Not that he'd reciprocate her attraction.

Knowing that, she was able to smile briskly. "Maybe you can take a jar home with you."

His gaze met hers. "Wouldn't be the same."

That wayward pulse in her throat leaped to attention once more.

The front door screen banged open suddenly, interrupting the quiet moment. Jimmy Ray stood at the doorway, looking between them, a suspicious frown covering his face.

Cassie withheld a sigh. Her oldest took his responsibilities as the man of the house seriously. Sometimes too seriously. His protectiveness was sweet, but hardly necessary. Blake Matthews hadn't exactly seemed overwhelmed by her presence. In fact, she doubted he thought of her as a woman at all. Which was fine, she told herself. She shored up her smile, directing it at her son. "Had enough studying for one night, Jimmy Ray?"

He moved closer, his stance clearly protective. "Just taking a break, Mama. I thought you might need something." His gaze challenged Blake, who seemed to catch the boy's inflection.

Blake looked first surprised, then amused. No doubt the thought of romancing her was ridiculous to him. She wondered why the thought rankled her slightly. What did it matter what a guest thought of her?

"No. I was just enjoying the quiet," she replied. "And Mr. Matthews came to see the fireflies."

"And now it's time to get back to work," Blake inserted, his voice once again all business. "I need to send for some battery packs for the computer, and modular connections for the phone. The hardwired dial phones won't accept my modem."

Cassie listened to the unfamiliar terminology, guessing that he meant that their house was hopelessly outdated. And now that his brisk, impersonal style was back, she also guessed that his earlier lapse had been a rare one. "I'm sure Jimmy Ray can help you out. He's always reading about computers. The school doesn't have the funds for one, but Jimmy Ray still keeps up on everything.''

Blake glanced at the boy. ''No computers in your school?''

''No, sir. But that doesn't mean I can't learn about them.''

''Of course not. I'll show you what I need. If you want to earn some extra money, you can set things up for me.''

Jimmy Ray's eyes brightened. He always jumped on a chance to earn something extra. ''Yes, sir.''

''Mr. Matthews,'' Blake reminded him.

Together they walked back inside the house. As the screen door banged behind them, flopping into place, Cassie heard their voices fading away.

It was best that Jimmy Ray had interrupted them. She didn't want to embarrass herself by acting like a schoolgirl who'd never encountered a handsome man. Although she wasn't sure Blake Matthews would even notice. The man seemed to live and breathe business. He might have had a brief nostalgic moment, but she guessed it had been the effect of the night air and the unaccustomed small-town atmosphere.

Still, she sat on the porch swing, listening to its rhythmic creaking as she rocked, wondering how other women would respond to a man like Blake Matthews. Knowing she needed to put the lock he'd started to open firmly back in place.

She was a mother, not a woman. And it wouldn't do to start thinking like one.

BLAKE STUDIED the new connections in his bedroom that Jimmy Ray had installed. He would now be able to use his computer, fax and modem. Impressed, Blake wondered again about these children. They were motivated, goal-oriented, respectful, and at first he'd thought they were Stepford children— programmed robots. But over the past few days, he'd discovered they were also fun-loving, happy kids.

Katherine Ann planned to be a doctor, Jimmy Ray wanted a career in computer engineering. Even ten-year-old David John had a goal—to be a professional baseball player…or an astronaut. But he, too, worked hard at school and home. They all pulled good grades, yet did their chores without complaint.

They also did odd jobs for extra money—from baby-sitting to yard work.

Blake's own sons had one goal. To have fun. Kevin, his fourteen-year-old, merely looked bored when Blake tried to tell him that he had to start concentrating on his schoolwork if he wanted to get into a good college one day. Kevin clearly assumed that Blake would pave his way into college with money. Not home enough to ride herd on him, Blake knew Kevin was still blowing off his schoolwork. And the identical nine-year-old twins, Mark and Todd, were just short of running wild. His latest housekeeper did little more than make sure they didn't burn the house down.

Blake had always heard that boys in fatherless homes were the ones in danger. Yet Cassie controlled her sons easily. Far more easily than he'd ever managed. If she had three pliable girls, he wouldn't have been as impressed, but he knew how much more difficult it was to keep boys in line.

Blake wondered how Cassie did it. She must surely be stretched thin herself, between housework, parenting, running a boardinghouse and taking in sewing and alterations, but still her children were well-rounded, happy. He knew she rose early and worked late into the night. Despite her overwhelming schedule, she created a warm feeling of family and home. Blake wished he could bottle her secret.

From what he could see, Cassie didn't have much of a social life, but he guessed she wasn't interested. Katherine Ann had revealed that Cassie was thirty-four—and didn't date. She certainly didn't dress like a woman trawling for men. But then it had been a long time after his wife's death before he showed an interest in women. He wondered how long it had been since Cassie's marriage ended.

Blake hooked the cables to his computer. Or maybe Cassie Hawkins was one of those rare women who didn't want or need a man in her life. Either way, it didn't concern him.

Because of the close atmosphere of the boardinghouse, he'd learned more about the Hawkinses than he expected. Cassie automatically drew everyone in the house close. Even though she said she wanted to treat her guests the way a hotel did, her natural hospitality flowed through, putting everyone at ease, making her home theirs, as well. She encouraged them to use the parlor, raid the refrigerator and take advantage of the huge, inviting yard.

Blake wondered, though, why none of her guests were regulars. He suspected most boardinghouses depended on regulars, rather than an occasional tourist. Even though there were only a few hotels in town, they could amply accommodate the normal tourist trade, except during Rodeo Days. And few people stopping overnight for just an evening sought out a boardinghouse. He frowned, wondering how the Hawkinses would fare once Rodeo Days ended. Personally, he planned to leave a generous bonus when he departed. After all, Cassie had saved him from sleeping in his car, and he could well afford the expense.

It was clear, from all the economizing he'd seen, that money was tight. Blake's suspicion that something else was going on deepened. The constant phone calls that left Cassie shaken, the expression of dread when the postman handed her the mail, the looks she exchanged with her children, which she thought no one noticed.

He'd also discovered that Cassie Hawkins was a very private person. Respecting that, since he was as well, Blake didn't pry.

After finishing up his computer installation, Blake, accustomed by now to wandering through the house at will, left his room, venturing downstairs to the kitchen to grab a sandwich. He began pushing open the swinging door, but then he heard Cassie's voice. From the one-sided conversation, it was clear that she was on the phone. Deciding to give her some privacy, Blake started to close the door but Cassie's voice stopped him.

"I've told you. I *will* come up with the money. You know my word is good."

There was silence as she apparently listened.

"Business is good right now, with Rodeo Days and—"

He heard another silence.

"I *know* Rodeo Days will end, but I'm hoping to find new boarders, and my sewing business is picking up, and—"

The silence was longer this time.

"If you could just see your way to extending the note—"

The interruption was brief.

"I will do anything to keep the house. If you'll just—"

The silence seemed to echo now.

"Yes, I know about my other outstanding bills. But when business picks up—"

The phone calls, letters and looks. The picture was coming together.

Cassie's voice was dull now. "Yes. I understand. But I'll find some way…. Yes. Goodbye."

Blake backed away from the door carefully. Making sure his feet were quiet against the wooden floor, he retreated upstairs. In her place, he wouldn't want anyone eavesdropping.

So, she was about to lose this house. A place that was clearly important to her. He wondered at the man who had abandoned them. An offhand comment from Jimmy Ray had told Blake his father neither visited nor sent any financial support. And now the Hawkinses were facing eviction.

Blake knew he could offer the money, or pick up the mortgage note himself. But he knew without asking that Cassie would never accept charity. Still, the thought of the Hawkins family losing their home was galling. A picture of her hardworking children flashed in his mind. It wasn't a fate any of them deserved.

It was difficult that evening to sit through dinner. Cassie was uncharacteristically quiet, even though she was as gracious and good-natured as always. Since he knew the truth, Blake wondered how she stood up to the pressure. The strain was visible in her face, especially in her eyes, but no one else seemed to notice. One of the disadvantages of knowing too much, he supposed. His appetite ruined, Blake ate little. Glancing around the table at the Hawkins children, who showed such promise, Blake couldn't stomach the thought of them homeless.

Placing his napkin on the table, Blake pushed back his chair.

Cassie glanced up, concern replacing the strain in her expression. "Is something wrong, Mr. Matthews? If you don't like the fish, I can cook—"

"That's all right, Cassie. Just not too hungry tonight. Besides, I have a lot of work to do."

She nodded, and Blake escaped before she could add anything else. He didn't want to blurt out her secret to a roomful of strangers.

Back upstairs, he stood in front of the bay window, listening to the swish of branches against the glass as he gazed at the quiet street below. Katherine Ann had confided that the house had been in their family for generations. And now they were about to lose it. Having had money all his life, including the trust fund that he had used to establish his business, Blake didn't know how it felt to stand on the edge of financial ruin.

His mind once again went over the possibilities. And once again he didn't come up with any he thought she would agree to. It was too bad she couldn't bottle the secret of her success with her children. Now *that* would be worth a fortune.

Straightening up suddenly, Blake turned from the window. She might not be able to bottle her success, but she could sell it. And he knew the perfect customer.

Him.

Chapter Three

Cassie knocked lightly on Blake's door, hoping she wasn't disturbing him. The light beneath his door always shone brightly late into the night as he worked, but Cassie thought perhaps he wasn't feeling well now. He'd barely touched his dinner. And he had been enthusiastic about her cooking since his first taste of her fried chicken.

The door opened suddenly, and Cassie offered him a tentative smile. "I hope you weren't napping. I thought maybe the fish really wasn't to your liking. I've brought something light. Soup and a chicken sandwich." When he didn't answer, she gestured self-consciously toward a small dish on the tray. "And rice pudding—that usually sets well on your stomach. The iced tea is fresh. Just made a new pitcher. It's sun tea, not boiled. Keeps it from being bitter." She tried smiling again.

A strange, inexplicable expression crossed his face, touched his eyes. But then he sighed, accepting the tray and putting it on the desk.

Cassie ran her hands down the legs of her worn jeans. He didn't turn around immediately, and she felt ill at ease, strangely awkward. "Well, I'll let you be. If you need anything else, just hol—just let me know."

Blake turned then, staring at her. Then he crossed the room in a few long strides. "Come in."

"I don't want to disturb you, and—"

Taking her hand, Blake pulled her inside and shut the door.

Cassie glanced nervously at him, very aware of the now closed door. "If you don't want soup or—"

"How can you be talking about food?" He shoved one hand through his hair. "Or be concerned that I didn't eat? With what you're facing, you need to be worried about yourself, not anyone else."

Cassie took a step backward and found herself against the door. He couldn't be talking about... She cleared her throat. "I'm not sure what you mean."

"I heard you this afternoon. On the phone. I didn't intend to eavesdrop. I was going into the kitchen to get a sandwich." His voice lost some of its aggressive gruffness. "So I know what's going on."

Cassie forced her voice to be steady. She knew she couldn't hide the truth forever. "I guess it doesn't matter. Unless I think of something fast, everybody in town will know. I haven't told the kids about how bad it is with the bank. They know about the other bill collectors, but I couldn't tell them about the house. I'd appreciate it if you wouldn't, either."

"And that'll buy you what? A few weeks? A month? What then?"

Cassie swallowed her desperation. "I don't know. But I'll think of something."

"I already have."

Puzzled, she stared at him, then remembered the closed door. If he thought she was that kind of woman, he'd learn in a hurry that she'd sleep in the street before she'd sleep with a man for money. "I don't know what kind of woman you think I am—"

"The kind who's a great mother. One who can raise kids that are respectful and motivated. One who can make a house into a home."

Cassie opened her mouth, but no sound came out. It had been a long time since she dealt with men, but this didn't sound like any kind of proposition she'd ever heard.

"That's your real talent, Cassie. It's not making you any money here. But it can somewhere else."

Confused, she found her voice. "What do you mean?"

"My boys need that kind of direction, discipline. They need a sense of home. And I'll pay you well to provide it."

"In Los Angeles?" Shocked, she could only stare at him.

His smile was amused. "Not much chance I'm going to move to Twin Corners."

"The reason I need more money is to keep my house. There's not much point in that, if I pick up and move across the country."

"You could rent the house out, catch up on your mortgage payments, get yourself back on solid financial ground. I'm offering you a year's employment contract, with an option to renew."

"Number one, I'm not moving to Los Angeles. Number two, you might not have noticed, but this part of Texas went flat when the oil business went bust. Nobody would rent the house."

Blake shrugged, as though that were a minor concern. "Then we'll think of something else."

"Are you serious? You want to hire me as a nanny?"

"Nanny, housekeeper, stand-in parent. I need someone who can keep my house running, get my children under control, give them what they don't have now."

Cassie could hardly believe his words. "You think you can hire someone to be the parent you aren't?"

"I want someone to help me with the children, not replace me." His tone was even, but she heard the flicker of pain he tried to repress.

Cassie felt that same mushy melting that struck her whenever she saw someone in need. She hadn't intended to hurt his feelings, but she realized she had. It was one thing to toss his offer back in his face, another to insult him. "I'm sorry. I have so much on my mind, and you took me by surprise. I'm honored that you think I could help with your children, but it's out of the question. Our life is here. I can't uproot my kids, drag them away from their home. I appreciate you wanting to help. And I'm not sure if that's not why you made the offer—instead of really needing a nanny. But the answer's no."

Blake didn't look like a man who had been turned down.

But she guessed that was because it didn't happen often. "What about when they don't have a home?"

She held on to her courage with the last of her shredding nerves. "I'll think of something."

He didn't look convinced. "You have time to think over my offer."

Cassie reached behind her for the doorknob. "I don't need to think about it. I'm not changing my mind." Not waiting for his answer, she escaped.

In the security of her own room, Cassie dropped her brave mask, sinking into the chintz-covered chair near the window. She didn't have a clue what she was going to do. Having tapped every financial source, taken on all the work she could find, she didn't know where else to turn. And with her limited education, the local jobs she could obtain paid barely minimum wage.

She glanced around the familiar room. Her eyes skipped across the bed, then returned slowly. So many of her memories were tied to this place. It had never occurred to her before that maybe not all of that was good. Her sense of failure was a clear memory. How often had she asked herself what she could have done to make the marriage better, more exciting? Then maybe Chuck wouldn't have left, and her children would have a father.

And maybe now she wouldn't be alone, misinterpreting a handsome man's offer.

Sighing, she threw the thoughts aside. Examining all the maybes wouldn't bring her the money she needed. She needed a solution. One thing was certain—it wouldn't be accepting Blake Matthews' offer.

BUT IN THE FOLLOWING DAYS, Cassie didn't find a solution. And the bank was losing patience. They absolutely refused to extend the note even an extra month, much less the time she needed to gather the money.

Blake Matthews hadn't repeated his offer, but she saw the questions in his eyes. Remembered the contract he'd offered.

Cassie decided to turn to the one person she could trust. Her mother. Not for financial assistance. Her mother lived on a small social security pension. But she always offered sound advice.

Martha Sanders opened the door, her face lighting up when she saw Cassie. Enveloping her only child in a hug, Martha fussed over her as they stepped inside. "You're looking peaked, Cassie. What's wrong, child?"

Cassie smiled tremulously, then poured out the entire story.

Her mother looked shocked. "Why didn't you tell me before?"

Shrugging, Cassie avoided her eyes. "I've been enough trouble to you. I didn't want you worrying."

Martha reached over to pat Cassie's arm. "You know as well as I do that that's what mothers are for. I wish I had the money—"

Cassie stopped her. "That's not why I'm here. I just need a dose of your common sense."

"You and the children can come here, of course."

Cassie glanced around the cottage, the home she'd been raised in. Her father had died when she was a baby, and her parents' plan to have a big family and move into a larger place had died with him. Martha had barely managed to scrape by. There had been times when she nearly lost the small house. And while Cassie was growing up, her mother had insisted that Cassie sleep in the one bedroom, taking the couch for herself. It had only been after Cassie married that Martha reclaimed the bedroom. When she divorced, Cassie had invited her mother to live with them in the larger home, but Martha had been insistent. She'd worked so hard to keep her little house that she didn't want to live anywhere else.

Knowing her mother's sacrificing nature, Cassie wouldn't have put it past her to once again give up her room for the children. Aside from the fact that she didn't want to crowd her mother from her own home, there simply wasn't enough room. Five people in the tiny house would be unbearable.

"Thanks, Mom. But it's not practical. I have to think of something else."

"No regular boarders yet?"

"Nope. Oil jobs are gone, and so are the people who worked them. The kind who wanted room and board instead of hotel rooms." Cassie stared grimly at the worn but clean carpet. "I haven't come up with any answers. Just a wild scheme from one of the guests."

"What kind of scheme?"

Grudgingly Cassie outlined Blake's offer. "But, of course, I can't do it."

"Why not?"

Cassie blinked. "I can't leave my home—"

"Which was Chuck's home, as well," Martha reminded her. "All of those memories aren't good. It's time you started making new ones."

"What about the children? They don't know anyplace other than here."

"Maybe it's time they learned. Maybe it's time you all learned." Martha leaned forward, taking Cassie's hands. "This could be a fresh start for all of you."

Cassie searched her mother's eyes, knowing what she was referring to, wishing they could both forget. "I'd be all the way across the country."

"With new people, making new memories. I think it would be good for you."

"But the kids would probably hate it. They won't want to change schools, friends—"

"Why don't you ask them?" Martha's tired but still pretty face softened. "If I recall, when you were their age, you dreamed about traveling to the far corners of the world."

Cassie managed not to flinch. "And look where that got me."

"Perhaps if you'd have had a chance to travel…"

Cassie looked at her mother uncertainly. "You really think this is a good idea?"

"Sounds to me like you're running out of choices. You can lose your house, or you can take a chance. Talk to the kids, Cassie. They might surprise you."

"Well, you certainly did, Mom."

Martha's generous smile matched her daughter's. "That's okay. I think you're going to surprise yourself, too."

CASSIE THOUGHT about telling her children that evening, but she kept putting it off until it was too late. Tomorrow was another day, she told herself. Right now, the kids needed their sleep.

Restlessly she prowled the front porch, too on edge to be content with the slower pace of the swing. Her mother's words had set off a chain of discontent, uncertainty.

The door opened quietly. Instinctively Cassie stepped back, into the shadows.

"Won't do any good to hide, Cassie. I've been watching you from the window."

Blake's words startled her. Not certain how she felt about him watching her, she pushed aside the warmth his presence brought. "Any special reason?"

"I wanted to see if you'd found your solution."

She steadied her voice. "And what did you decide?"

"That you really need to take my offer."

Deflated, she sank against the railing. "I haven't stopped looking for another way."

His face was in the shadows, but Cassie guessed it was covered by a disbelieving look. "What if I up my offer?"

"Excuse me?"

"I'll catch up your back payments."

"How did—"

"Banks seldom foreclose on current loans. In addition to your salary, you and your family can live in the guest quarters of my house. No rent, Cassie. The salary will be all yours. And if you rent your house, that will pay the mortgage. If not, you'll have plenty of salary to handle it."

It was a more-than-generous offer, one she wasn't sure she could refuse. Still, her pride surged forward. "I don't want to show my children that the answer is to run away."

"You're not running away. You may not have noticed, but in this century people often relocate to take a better job." Blake moved closer, cornering her. "And while you're thinking of your pride, perhaps you should think about your children instead.''

Anger and resentment flared, but he didn't allow her to voice either, cutting her off before she could.

''Yes, I know you love your children, but what are you offering them? A second-rate education? And they're all hoping for scholarships to colleges that want the best of the best. You think Katherine Ann can compete with other students to get into medical school with the background she gets here? And Jimmy Ray. The kid's dying to get his hands on a real computer. With his mind, he could run rings around the competition. Instead, he's poring over outdated books and magazines, trying to get a taste of what he wants. In L.A. he can take his pick of computer courses. You're lucky enough to have kids who are motivated, with goals they *could* achieve…with the right tools. Are you going to give them those tools, Cassie? Or are you going to tie them to this town?''

Stunned, Cassie swallowed against the lump in her throat. Was he right? Was her blind pride robbing her children of a lifetime opportunity?

Overwhelmed, she stared at him, hardly able to find her voice. ''I haven't even talked to my kids yet.''

Blake turned to the door, reaching for the handle. ''Don't wait too long, Cassie. I don't want to see you lose your house.''

HIS WORDS RANG IN HER EARS all the next day, as she cleaned the house, then tackled a huge pile of alterations and mending. Automatically she went through the motions of her work, once again turning over the alternative solutions to their problem in her mind, realizing there really weren't any.

Resigned, she called a family meeting that night, after the supper dishes had been washed.

The kids looked at her expectantly, and for a wild moment she wished she could assure them that she had everything under control, that their money problems were over. But reality reared its ugly, insistent head, and Cassie outlined Blake's offer instead.

"Los Angeles?" Jimmy Ray questioned. But there was more curiosity than dismay in his voice.

"Isn't that where the movie stars live?" David John asked.

"And where some huge medical centers are," Katherine Ann chimed in.

Cassie studied her children's faces. None of them looked as upset as she expected. "This would mean changing schools, leaving your friends behind. It's a whole different world in the city."

"That's where Disneyland is!" David John suddenly remembered, nearly toppling over his chair.

"We would be moving to the city, not to Disneyland," Cassie reminded him.

"Then you're really thinking about this, Mama?" Jimmy Ray asked.

Was she? She glanced around the circle of dear faces. "I'm telling y'all about the offer. Now I want to know what you think."

"Is there any way we can pay the bank?" Always practical, Katherine Ann went straight to the heart of the matter.

"I haven't thought of anything yet. That doesn't mean I've given up. This isn't our only choice."

"Sounds like it is, Mama," Jimmy Ray added seriously.

"I can look for more work," Cassie answered, wondering where that work would come from.

"You can't work more, Mama. You're worn-out now." Jimmy Ray's gaze remained steady, unblinking, although his Adam's apple bobbed. "I could take off from school for a while, get a regular job."

Cassie's heart nearly skidded to a stop. Whatever else was wrong with her life, she'd been blessed with the best kids in the world. "No, Jimmy Ray. I won't ever let you do that." Her gaze moved slowly around the table. "If you're all in agreement, I'll see if the house can be rented. I don't think so, but if it does, then I'll tell Mr. Matthews we'll go."

One by one, her children voiced their agreement. Sucking in her breath, Cassie realized they could be changing their lives forever.

"When will we know, Mama?" Katherine Ann asked.

"Probably soon."

"I sure hope we can rent the house!" David John declared, obviously still entranced by visions of Disneyland.

"I'll try, but don't get your hopes up. I don't think anyone will rent the house."

BUT CASSIE WAS WRONG. She'd barely put the notice in the county paper and on the bulletin board at the grocery store when the phone rang. The young couple who rushed over loved the house and its huge windows. Both were artists who had fled the big city for country life. They said the house would be perfect—after they converted two of the bedrooms into studios. They agreed to rent the house furnished, and store the extra things in the basement.

Almost before Cassie could think, the couple had given her the first month's rent, anxious to move in immediately. The reality of what she'd done sank in as she gazed around her home. Soon to be someone else's home.

She was still dazed when Blake returned from his last meeting. He'd started to walk past the parlor when he glanced at Cassie, sensing something different. Entering the room, he saw that she looked like a shell-shock victim.

"Cassie, is something wrong?"

Dumbly she held up a piece of paper.

Staring at it grimly, he guessed it was her foreclosure notice.

"I rented the house," she said, her voice empty except for a sense of wonder and disbelief.

"You what?"

"I rented it. I didn't think I could, but I did."

He grinned. "Then you're accepting my offer?"

Dazed, she met his gaze, still blinking in astonishment at herself. "California, here we come."

Chapter Four

Cassie, her children and their dog stood in the curving driveway and stared at the huge house, a mansion right out of "Lifestyles of the Rich and Famous." Stunning, the sleek contemporary building seemed to rise on the hill, supported by massive banks of windows and the thrust of its towerlike design. Lush greenery tumbled over the manicured lawn, and glossy, exotic flowers bloomed, intense bursts of color against the stark white house. It was the sort of place Cassie had seen in magazines, so perfect it didn't seem real.

She turned back to the taxi driver who was unloading their luggage from the trunk. "I'm sorry, sir. This must be the wrong address." She handed the man a slip of paper with Blake's address written on it.

He glanced at it briefly. "This is it, lady. And the cab voucher covered the ride. So I'll be on my way."

"But this can't be—"

Katherine Ann tugged on her arm. "Look, Mama."

Cassie glanced at the discreet carved brass sign that rested beneath the ornate sconce at the front door. Matthews was engraved beneath the numbers. It *was* his house. Why hadn't he warned her?

This wasn't at all what she'd expected. It struck her swiftly that she was completely ill equipped to handle anything to do with this mansion...or the man who owned it. Cassie turned, ready to call the taxi driver, to run back to Twin Corners. But the employment contract she'd signed burned in her thoughts. She might want to run, but for the next twelve months she couldn't.

Cassie glanced down at the plain flowered cotton skirt and serviceable blouse she wore. They had seemed like practical choices back home, especially considering the skimpy wardrobe she owned. But here in the city she felt dowdy and out of place.

Gulping back a nervous titter, she tried to act as though she were accustomed to just such a situation, instead of looking like a gawky country girl who'd fallen headlong into the big city. Which was exactly how she felt.

"Okay, everybody, let's get our suitcases." Gripping her own as if it were a lifeline, Cassie led the way to the front door and rang the bell. "I wonder if this is how the Beverly Hillbillies felt," she muttered under her breath.

A young woman in a crisp uniform opened the door and stared at them curiously.

Cassie took a breath. "Hi. I'm Cassie Hawkins, and these are my children, Jimmy Ray, Katherine Ann and David John."

Clearly puzzled, the woman stared down the line of faces, her gaze finally landing on the dog, who thumped his tail in a friendly fashion. "*¿Qué?*" Then she shook her head. "I'm sorry.... What?"

"Cassie, that's right." She smiled, wondering if the woman planned to keep them standing outside. "Mr. Matthews is expecting us. I'm the new nanny."

"*Si*, yes." The woman opened the door wider and ushered them inside.

Cassie stared upward at the ceiling, which soared more than two stories high. When Blake had assured her that he could more than afford her salary and the expense of moving the family, he hadn't exaggerated. But she'd never expected anything like this.

The woman switched to English. "Señor Matthews is in his office." She pointed to double doors at the end of the huge hallway.

Cassie tore her eyes from the eye-popping interior. "Thank

you." She turned to her children. "I'll talk to Mr. Matthews first."

She heard distracted murmurs of agreement, realizing the kids were as overwhelmed as she was. Taking a deep breath, she smoothed perspiring palms against her cotton skirt and approached the formidable-looking doors, knocking lightly.

When she didn't hear an answer, she leaned close to knock again, but the door suddenly opened. Nearly falling into his arms, Cassie met Blake's face, inches from her own. Trying to regain her equilibrium, she rocked back on her practical flat shoes.

"You're here," he commented unnecessarily.

"So I am."

He held out a hand. "Welcome."

Awkwardly she accepted the handshake, feeling a tremor of awareness at his touch. To dispel it, she made her smile overly bright. "You want to say hi to the kids?"

"Sure, sure." He glanced back briefly at the overloaded desk in his study, then moved with her down to the hall, greeting the children, hearing snatches of their excited talk about riding in an airplane, then seeing L.A.

He looked taken aback when the dog licked his hand and waited to be patted. "Uh...I didn't know you were bringing Gulliver."

"He's part of the family," David John announced.

The dog barked in agreement as the children all tried at once to tell Blake about their trip. When the babble finally died down, they glanced at him expectantly.

Blake returned their glances. "Oh...you need to know where you're staying. Maria has cleaned your rooms. Did you meet her?"

Cassie smiled at the young woman. "Yes."

"Good. She can show you the way." He turned back to the study. "I'll see you after you get settled in."

"Sure." Wishing he was the one showing them their new home, Cassie followed Maria up the curving marble staircase, trailed by her children and Gulliver.

It was silly to be disappointed. What had she expected? For

him to fling her into his arms, thrilled to have her there? Maybe not. But it would have been nice to have him a bit more concerned about their arrival.

She considered kicking herself, but she was too loaded down with suitcases to even try. Before leaving Texas, she had lectured herself sternly. Now that Blake Matthews was her employer, she intended to squelch any stirrings of attraction. It was one thing to have a few giddy feelings for a handsome guest in her own boardinghouse. It was another to entertain those feelings for her employer. Especially when he'd given her the first opportunity she'd had to provide her children with a future. There was no way she was going to blow this by going all moony-eyed over him.

No, that had come to an end.

Maria stopped at a light, airy room decorated in delicate shades of yellow. The bleached oak furniture was both tasteful and inviting. Maria pointed inside. "This room is for the girl."

Katherine Ann gasped. "For me?" Although she'd always claimed to be more interested in learning and studying than in other, more feminine pursuits, Cassie knew it was because they hadn't had the means in Texas to explore any other interests. Katherine Ann walked into the room slowly, trailing her hands over the furniture. "It's beautiful."

Cassie moved inside to give her daughter a small hug. "Why don't you get settled in? I'll be back later."

Katherine Ann was distracted, already lost in the wonder of this new world. "Okay, Mama."

Cassie and her sons followed Maria down the hall. "These rooms are for the boys." Maria pointed inside. "They're connected with a bathroom. The one on the other side is for the young one."

David John raced inside, while Jimmy Ray moved more slowly. Sleek contemporary furniture filled the room, including bookcases and a curving desk. But it wasn't the furniture that drew Jimmy Ray. Cassie withheld a gasp.

On the desk, a gleaming computer setup waited. Jimmy Ray walked to it slowly, tentatively touching it, running his hands over the smooth surface, before turning to his mother. "Do you think it's a mistake, Mama? That it's supposed to be some-where else?''

Cassie had seen a computer on Blake's desk. "I don't know. You'd better ask Mr. Matthews.''

"Sure, Mama." But his eyes hadn't left the computer.

Cassie hoped the computer was indeed meant for Jimmy Ray, especially since Blake had been so adamant about her son's computer education. But she guessed the expensive com-puter belonged to Blake's children. Still, if Jimmy Ray could just have access to it… Wiping an unexpected bit of moisture from her eyes, she turned to Maria. "I guess I'm next."

"Down this way." The hall curved, and a skylight poured sunshine into the area, highlighting a beautiful arrangement of fresh, vibrant flowers. Trying to keep her eyeballs attached, Cassie followed as the hall wound around toward the other side of the house.

They passed a few closed doors, and Cassie couldn't contain her curiosity. "Maria, what are these rooms?''

"Some are guest rooms. Also the library, sunroom and mu-sic room.''

"I thought one of the guest rooms was mine.''

Maria smiled. "The one Señor Matthews picked out for you is larger than these—a suite. We're almost there.''

Cassie digested that. "There was no need to make a fuss." She couldn't help craning her neck back, looking longingly toward the wing her children's rooms were in. Feeling home-sick and disoriented, she wished her room was closer to theirs.

Maria stopped, then turned with a smile. "And this is your room, *señora*.''

Stepping inside, Cassie withheld a gasp. A Queen Anne–style cherrywood four-poster bed dominated the center of the bedroom, and a sheer, gauzy white canopy seemed to float above the bed. Fragile curtains of the same gauzy white ma-terial were pushed back to reveal a triple-paneled set of French doors. Instinctively Cassie stepped closer, seeing that the doors led to a flagstone terrace. Turning around, she saw that match-ing pieces of cherrywood completed the furniture.

She moved farther inside, still staring. The sitting room, separated by an arched open doorway, was also furnished in traditional pieces. A love seat and wing chair faced the huge white marble fireplace. The mantel was also carved from rich cherrywood. It struck Cassie that this was the only room not decorated with stylish but almost stark modern furniture. The familiar style warmed her chilled, nervous heart.

Turning back toward the bedroom, she saw that a beautifully crafted Persian rug covered the wood planked floor, adding a splash of color. Her gaze skipped to the nightstand, which held a vase filled with more exotic blooms. The room was at once elegant and inviting.

Impulsively Cassie turned to the woman who waited near the doorway. "This is beautiful, Maria."

"*Sí*, yes, *señora*."

"Cassie, please. We'll be working together now."

Maria smiled. "Cassie."

"Is your room close by?"

Maria shook her head. "We're in the separate houses." At Cassie's puzzled look, she explained. "Behind the big house are servants' quarters. The staff lives there. Pedro—the general handyman—and his wife, Isabelle, who's one of the maids. Albert, the driver, and Dora, the new maid."

"Oh. Still, this room, and my children's rooms, seem awfully nice for hired help." Cassie glanced again at the scrumptious furnishings.

Maria shrugged. "Señor Matthews is a nice man."

He'd certainly pulled her bacon out of the fire, Cassie agreed silently.

Turning toward the hall, Maria shrugged again. "This part of the house is usually for guests, but maybe he doesn't think of you as staff."

Startled, Cassie met the woman's warm brown eyes. "You don't…mean…."

Maria lifted a casual shoulder. "You are to be in charge of his children. That is a special job."

Relieved, Cassie managed a smile. "I guess so."

Maria moved toward the doorway, then paused. "Welcome, Cassie. I hope you're happy here."

"Thanks, Maria. Me too."

After the woman left, Cassie turned back to the incredible room, gave in to the urge that had been plaguing her, and pinched herself. But the room didn't fade away. Laughing aloud, she dropped back on the downy comfort of the bed. She was truly in paradise.

PARADISE had a lot of faces, Cassie discovered. And the three belonging to Blake's children held expressions ranging from disinterest to dislike to disrespect.

Blake had briefly introduced them. The oldest, fourteen-year-old Kevin, challenged her with a single glance. The nine-year-old twins, Mark and Todd, imitated their older brother's belligerent actions. Before she could take in any more about them, Blake fled to a meeting.

The boys were as bad as he'd described. Mouthy, disdainful and uninterested, they scattered as soon as their father was out of sight. Cassie decided not to pursue them until she knew the house and her job a little better.

Acquainting herself with the huge kitchen, Cassie looked for enough essentials to prepare dinner. Pulling open the refrigerator, she rooted through the sparse contents. Frowning, she decided that no one had gone shopping since the previous housekeeper left.

Uncovering tuna and noodles in the pantry, she put together a casserole. A search of the freezer yielded enough frozen entrées to last a month, but no vegetables. A further search through the pantry provided enough of the basics to make biscuits and a yellow cake. For all the kitchen's designer style and modern conveniences, it wasn't stocked to feed a family.

Hands on hips, Cassie surveyed the bountiful counter space, the island workstation and the adjoining breakfast room. The room curved invitingly around a huge bay window that revealed a burst of colorful, exotic flowers and lush greenery landscaping the yard.

Katherine Ann shyly poked her head into the room, finally having left the sanctuary of her room.

"Just in time, Katherine Ann. I could use some help setting the table."

"Sure, Mama." Automatically she accepted a stack of plates.

"Did you get settled in?"

Katherine Ann clutched the plates, a dreamy expression on her face. "Did you see how beautiful the room is? I had to pinch myself so I'd know it was real."

Since Cassie had done the same thing, she could only nod in agreement.

Katherine Ann all but twirled. "It's just like out of the magazines. Do you suppose people get used to living like this?"

Cassie reached out to tuck a wayward strand of hair behind her daughter's ear. "I'm not sure. But I don't think we should."

Katherine Ann looked both crushed and incredulous. "Why not?"

"My contract's only for a year. I hope the job will work out, but I can't make any promises. It would be awfully difficult to return home if we forget our roots."

Katherine Ann studied the toe of her shoe for a moment. "I don't think we'll forget what you've taught us, Mama. The important things. But is it wrong to want nice belongings?"

Seeing the earnest, troubled expression on her child's face, Cassie smoothed a hand down her soft cheek. "No, sweetie. As long as we don't forget that things aren't more important than people."

Katherine Ann's expression cleared. "That won't ever happen, Mama."

This child, so close to her heart, was at once both her most difficult child and her most perceptive one. Probably because Cassie saw too much of herself in Katherine Ann. The desire to succeed, the yearning to have more than life had allotted, the capacity to be swayed by the lure of new, distant places.

None of those ambitions had turned out the way Cassie once thought they would. Now she hoped for peace, the children's happiness, and relief from their financial burdens. As she glanced around the magnificent room she stood in, Cassie knew that a portion of her hopes had been realized. Provided Blake Matthews liked the way she performed her job.

Cassie checked on the tea and saw that it had steeped long enough. "What are your brothers doing?"

Katherine Ann put the last plate on the table. "Jimmy Ray's glued to that computer, and David John was bugging the twins."

Cassie stilled her hands. "Why?"

Katherine Ann shrugged. "Why not?"

"This is going to be our home for the next year, and I want you and your brothers to get along with the Matthews."

The thin shoulders bobbed up and down again. "I like Mr. Matthews fine. But the boys are the worst."

Considering how tired she was, Cassie didn't feel this was the time to launch into a lecture. Right now, she just wanted to get through this first long day. "The silverware's in the first drawer on the left."

Katherine Ann nodded, efficiently setting the table.

Pulling the casserole from the oven, Cassie glanced up as Blake came in through the back door. His puzzled face pulled together in a question as he looked at the clutter of bowls in the sink, then at the big round table in the breakfast room, which had been set with eight places.

Cassie smiled at him as she put the casserole on a trivet. "Good, you're just in time. Supper's almost ready."

"Supper?"

"Well, I suppose you call it dinner. It's not much. I couldn't find hardly anything in the kitchen." She smiled, feeling ridiculously nervous, like a student trying to impress the teacher. "Could say the cupboard's bare. I'll have to go shopping tomorrow."

"Sure. Household money's in a canister on the top shelf." His face drew together again. "I didn't know you were going to all this trouble...."

"Why, sure. That's why you hired me."

Kevin and his brothers raced down the stairs, headed for the back door.

"Whoa!" Cassie held up her hand, staving off their escape. "Where do you think you're going?"

"Out," Kevin answered for them.

"Not now. We're ready to eat supper."

The boys looked at the table, and Kevin said, his voice dripping with disdain, "*Supper?* What's *that?*"

Cassie leveled them with a look that never failed to make her own children straighten up. "It's called sup—dinner. You know, when members of the household sit down at the table together, pick up forks, put food in their mouths, chew, swallow. It's a wonderful experience. Try it. You'll like it."

The boys turned to Blake. "Dad, we don't have to stay, do we? We were going to grab some burgers, then hit the arcade."

"Mrs. Hawkins went to a lot of trouble. Wash your hands and sit down."

Three rebellious faces glared at Cassie. Dragging their feet, the boys crowded into the bathroom beneath the back stairs. Hearing the amount of splashing, Cassie suspected they were covering the room in water.

As the boys returned to the kitchen, Kevin sniffed the air. "Smells like something died in here. Or maybe that's… *supper,*" he said, drawing out the word, mocking her drawl. "Come on, *y'all.* Let's pull up to the chuck wagon."

Cassie held on to her temper. She didn't want a scene on her first day. Blake returned, his jacket and tie gone. Her own children were on his heels, and she breathed a sigh of relief. Allies in the enemy camp.

Once everyone was seated, Cassie glanced around the table. Blake looked resigned, his children rebellious, and hers uncomfortable. Oh, this was going well. Her gaze went back to Blake as she folded her hands and looked at him expectantly. His eyes fell on her hands, and he nodded to her.

She uttered a brief blessing and then raised her face, meeting three disbelieving pairs of eyes. A little disconcerted, she smoothed her napkin before offering the plate of biscuits to Katherine Ann. Then she picked up a serving spoon. "Kevin, if you'll pass your plate, I'll serve. The casserole dish is pretty hot."

He sent a sulky look in his father's direction, then thumped the plate into her hands with more force than necessary. Cassie spooned a portion onto his plate and handed it back.

"What *is* this?" Kevin asked, staring at the casserole as though she'd served him cow patties.

"Tuna casserole," she replied, filling the twins' plates.

"Yuck," Mark responded.

"I hate tuna," Todd chimed in.

"The pantry was full of tuna. I thought it must be one of your favorites," Cassie replied, automatically accepting Blake's plate as she looked at the rebellious trio of faces.

"That would be Mrs. Thompson," Blake replied. "The former housekeeper. The boys and I either eat out, have dinner delivered, or put something in the microwave."

Which explained the contents of the freezer.

Cassie hid the uncertainty trembling inside her. She had two choices. Cave in to their routine, making it easy on the Matthews men. Or do the job she'd been hired for.

"Luckily you won't have to do that anymore. Tomorrow I'll go shopping." She glanced at Blake's sons. "After I find out what you like to eat. Then we can make sure that su—dinner is a family affair. If you don't like tuna, I could scramble some eggs."

Mark looked briefly interested, but Kevin elbowed him, and he set his face in a mutinous line, as well.

"I *want* a burger," Kevin retorted.

"I'm afraid we don't have any hamburger," she replied, precariously hanging on to her temper. It had been a long, trying day, and her patience was wearing thin.

Blake glanced between his sons and Cassie. "Try the tuna. If you still don't like it, I'll call for some burgers. You'll learn that Mrs. Hawkins is a wonderful cook. Her fried chicken's the best I ever had."

"I like chicken," Todd offered.

"From the Colonel," Kevin added.

"Mama's is better," David John said defensively.

Kevin rolled his eyes. "Then why doesn't she own the franchise?"

"That'll be enough," Blake inserted. "Just try the casserole."

Kevin made one half-hearted stab at the tuna, before announcing he didn't like it. Mark and Todd followed his lead.

Cassie met Blake's eyes and read defeat there. Resigned, she didn't say anything as he ordered the burgers. She and her children resolutely ate the casserole, even though Blake offered them burgers, as well.

Seeing the fatigue on her children's faces, Cassie ended the meal quickly. When the burgers came, Blake's sons disappeared with the food, not bothering to even attempt an appearance in the breakfast room.

Cassie started to clear the table just as Maria entered the kitchen.

"You should have told me you were cooking," Maria gently scolded her. "The clean-up is my job."

"But—"

Maria shooed her away. "Go, you're tired."

Cassie couldn't argue with her logic. "Thanks. I'd like to check on my kids."

It didn't take long to see that they were settled. Exhaustion and excitement had taken their toll. And tomorrow they had to enroll in new schools. Suddenly, the whole process seemed overwhelming. How in the world was she going to find their schools, even the grocery store, in this unfamiliar city? All of Twin Corners would fit in just this neighborhood.

Distraught, but too restless to sleep, Cassie wandered back downstairs, seeking out the patio near the pool that she'd seen from her terrace. She needed the comfort of the outdoors, the pretense that she was in her own swing on her own porch.

What had possessed her to move across the country, leaving everything familiar behind? She no more belonged here than her old-fashioned notions did. She wasn't any more suited to the big city than the Matthews boys were to tuna casserole.

Kicking off her shoes, Cassie rolled up the legs of her jeans, dropping to the side of the pool to dangle her feet in the water. The dramatic patio lighting reflected on the pool, making it look like a dark, rippling diamond. A jewel that nearly matched the starlit sky.

Sighing as she gazed upward, Cassie remembered a time when her every fantasy had centered around traveling to new, exciting places. But somehow those fantasies had never contained tuna casserole or resentful children.

A sudden splash of water startled her, dragging her attention back to the pool just as Blake surfaced directly in front of her. She gasped at the seeming intimacy of his face positioned between her knees. Jerking her foot backward, she was startled when Blake grabbed that same foot.

"Oh, no, you don't. I thought sure I'd captured a mermaid."

Despite the sudden thumping of her heart, Cassie managed a laugh. "You think my legs look like a fish tail?"

"You have a way of twisting words, Cassie...." He levered himself up a bit on the side of the pool, a sheet of water pouring from his chest.

Cassie's throat tightened. She hadn't been wrong about those muscles. She'd simply underestimated them. Deliberately, she lifted her eyes away.

He yanked gently on her foot. "You're about a million miles away. Something on your mind?"

She shook her head, then let her gaze drift back toward him. "It's just been a long day."

Blake studied her face for a moment, then pulled himself up and out of the pool. Cassie stared at the ripple of muscles, the deeply tanned skin, then the intriguing vee of dark hair that led to his brief trunks. She'd only seen men in swimwear like that in the movies or in magazines. And those men hadn't been beaded with water, as Blake was, making his every move beneath the moonlight that much more sensual. Cassie averted her gaze, drawing on her inner strength to recover her equilibrium.

Blake reached up to slick back his hair, then looked again at Cassie, his eyes darkening in the diminished light. She wished there was something other than the pool to disappear into. She didn't especially want to drown, rather than face him.

"Probably feeling a bit overwhelmed," he guessed accurately. "And wondering why you ever agreed to come here."

Cassie managed to look at him. "How did you know?"

"It's not so difficult. I plucked you out of one world and dropped you into another. I'm guessing you feel like you've landed on another planet and there's no shuttle to take you back home."

Cassie smiled reluctantly. "Pretty much. Things are different here. And it's only our first day. I'm kind of dreading tomorrow."

"L.A.'s no town for beginners. Albert will drive you."

"But—"

"You have two schools to find, along with the shopping center. I can drive myself, and I'll tell Albert to show you the basics of the city. You won't learn all of L.A. in one day, but you'll know enough to get where you have to go. The rest will come later."

Relieved, she dared a glance at him, trying to ignore the wealth of bare skin. "Los Angeles is bigger than Twin Corners, I'll admit that. I wasn't looking forward to getting lost."

He glanced at her quizzically. "Then why didn't you ask for help?"

She folded her hands, staring again at the water. "Asking doesn't come easy to me."

"I should have remembered. Pride's important, Cassie, but needing other people is important, too."

He reached over to tip up her chin, and Cassie nearly bolted. An unexpected trembling attacked her vulnerable insides, and she wondered if it was visible.

"You're no quitter, Cassie." He dropped his hand, but the imprint still burned her skin. "I know my boys didn't make it any easier, but they'll come around. You've got the touch." He waggled his eyebrows. "And now I've got to finish my laps."

Standing, he dived cleanly into the water.

He was wrong, Cassie thought distractedly, lifting her fingers to the jaw he had bracketed. She didn't have the touch. He did.

Chapter Five

The following days flew by. Cassie learned her route to the schools and the shopping center. White-knuckled at first, then with more ease each day.

To her amazement, Blake left the country on her tenth day in L.A., briefly explaining that the two-week business trip couldn't be avoided or postponed. She had expected him to be around during this transition time, knowing it wouldn't be easy for the two families to meld. The Matthews boys, who'd been settling down—a little—resumed their obnoxious behavior, escalating their antics, since they knew she had no one to turn to for support.

Still, she insisted they sit down to eat dinner each evening, refusing to relinquish the family hour. Although they kept up their sarcastic comments, she noticed they were eating more of her cooking.

Mark and Todd were easier to deal with than Kevin, especially when their older brother wasn't around. It wasn't difficult to uncover the twins' likes and dislikes. And although they tried repeatedly to fool her about who was Mark and who was Todd, she had been able to tell them apart since the second day. She couldn't have explained how she knew, but it was something in the eyes, and their expressions. They were disappointed that the switching act didn't work. Apparently, they'd used it successfully on past housekeepers. Yet she had a sneaking suspicion that they were secretly pleased that she paid enough attention to them to tell them apart. Despite their swaggering bravado, they were still only nine years old and in desperate need of attention.

The relationship between Jimmy Ray and Kevin was a difficult one. A year older than the more sophisticated Kevin, Jimmy Ray resented the other boy's superior attitude. And Kevin enjoyed needling Jimmy Ray, reminding him at every opportunity that he was a hick. Because Cassie had asked him to keep the peace, Jimmy Ray chose to retreat to the computer Blake had assured him was his, rather than fight. But Cassie knew her oldest son was about to blow if Kevin kept up his taunts.

Katherine Ann was the only one who was able to get along with them all. Treating the twins much as she did David John, she regarded them as little more than a nuisance—like the bane of one's existence that was any younger brother. And, oddly, Kevin didn't treat Katherine Ann the same way he did Jimmy Ray. While he wasn't overly friendly, he didn't go out of his way to torment her.

Reflecting on all this one afternoon, Cassie stirred a bowl of cookie dough, adding more chocolate chips. It was still too early to tell whether they could all get along peaceably. One thing continued to amaze her. Even though he was half a world away, Blake had called only once to check on his children, and then he'd sounded distracted.

Frowning into the mixing bowl, Cassie added more nuts, as well. True, she had Blake's itinerary, but she had thought he would want more contact with his children. Beneath their tough attitudes, she sensed, they were crying out for attention. Not ready yet to take that attention from her, the boys clung to their rebellious ways.

Hearing the back door open, Cassie smiled at David John and the twins. Though certainly not yet friends, the three had come to an uneasy alliance. Since the older kids got home later, they tolerated one another in the early afternoons.

"Whatcha making, Mama?" David John asked, climbing on a tall bar stool to watch.

"Cookies...chocolate chip."

The twins edged a bit closer. She knew it was their favorite. She'd also discovered that they usually filled up on candy and chips. By stocking up on fruit, yogurt and healthier snacks, she was trying to subtly change their habits.

"Make you guys a deal. Do your homework at the table in here, and when you're finished we'll have hot cookies."

Todd licked his lips in anticipation, but Mark frowned. "I'm hungry *now*."

She tossed him an apple. "That should hold you."

He still looked disgruntled, but in a moment she noticed that he was biting into the fruit. While she knew David John would complete his homework, whether in the kitchen or in his room, the twins weren't as dependable. Left to their own devices, they would watch TV in their rooms and then mumble evasively about their homework.

Backpacks hit the breakfast room table, and the top was quickly covered with books and papers as they settled in to work. And in a short while, they were busily finishing homework, spurred on by the aroma of fragrant cookies filling the air.

The twins might be sophisticated city kids, but a chocolate chip cookie was a pretty effective equalizer. They all munched contentedly, matching milk mustaches decorating their upper lips.

Cassie had been horrified to learn that the Matthews children drank soda instead of milk. She wondered why all their teeth hadn't fallen out. There had been plenty of grumbling at first, but nothing washed down a freshly baked cookie like a glass of milk.

"I'm making Chinese food tonight," Cassie told the boys as they finished the snack. "It's a special recipe."

"We have frozen egg rolls," Mark told her.

Cassie put another tray of cookies into the oven. "They aren't quite the same as homemade."

Todd shrugged. "And China Platter delivers."

David John grinned at her. "Wait'll they taste yours. They won't want any more dumb frozen stuff."

Cassie rumpled his white-blond hair. "Thanks, pal."

By evening, the house simmered with the delicate scent of wonton soup and chow mein. Deciding to be festive, Cassie donned a silk blouse that dipped over her shoulders, one she'd purchased on her first shopping excursion in the city. She brushed her long hair into a smooth wave and disregarded her usual barrette.

A refreshing breeze lifted the curtains at the window, sending in the sweet smell of orange blossoms. Cassie hummed as she checked the table, leaning over to light the candles.

The humming masked the sound of the door opening and Blake's startled exclamation when he saw her.

The flare of the match illuminated her flawless skin, casting her delicate features in pleasing relief. As she bent over, the low neckline of her blouse revealed intriguing curves Blake hadn't known she possessed. His gaze roamed over her, taking in the effect of the blouse that skimmed over her shoulders, baring just enough skin to make him want to see more.

Her hair was different somehow, too. In the candlelight, it resembled burnished wheat as it swung unhindered over her shoulder. Long eyelashes shadowed her cheeks as she studied the table, straightening the silverware, then rearranging two of the platters. Had she changed that much? Or had he simply failed to see her before?

He stepped closer, and she looked up, surprise filling her smoke-colored eyes. One hand flew to the delicate hollow of her throat. "I...I didn't expect you."

"I do live here," he reminded her gently, watching the confusion play over her face. "And I decided to come home a day early."

"The boys will be glad you're back. And your timing's perfect. We were about to sit down to dinner."

She didn't even stumble over the word, he noticed. Before, she'd always started to call the meal *supper*. Another change.

Gulliver's toenails clicked over the tile floor as the dog rushed to greet him. While he hadn't wanted them to bring the large animal, Blake had to admit that Gulliver was growing on him, especially after a two-week break from the dog.

"He likes you," Cassie commented softly. "And he's pretty picky."

That was it. The softness. Whenever he thought of Cassie, it had been entwined with the image of steel, a backbone that wouldn't buckle under a ton of pressure. It hadn't occurred to him that she could be soft, too.

She glanced at him, with a curious look that unsettled him. Reflexively he held up his briefcase and garment bag. "I'll put these away and be ready in a few minutes."

She nodded. "There's no hurry. It's not the kind of meal that's timed down to the second. It'll stay warm till you're ready."

"Uh-huh." Backing up, he nearly toppled Katherine Ann as she came into the kitchen.

She smiled, in a shy imitation of her mother. "Hello, Mr. Matthews. I'm glad you're home."

"I am, too," he replied, pushing open the swinging door.

It was jet lag, he decided. That accounted for the imagined changes in Cassie. He was sure that by the time he returned to the breakfast room, everything would be back to normal.

But it wasn't. Not only were his children not close to gnawing each other to bits, but Cassie still looked different. While the kids were hardly acting like the Waltons, they were being civil. And apparently they had grudgingly accepted the dinner ritual.

Although the meal was delicious, he barely tasted it. Instead, he watched Cassie. How had he managed not to notice until now that she was a woman? He supposed that somewhere in his brain he'd cataloged that fact. After all, she couldn't be a mother without being a woman.

But there were women. And there were women.

Somehow, while he was out of the country, she'd slipped from one category to the other.

The tight, pinched expression, along with the worry that had prompted it, was gone from her face, he realized, making her look younger, more vibrant. Now she certainly didn't look old enough to have teenage children. Blake watched her quiet competence, the ease with which she presided over the meal, drawing out each of the children. Yet he wondered about the slight flush of her skin, the brightness of her eyes.

And the kids were cleaning their plates, he noticed. No requests for burgers or pizza this time. And they dug into the fruit-filled dessert with equal enthusiasm. Another one of Cassie's transformations?

Cassie turned to Jimmy Ray. "I haven't had a chance to ask you. How'd the computer project go?"

"Pretty good, Mama. It's going to be in the science fair."

Cassie clapped her hands together. "That's wonderful. And to think you were more than a year behind the other kids in the class!"

Blake thought it was nothing less than amazing. He wished his own executives possessed as much drive as this teenager.

Kevin snorted. "Yeah, but if you're in the science fair, you have to waste a whole Saturday sitting around with a bunch of science geeks."

Blake cleared his throat. This was treacherous territory. While he wanted to instill motivation in his kids, he didn't want them to resent being compared to the Hawkins children. At the same time, he didn't want Jimmy Ray's accomplishment to be ridiculed. "What's fascinating to one person can be boring to another. Jimmy Ray might not like spending a day at the beach. He might prefer something else...." Blake searched his mind. "Like a day at the museum."

Both Kevin and Jimmy Ray looked at him as though he'd lost his mind.

"That was just an example," Blake finished hurriedly, realizing he was sinking rapidly. Avoiding their stares, he made the mistake of looking at Cassie instead. And found himself feeling even more unsettled.

A tinge of pink still dusted Cassie's cheeks, and her tongue flicked to one corner of her mouth. Why hadn't he noticed before how full her lips were? Or their deep rose color, without benefit of lipstick?

She glanced up at him, and he saw the silver of her eyes deepen before she reached for the pitcher of tea, refilling glasses. He wondered what had prompted her sudden solicitousness. Competence, or nerves?

"Mr. Matthews is right. You boys both have things to be proud of. Kevin, did you tell your father what you made on your English assignment?"

Kevin mumbled something unintelligible.

Blake watched as Kevin uncharacteristically kept his gaze directed at his plate. This was his quick-comeback kid, without one shy bone in his body. "I didn't hear you, Kevin."

"I made a 'B,' okay?" he responded defiantly.

Considering that his average generally hovered between D and F, it was remarkable. More treacherous ground. Blake didn't want to unseat his progress with too much false-sounding enthusiasm.

"Sounds good to me," he replied mildly. "Is this unit something you're interested in?"

"Sort of."

Blake wondered if digging for gold was as difficult as this. "What was it?"

"A book report."

Which usually earned Kevin a zero, since he hated to read.

"Must have been an interesting book," Blake said carefully.

"It was okay. I'm done eating. I need to meet the guys."

"What do you have planned for the evening?" Cassie asked Kevin as she spooned more fruit into the twins' dishes.

"Just hanging out at Brian's, videos and stuff."

Blake watched in silent amazement as the exchange continued. Kevin never gave him any details. In fact, he was usually hard-pressed to get him to answer at all.

"Is all your homework done?" Cassie asked. "You have a math test Friday."

"Yeah. It's done." Kevin was scooting his chair backward, scraping it against the tile floor. "I gotta go. The guys are waiting."

"If your father says it's all right…"

Kevin looked imploringly at his father. "Dad?"

Clearing his throat, Blake found his voice, realizing he had a part in this after all. "Sounds okay."

Kevin popped up, not waiting for any second thoughts, grabbing his plate and heading toward the kitchen.

"Be home at nine," Cassie cautioned him.

"Yeah, yeah. Later."

The twins quickly finished their fruit and, along with David John, jumped up, pushing their chairs back noisily.

"Mark, you didn't finish your milk."

"I'm Todd," he replied shortly, ignoring the glass.

"No, you're not. And you usually drink all your milk, Mark. You feeling okay?"

"Yeah, I'm just full." He squinted at Cassie. "You sure I'm Mark?"

"Very sure."

He shrugged his shoulders as he sent his identical twin an exasperated glance.

Blake stared between Cassie and the twins. None of the other housekeepers had managed to tell them apart after months of being with them. "You can already tell Mark and Todd apart?"

She glanced at him quizzically. "Of course." Then she turned her gaze on D.J. and the twins, who were scurrying away. "And what are you three up to?"

"We're making something," David John confided, just as Mark elbowed him sharply.

"Come on, D.J., we gotta ditch," Todd inserted.

Cassie's eyebrows rose, but she didn't question them. "Take your plates into the kitchen."

Turning back to the table, they obliged, disappearing quickly.

"D.J.?" Blake questioned.

"His new identity," Cassie replied with an ironic twist of her lips. "Says David John is a Texas name, and he's an L.A. *dude* now."

Blake couldn't resist a chuckle.

Jimmy Ray and Katherine Ann were rising, as well, automatically gathering their plates, along with the serving dishes. They trooped into the kitchen, and then footsteps clattered up the back staircase. In an instant, the crowded table had emptied, leaving only a twosome.

The candlelight still flickered between them, and the scent of orange blossoms from the open window wafted through the air.

"Well…" Cassie began.

"So…" Blake said at the same time.

Laughing awkwardly, then letting that fade into silence, they glanced at one another, then away. Cassie folded and refolded her napkin, then ran her fingers up the glass, drawing swirls in the condensation that beaded its exterior.

"The children seem to have taken to you," Blake said finally, wondering why he, too, had suddenly lost his usually glib tongue.

Cassie shrugged, not drawing her hand away from the glass. "I'm not sure I'd say that. We're still getting used to one another."

"It usually takes an act of Congress to pry anything out of Kevin, but you know about his schoolwork, where he's going."

Cassie glanced at him in surprise. "I don't believe in not knowing where my kids are. Kevin pointed out that he wasn't *my* kid. So, I told him if he didn't tell me, I'd follow him. Everywhere he went, I promised to be his shadow. I guess he thought that could be pretty embarrassing, especially in front of his friends."

Blake tried not to let cynical amusement color his tone. "I guess it would be, at that. How'd you come up with that plan? It would never have occurred to me."

"I've been taking care of my children on my own for a long time now. I've gotta be smarter than them, or they could run over me. Especially boys. They tend to listen to a man more than a woman. Knowing I didn't have a man around, I couldn't let go of my control. Since Kevin wasn't already in my control, I had to be a little more ingenious."

Her eyes had that tough fierceness in them again. Still, they resembled smoke in the diffused light. Blake lifted his glass, saluting her. "However you managed it, I'm glad. You might have noticed that the boys are headstrong."

She pursed her lips as her eyes widened a fr⸺
you could say that."

"You thinking I'm the master of understatement?" he asked, unable to repress a grin.

A smile tugged at her full lips, and she tossed her head back, allowing the candlelight to warm the burnished wheat of her hair. "So you're not convinced that your children are perfect?"

"Far from it. Otherwise I wouldn't have needed you."

Another silent moment lumbered between them. He hadn't meant to phrase the words quite that way. Need was a powerful emotion, one he hadn't allowed himself for a long time.

"My children are glad you needed a nanny. The city's like another world to them," she answered softly.

"What about you, Cassie? Is it another world to you, as well?"

She played with the glass again, circling the beads of water with her fingers. "It *is* different. I used to think about exploring new places."

"Why'd you stop?"

Her face tightened, driving away the softness. "I grew up," she replied shortly in a brisk voice. She rose in a sudden movement. "I need to get this cleared away."

"That's Maria's job."

"Where I come from, everyone pitches in. I don't expect anyone to do what I won't."

Puzzled, he wondered at the change in her. All the softness was gone. Yet she still looked different. Too different for comfort.

"But I'm spending most of my time with the kids," she continued. "They're not lacking for attention. It's just that I can't stand leaving a mess for Maria." She held out a hand to stop an expected protest. "And, yes, I know it's her job, but that's just how I am. You probably know that by now, though. And I can't change my spots or—"

"I give in," he managed to squeeze in. "Didn't mean to start another speech."

She flushed, suddenly embarrassed. "I'm rattling on again, aren't I?"

He shrugged. "I wouldn't want to go after those spots of

Cassie wished she possessed just a shred of decorum. But around him, she seemed to lose what little she had. Deliberately, she made herself be brief. "Right."

The back door opened suddenly, surprising them, since the kids were all in the house. Cassie watched as a tall, beautiful woman swept inside, heading directly for Blake. In an instant, she crossed the room and launched herself into his arms.

Cassie felt every inch the country hick as the elegant, stylish woman attached herself to Blake, kissing his cheek as a silvery laugh erupted from sensuous lips. "Oh, darling. This European jaunt's taken its toll on you. You seem positively *domestic.*"

Blake gently disengaged himself. "I wasn't expecting you, Daphne."

She raised dark, skillfully arched brows. "Of course not, it's one of my talents—delivering the unexpected." Her dark gaze flickered toward Cassie and rested on her briefly, the quick look assessing, then dismissing.

Feeling light-years away in sophistication, Cassie wished she could fade quietly into the background. But Blake brought her forward instead.

"Daphne, this is the boys' new nanny, Cassie Hawkins."

Cassie automatically stretched out her hand.

"Cassie, this is my sister-in-law, Daphne Kerara."

Daphne didn't completely ignore Cassie's outstretched hand, but instead of taking it, she offered a limp semiwave. Cassie lowered her hand, trying to disguise her awkwardness with an overly bright smile. "Glad to meet you, Mrs. Kerara."

"Ms.," Daphne replied. "No attachment implied or taken, right, Blake?"

"She's between divorces," Blake offered, for Cassie's benefit. "But I imagine she's got her eyes set on some poor, unsuspecting slob."

Looking between them, it took only a few seconds for Cassie to guess just who that unsuspecting slob was. She managed to smile, in spite of the unreasonable pain that discovery caused. She directed her words at Daphne. "I'm divorced myself. I guess we have something in common."

A look of disbelieving distaste crossed Daphne's perfect features. "Um."

"Cassie's from Texas," Blake offered.

"I didn't think the accent sounded local," Daphne replied, her tone indicating barely concealed disdain.

Cassie's smile dimmed a few watts.

"Cassie has three kids of her own, two boys and a girl," Blake inserted in the awkward pause.

"Guess you need to be getting home to them," Daphne replied, her eyes still measuring Cassie—obviously an automatic predator's gesture.

"They live here...with me," she answered quietly.

"You mean *six* kids live here now?" Daphne turned her disbelieving gaze on Blake. "Are you crazy? Three was too many!"

A slight tic in Blake's jaw was the only indication of how her tactless words affected him. "Only in your opinion. Elizabeth and I were thrilled that the two planned babies turned into three."

"My sister, bless her, had some unusual likes and dislikes." Daphne's glance turned coy as she directed it at Blake. "Of course, some of her choices were first-rate."

Cassie felt as though she were watching a very wily cat stalking a hapless canary.

Blake laughed. "You're only saying that because you know I'm safe. With three kids, I'm not on your eligible list."

"There's always a prep school waiting in the wings," Daphne replied.

Blake's easy grin tightened slightly. "And you know that's not an option. Besides, I'm mere family. You're hunting big game this time."

Daphne scarcely hesitated before issuing another silvery laugh. "You know me too well, darling." She turned a pointed glance on Cassie. "But I did have some things to discuss with you."

Taking the weighty, obvious hint, Cassie stepped toward the doorway. "If you'll excuse me—"

"That's all right, Cassie. I don't think you finished what you wanted to do in here." Blake's gaze rested on the still-cluttered table she had insisted on clearing. "We'll go into my office."

"Oh, let's make it the den," Daphne suggested in her throaty voice. "It's so much…cozier."

Watching the woman all but glue herself to Blake's side, Cassie couldn't help comparing her to the image she'd formed of Blake's deceased wife. Daphne had shattered that image completely.

Mark skidded down the stairs. "We need some glue."

Automatically she turned to the pantry and reached inside. "Just don't glue anything you're not supposed to."

"Yeah." He reached for the white tube she held out.

But Cassie didn't release it immediately. "Your aunt Daphne's here. I imagine you and your brothers will want to visit with her."

Mark pulled a disgruntled face. "How come?"

Surprised, she stared at him. "Well, because she's your aunt."

"So?"

Cassie couldn't understand his reaction. "She's your mother's sister. I thought you'd—"

"She's nothing like Mom. She doesn't even like us."

"Oh, I'm sure you can't mean that," Cassie replied, automatically reaching out to smooth his troubled brow.

Mark jerked back a bit, and Cassie let her hand fall away, knowing he wasn't ready yet for a stand-in parent.

"Daphne only comes here to see Dad. She thinks we're in the way."

Realizing that Daphne had known Blake was in Europe, yet hadn't stopped in to visit her nephews, Cassie guessed that Mark might be right. Knowing better than to argue a point she wasn't sure of, Cassie handed him the bottle of glue. "Well, your dad certainly doesn't feel that way about you guys."

"Yeah, I guess. He's busy at work a lot, but he can't help that." His look was more than a touch defensive.

Cassie felt an unexpected tugging. Despite his brave front, Mark needed reassurance that he was wanted by his father. "That's why he hired me, Mark. He hates that he can't be with

you and your brothers more, and he wants to make sure that
you have someone around who cares about you.''

His look was suspicious. ''Why should you care?''

She took a deep breath. ''It's just who I am, I guess. Just
like how I know you're Mark and not Todd. I know you
haven't had a lot of time to get to know me, but this is more
than just a job to me. It's a new opportunity for my kids, too,
something that makes them happy. We're doing each other a
favor. I can be around when your Dad can't, and we get to be
part of your family.''

Mark shrugged, and she could sense his internal struggle.
''Yeah, well, I gotta get back with the glue.''

''Sure. You want to take some cookies with you? For you
and the other guys?''

''Yeah, I guess so.'' But despite a show of disinterest, he
trailed her to the counter and accepted the plate of homemade
cookies.

She made one final effort. ''Will you tell Todd that your
aunt is here?''

Mark headed toward the stairs. ''He won't care, either.''

Even though she knew that Maria would clean the kitchen
at the end of the evening, Cassie rinsed the dishes and stacked
them in the dishwasher. Then, taking nearly another hour, she
straightened and cleaned the kitchen, needing the familiar sense
of order. It had surprised her to feel an unexpected pang of
jealousy when she saw Daphne wrap herself around Blake.

She'd thought her reactions to him earlier were the result of
the length of time that had passed since she had any interaction
with a man. She hadn't counted on there being something more
to those feelings. Certainly not jealousy, or the emotions that
prompted it.

She glanced longingly out the window at the huge swimming
pool, wishing she could diffuse some of her sudden tension by
swimming endless laps. Even if she had a decent suit, she
wouldn't put it on with Daphne around. She felt inferior
enough without putting herself on display for more condescen-
sion.

Hearing adult voices, Cassie pulled her apron off, planning

to disappear up the stairs and avoid another encounter. But the door opened just as she reached the first step.

"Oh, if it isn't Mary Poppins," Daphne commented, in that sultry voice of hers.

Cassie felt her backbone stiffening. She might be an employee in this house, but she didn't intend to be treated like an eighteenth-century scullery maid.

"Glad you're still here," Blake said before she could reply. "You can tell Daphne how well we're all getting on."

Briefly Cassie met his eyes and saw him signal silently for her agreement. She paused for only a moment. "The boys are quite content."

"I'm only concerned about their welfare," Daphne replied, an obvious challenge lurking beneath the innocent words.

So much that you didn't call once when their father was out of the country, Cassie thought to herself, seeing through Daphne's barely veiled machinations.

"That's why Cassie's here—to provide the right kind of care."

Daphne tapped perfect French-manicured nails on the counter. "I really should see more of them."

With a sinking feeling, Cassie guessed that the woman intended to appear often, staking a claim to her late sister's husband.

Blake took Daphne's elbow. "Thanks for your concern. And for stopping by. Sorry I don't have more time, but—"

"I know. Business calls. But you have to admit, it doesn't have a voice like mine."

"No argument there." He kissed her cheek, and she lingered in the doorway.

"Good night, Ms. Kerara," Cassie added.

The other woman barely glanced her direction. "Yes. Good night." Daphne looked as though she desperately wanted to stay. Instead, she sidled her slinky body out the door, deliberately leaving a provocative image behind.

Stepping down from the landing, Cassie reached for the apron she'd hastily tossed on the counter, intending to fold it. "I'm finished in here. I'll let you get to your work."

"Not tonight."

"But you said—"

"Daphne's rather insistent. A white lie's more diplomatic than the truth."

"Which is?"

"She's a very wearing person."

Cassie chose her words carefully. "Then she's not that much like your wife was?"

Blake laughed—a hearty disbelieving sound. "They couldn't be more different. Daphne was several years older than Elizabeth, the child of their father's first wife—the original dragon lady. Elizabeth was born when their father was older and apparently wiser. And Elizabeth's mother had the same sweet quality she passed on to her daughter. So Elizabeth had better odds of turning out right."

"Were the sisters close?"

"In her own strange way, Daphne was very fond of Elizabeth. Even though she resented her father taking a second wife, Daphne liked having a younger sister who idolized her." He smiled wryly. "You might have guessed that she's not averse to a little goddess worship."

"Or a lot."

"So you did notice."

Cassie placed the folded apron is a drawer. "Hard to miss. But I shouldn't be criticizing your family."

"With a moving target between your sights, it's hard to not take a shot."

"Still...I won't do it again. Next time she's here, I'll be especially gracious."

Blake laughed. "Don't hold your breath. She drops in about as often as Santa Claus and the Easter Bunny. Occasionally the tooth fairy, as well."

Cassie kept her opinion to herself. From the message that had flashed in Daphne's eyes, she suspected that the other woman had decided it was time to move in for the kill. And, unprepared and unsuspecting, Blake was ripe for the taking.

Chapter Six

Cassie parked the sporty candy-apple-red Firebird in the garage, next to the other cars. Although she'd originally protested the practicality of the vehicle Blake had put at her disposal, she secretly loved the flashy, fast-moving car. It was easy to pretend that, behind the wheel, she shed a decade of both age and responsibility.

Although initially terrified of the crowded, bustling city, she was growing to like it. At first she'd felt as though she'd been dropped inside an anthill that had been stirred with a big stick. She'd seen more people the first week in L.A. than she had in her entire lifetime. But she was beginning to appreciate the city's diversity, and its anonymity. Twin Corners hadn't offered either.

Nor had her hometown possessed a fraction of the shopping L.A. did. Although her practical side wouldn't allow her to waste money foolishly, she absorbed the sights and the nuances of the fashion-conscious. Along the way, she was developing an inner sense of style that was subtly changing her appearance, mannerisms, even her speech.

And the past month, while Blake remained in L.A. instead of leaving the country again, she'd also given a lot of thought to the ridiculous attraction she was developing for him. Telling herself in no uncertain terms that it was inappropriate, and that she was going to slam the door shut on those thoughts, she still found her gaze wandering toward him. And she'd taken far too much interest in his social life. She knew a handsome, sophisticated man like Blake must have women hanging all over him, yet she wondered. And Daphne hadn't left her thoughts, especially since she'd had dinner with Blake twice in the past few weeks.

With an instinct that was purely feminine, Cassie knew the other woman resented her presence, especially since she'd discovered the proximity of Cassie's and Blake's bedrooms. Although she'd claimed to have wandered into Cassie's bedroom by mistake, it was difficult to believe that Daphne's every move wasn't calculated. Especially when feline anger glowed in her gorgeous eyes.

Inordinately pleased to have unsettled such a formidable woman, Cassie couldn't help wondering what it would take to completely intimidate her. She also couldn't help wondering whether it bothered Blake to sleep in the bedroom across the hall from hers. Initially entranced by the beautiful suite, she hadn't realized that his bedroom was so close to her own. Now that fact was never far from her thoughts. And she couldn't help thinking about why he'd assigned her the suite of rooms directly across from his. The wing was distinctly set apart from the other bedrooms, and that made it seem private. Almost too private.

Glancing at her watch, Cassie saw that she had some time before David John and the twins would be home. *D.J.*, she reminded herself, knowing how important it was for him to establish his new L.A. identity. Since she already had the children's afternoon snack prepared, she could steal a few moments for herself.

Cassie stopped first in Katherine Ann's room to drop off the largest shopping bag. The usually easy-going Katherine Ann had dug in her heels about getting new school clothes. Although shorts and T-shirts were a fairly universal wardrobe-stretcher, there were other things she needed to update her rural clothing to the big-city look. And, she'd informed her mother, she didn't want to look like a geek. And Cassie could only agree. It was difficult enough to be a teenager. Add relocation, and that upped the stakes. Add coming from Twin Corners to

L.A., and those stakes zoomed to a mathematical equation beyond her expertise.

Cassie smiled as she deposited the bag on the pretty makeup table by the window. For all Katherine Ann's protests that she wasn't influenced by anything else in the new city culture, she'd accumulated some makeup on their past shopping excursions. It wouldn't be long before her little bird dusted off her plumage and started to fly.

Cassie continued to smile as she entered her own room. Opening the shopping bag, Cassie withdrew the small bit of material. While the most conservative bathing suit she could find, it still seemed skimpy to her. But she was dying to try the pool. She'd always loved to swim, if only in the neighbor's pond, and had been drawn from the start to the pristine, oversize pool. While her children had all quickly tried the pool and now used it regularly, she'd held back.

But today she'd seen the swimsuit sale. Her own faded, stretched-out suit had been thrown away when she packed. She'd regretted its loss ever since she first spotted the pool. Today, on an impulse, she'd bought the new suit, after checking out every style on the rack, some of which had her small-town eyes nearly bugging out. And although the suit wasn't as conservative as she would have liked, she had to admit that it was the most stunning one she'd ever owned.

Deceptively simple, it had a unique cut that made it stand out from the rest. Her entire back was exposed, as the suit dipped precariously low, then hugged her curves. Rather than the expected black or hot flash of color, this suit was white.

Anxious to try the pool, Cassie quickly shed her clothes, then stepped into the suit. Not wanting to risk a look into the mirror, she shrugged on the terry cover-up the persuasive saleswoman had talked her into. Grabbing a towel from the bathroom, she bounced down the stairs, feeling like a kid let out of school for the summer.

She slipped out the French doors and approached the pool. The water sparkled invitingly, and Cassie didn't need a second invitation. She dived in, then fell easily into a pattern of laps. If things had been different in high school, she could have stayed on the swim team. Now, it was sheer bliss to have a pool right in the backyard. Her strokes cut the water smoothly with the precision she'd once learned, then perfected.

After a respectable distance, she felt invigorated, rather than winded. Apparently, chasing the children had kept her in better shape than she realized. Glancing at the three staggered diving boards, Cassie felt their lure. At one time, she'd been torn between swimming and diving, not certain which one to concentrate on. She had leaned toward diving, and had hoped to win a scholarship with her skill, but college was another dream that had bitten the dust.

Shaking away unpleasant memories, Cassie started first with the low board. Executing a flawless dive, she felt a resurgence of confidence. She duplicated her effort on the medium-level board and then decided to tackle the high dive.

Tie pulled askew, jacket flung over one shoulder, briefcase in hand, Blake took a shortcut from the garage through the terrace that surrounded the pool. As he glanced upward, his gaze came to a halt on Cassie.

Like a sleek white column, she dominated the highest diving stand. Her long blond hair was skimmed backward, accenting her lovely facial structure. Her head was erect, lowered only enough so that she could see the end of the board. A body that he had never dreamed she possessed was posed in a classical form. Had she purposely hidden it behind loose-fitting T-shirts and jeans? Considering how dry his mouth suddenly was, it had probably been a wise move.

Realizing she planned to dive, he opened his mouth to shout a warning. The high platform was only for experienced divers. A novice like Cassie could get seriously hurt. But before he could yell, she stepped, sprang, then arched into an unbelievable curve followed by a series of complicated moves before cleanly entering the water, scarcely leaving a ripple as she executed a flawless entry.

The warning forgotten, Blake felt his mouth hang open. Her dive had been a flowing cascade of seemingly effortless elegance and grace. Surfacing, she deftly pulled herself from the pool and walked toward the board again.

Feeling like a voyeur, Blake watched every move, from her deceptively long legs to the generous cleavage her suit revealed. Water beaded and skimmed over her honey-colored, luminous skin. She slicked back her generous length of hair, and his gaze dwelled on the slope of her beautiful shoulders and the sweep of her bared back.

She climbed the ladder quickly, legs that stretched from here to Dallas moving her quickly. Then she executed another complicated dive. He knew the degree of difficulty in her dives. Where had this unexpected talent sprung from?

Remembering where she'd surfaced before, he dropped his briefcase and jacket, then moved quickly to that spot at poolside. When her head broke through the water and she reached out to the edge to pull herself up, he grasped her hand. Surprise ricocheted across her face and then rippled in the sudden tension of her body as she gracefully rose from the pool, the water sluicing over her, accenting each curve.

"What…? When…?" she began, obviously ill at ease.

Amused, Blake didn't release her hand, instead feasting on the closeup view. "At a loss for words? That's not like you, Cassie."

"I thought you were at work."

"Just one of my periodic raids to check on the staff," he replied.

"This is my free time," she said, fumbling. "I have the boys' snacks all ready and Albert won't have them back from school for nearly an hour, and dinner is planned. I went to the market, so everything's fresh. And—"

He held up one hand. "I was kidding. I'm home because I just finished a killer deal and I need to relax. Thought I'd get in a few laps."

She gestured nervously toward the pool, and he realized she was vastly uncomfortable. "The pool's all yours. I was ready to get out, anyway. I should be changing so that I'll be ready when the boys get home." She inched backward as she spoke.

Blake suspected she was ready to turn and flee. "You just said it'll be almost an hour until they get home."

"But—"

"And you also said their snack's ready. Go ahead and swim. I'll change in the cabana and join you."

"But—"

"Don't want to disappoint the boss, do you?"

Her face clouded. "Well, no. But—"

"Then don't. Won't take me a minute to change."

She tried again. "I'm sure you'd rather swim alone."

"I can swim alone anytime. I'd rather not right now."

Her sigh echoed like the ripples cresting the pool. "If you say so."

"I do." Purposely brisk, he didn't allow her any reprieve as he changed quickly into the suit he kept in the cabana, then returned to her side. "Do you have any more professional dives in your bag of tricks?"

She shuffled her feet uneasily. "It's just something I play at."

"Not with *your* form," he replied bluntly, wondering why she didn't want to talk about her diving. "I'd like to see another dive."

She nodded, but this time her legs didn't travel as swiftly up the ladder. Yet, once in position, she fell into the concentration that was crucial. And once again, she executed a flawless, complicated dive. To join her, Blake dived in from the side of the pool, waiting where he expected her to surface.

To his surprise, her face bobbed up across the pool from him. She certainly was a quick study. Already on to his tricks, she wasn't easily fooled. And she hadn't wanted to surface in his grasp.

She was smart, and obviously talented, and, to his amazement, she had a body most of the women in Beverly Hills would kill for. And hers wasn't the result of a clever plastic surgeon. Yet she seemed uneasy about the lot of it. He wondered why.

Lazily he swam toward her, his strokes broad and easy. He saw the trepidation in her expression and decided to push her boundaries, to see what lay behind the carefully maintained front.

Diving beneath the water, he grabbed for her leg. But she'd

already swum away. Apparently anticipating his move, she'd countered first. She *was* a clever girl.

Blake flipped onto his back, slowly backstroking away from Cassie. Out of the corner of his eye, he could see Cassie watching him suspiciously. Good—he'd unsettled *her*.

It was clear that she was a woman of many hidden talents. His gaze roamed over her as she stepped from the pool and approached the mid-level diving platform. Many, many hidden talents.

He wondered if all the men in Twin Corners had been blind. *You didn't notice either,* a mocking voice reminded him.

But he was noticing now.

Her dive was once again clean and flawless. But he didn't race to a spot where he thought she might surface. Instead, he continued his lazy backpedaling motion. It was clear from her expression that she expected a surprise attack. Some of the tension faded from her rigid posture.

"You up to some distance?" he called out.

Her hands reached up to slick back her hair. "Sure."

"What's your handicap?"

Her grin flashed unexpectedly. "Three kids, and as many extra years."

"Feel free to use your cane or walker," he replied, instantly liking this side of her.

"I'd opt for a wheelchair, but it might weigh me down," she replied saucily.

"Or rust out before I get winded."

"Think you're pretty hot stuff, don't you?"

He lifted one shoulder negligently. "Just facing facts."

"Then face this. I'm out of practice, but I'll take you on even. No head starts, no handicaps."

"Remind me not to take you to the track. You'd lose your shirt." The words were barely past his lips when he envisioned just such an event. And the picture in his mind made his mouth go suddenly dry.

She tossed her head back. "Unless you're afraid to take me on..."

"This, woman, is war."

"You picked a soggy battlefield," she volleyed back.

"And you picked the wrong opponent." He thought of the swimming medals from high school and college that were tucked into one of his drawers. It wasn't the only sport he'd excelled at, but it was one he'd continued long after school.

"Maybe, maybe not," she mumbled in response, taking her position next to him.

"Two hundred yards?" he questioned, slipping into swimmer's vernacular, measuring the pool in distance rather than in laps.

"Make it five hundred," she replied, already settling into a starting position for the twenty laps.

They both started quickly and efficiently, but she had the initial advantage, using an effective grab start. Despite Blake's superior strength, they were evenly matched. Even though Cassie no longer had access to a regulation pool, she swam regularly in the pond. Hitting the wall for fast touch turns came back to her as though she'd never left the sport.

But it wasn't until the last two laps that Cassie began to suspect that Blake was holding back. When they arrived at the edge of the pool nose-to-nose at the end of the distance, she was sure of it. She wasn't sure whether to be flattered by his gentlemanly gesture, or irritated.

Choosing to escape rather than to decide, she grabbed the edge and vaulted upward. But she didn't count on Blake's immediate response. In a flash, he grabbed her leg, pulling her back into the pool. Off balance, she all but landed in his arms. A fleeting but intense sensation of heat and muscle unbalanced her insides, as well.

Cassie felt as weak as though she'd just completed a marathon, instead of five hundred easy yards. Meeting Blake's eyes, she saw that his teasing glint had disappeared, replaced by a darker, more intense emotion. She intended to distance herself, to push away. Instead, she lingered in the circle of his arms.

Close up, she could see the clean, strong angles of his face, the dark shadow of his jaw, the fan of laugh lines near his eyes, and lips full enough to be sensuous. Sensuous enough to be dangerous.

For a moment, she forgot that she was in a pool. The sensation of floating was so strong, she couldn't be sure whether it was physical or emotional. And still she didn't move.

Neither did he.

Their eyes met again, and he broke the stillness, edging toward her, his gaze focused on her mouth, his head tilted toward hers.

"Mama!" D.J. shouted on the run.

"Hey, Dad!" Todd yelled in surprise. "What're you doing home?"

"Yeah," Mark chimed in, running with his twin to grab a suit from one of the cabanas.

Cassie scrabbled for and then found her voice. "What are you doing home from school so early?"

D.J.'s muffled voice emerged from the cabana. "It's not so early. We only got out thirty minutes ahead of time. It was teacher prep day."

Having moved away from Blake, Cassie reached upward, grasping the edge, intending to escape. But D.J. emerged at that moment, running toward the pool.

"Don't run," Cassie warned him.

He slowed down, then jumped in beside her, making a huge splash. The twins weren't far behind. The seeming intimacy of the pool was transformed instantly into a noisy, splashing crowd. The twins took the opportunity to gang up on their father, double-teaming him, trying to dunk him. D.J. joined the twins, and the three boys resembled overeager puppies as they finally dunked Blake. Sputtering effectively, he managed to look outmatched.

Blake took their teasing good-naturedly, in turn yanking each of them under briefly, watching as they emerged laughing and trying to catch him again.

It was a side of Blake that Cassie had never seen before. She had begun to wonder if he ever took much of a role in his children's lives. His main concern seemed to be his business, his attention lavished on its corporate heart. And that business appeared to fulfill all his needs. It was reassuring to see that he had reserved some of his affection for his children.

She wondered where he spent the remainder of that affection, and whether perhaps the lovely Daphne would capture it.

Shaking her head at the unwanted thoughts, Cassie climbed from the pool, unnoticed by the boys, who were splashing nearly as much water on the terrace as remained in the pool.

She turned and looked back, feeling a catch in her throat as she watched David John play with Blake. Her son had never had the opportunity to engage in horseplay such as this. In fact, there'd never been a father figure for him. Her ex-husband had been long gone by the time David John was old enough to want a daddy. And that was the one thing she'd never been able to be for her children. A father.

Cassie took one last glance, her stomach clenching as she realized the path her thoughts had taken. Blake Matthews was her employer. In some ways, he'd been her savior. But under no circumstances could he be anything else. She thought of her children's lives if she had to take away the bright future Blake had offered them. Deliberately she shoved aside the attraction she felt for him. Gritting her teeth, she flashed on the pain of her past, needing that reminder, as well. No, Blake Matthews could never be anything else to her.

Chapter Seven

Blake strolled along the sunny, immaculately maintained sidewalks of Rodeo Drive. Although most people's eyes were on the intriguing exteriors of the famous stores, his gaze was fastened on Cassie. Watching her reactions was far more interesting. And more appealing than the casual see-and-be-seen tactics of many Rodeo Drive regulars.

From the welcoming espresso bar amid the exquisite clothing in Fred Hayman's to the classy yet sterile domain of Chanel, they examined the exclusive, pricey stores. And Cassie hadn't stopped staring. Not since they left the car to be valet-parked at the Beverly Hills mall.

"I didn't know malls had valet parking," she had whispered as the attendant drove away. From that moment, she resembled an inquiring sponge, examining, then absorbing, the sights.

But she hadn't reacted to the lavish display of designer clothing as he'd expected. Most women would have lingered over each rack, but Cassie hadn't. He had planned to buy her whatever pleased her the most, but she hadn't expressed any special interest so far. Not that she was uninterested. But there hadn't been any typical female swooning. Instead, she seemed to be registering the sights and sounds. It was almost as though he could see a silent recorder click on, the reels spinning.

They paused in front of the Escada store, and indulgently he watched as she examined the mannequins.

"Do you like the dress?" he asked.

She nodded, then started to move on.

"Would you like to try it on?"

Surprise flitted over her face, followed quickly by the look he recognized as one she used on the children when they suggested something particularly outrageous. "I think we have better things to do with our time."

Amused, he tried not to let it show. "Such as?"

She held out her hands in a widespread motion. "It's *your* city. I'm sure there's more to it than just fancy stores."

"So there is. You ready to leave Rodeo Drive?"

"More than ready. If we don't hurry, the ransom to get the car back from that fancy valet parking will cost more than a month's mortgage."

The laughter escaped before he could prevent it. "You're priceless, Cassie."

Her voice was dry. "But the parking isn't. Did you see how much they charge for every thirty minutes? That's more than most people in Twin Corners earn an hour at their jobs."

"But the parking in Twin Corners is free," he reminded her, the laughter still lurking in his voice. "Keeps costs down."

"Most people back home wouldn't pay highway robbery so they could park their cars, just for the privilege of shopping at overpriced stores."

"You weren't impressed?"

She shrugged. "It's all flash and splash. Wrapped up in a real pretty package, but still all flash."

Since he privately agreed, Blake could only smile at her observation.

But, seeing his smile, she frowned. "Is this where you go to shop?"

"You can wipe the disapproval off your face. No, it's not. But I thought you'd like it."

"Because most women you know do?" she guessed astutely.

"Something like that. Plus, it's something different, something a lot of people want to see when they come to L.A."

"I like doing lots of touristy things," she admitted. Her smile flashed. "I'm dying to put my feet in the prints at Grauman's Chinese Theater."

"Mann's," he corrected gently. "Change of ownership. We can go there. It's not far from here."

Her face wavered as she consulted her watch. "Kids are still in school, and the younger ones have a den meeting right after."

Blake could still hardly believe she'd talked the twins into joining the Cub Scouts, but despite their grumbling and superior attitude, he suspected they were secretly loving it. "I think Albert can handle getting them there and back."

Still, she hesitated. "Today's a long meeting. They're taking a field trip."

"Even better." He pulled out his cell phone, and in a few moments the matter was handled. "Now the afternoon is free."

"But I don't want to take up your whole day."

"I told you I'd give you a tour. I hadn't planned to wait this long." Blake didn't add that he'd been compelled to spend more time with her. He didn't want to examine why he was so drawn to her, or how he'd found himself daydreaming about Cassie, instead of concentrating on cost projections. He simply knew he had to spend more time with her, away from six pairs of scrutinizing eyes. Today had fallen into his lap—beginning with the unexpected cancellation of a daylong meeting and Cassie's offhand remark that she'd like to see more of L.A. And Blake wasn't regretting a moment of the stolen time.

It didn't take long to retrieve the car, then glide into the perpetually busy streets. Accustomed to the traffic, Blake navigated easily toward Hollywood. Cassie sat upright, enthralled by the sights on Hollywood Boulevard. As they crossed the intersection at Vine, she let out an excited squeal.

"Hollywood and Vine! Can you believe it? Just think. This is where Schwab's drugstore is—where Lana Turner was discovered." She glanced around excitedly, her eyes flicking past the Capitol Records Tower. "Where is Schwab's?"

"It was torn down in the eighties."

She made a moue of disappointment. "How could they tear down a landmark like that?"

"Progress. I hate to burst your bubble, but Lana Turner wasn't discovered at Schwab's."

Cassie glanced at him suspiciously. "Is that what you tell the tourists?"

"Actually, most of the tourists still think she was. Just more Hollywood hype. But then, it's all part of the legend."

"I don't care if it's hokey." Her gaze roved over the shabby yet bustling street. "Can we stop and see the stars on the sidewalk?"

"Sure. There's a parking lot right next to Mann's."

"More valet parking?"

He laughed. "Not here."

As anxious as a child at a playground, Cassie eagerly devoured the sights of the famous hand- and footprints. And as she'd said she would, she placed her feet into the impressions made by the female stars.

Teetering in Marilyn Monroe's footprints, Cassie looked askance at him. "These women must have had awfully tiny feet. All of them. I look like a giant next to them."

Blake gestured toward the small, precise impressions. "Look again."

She cocked her head, studying the prints, still puzzled.

"She was wearing high heels, very high heels. So were the rest of the women. That's why the prints look so small."

Cassie thumped the side of her head. "Of course. With the high arch and the tiny spike heel…" She met his gaze and that smile surfaced again, a flash of pure sunshine. "Thanks for not making me feel like an Amazon."

He couldn't help the sweeping glance that took in her endlessly long legs and deceptively slim figure. She was no Amazon. Having seen her in a swimsuit, he could testify that she could compete with any of the stars she was comparing herself against.

Then she was flitting again, darting over to the slab of concrete with Betty Grable's scrawled signature.

"Look," Cassie practically breathed. "She put her whole legprint in cement. Her million-dollar leg!"

Cassie's total and innocent captivation with things Blake found commonplace continued to charm him. Instead of being disappointed that the glamour of Hollywood Boulevard had grown seedy, she had easily forgiven the changes, thrilled by the stars' walk of fame, then enchanted with the famous theater and its equally famous sidewalk of hand- and footprints. He had expected this degree of excitement at the wealth and extravagance of Rodeo Drive, not at this familiar landmark. But she'd turned the familiar into something that was new again. It had been a long time since he viewed the sights of L.A. with fresh eyes.

When she finally gave up her inspection of the sidewalk, her sigh was heartfelt. "That was wonderful."

When they reached the car he glanced at her, seeing her genuine contentment. "There are as many sides to the city as there are freeways."

"There can't be *that* many," she replied dryly.

After closing her door, he slid into the driver's seat. "We haven't even begun to touch on a fraction of them. For every part of the city you've seen, there are dozens more."

She twisted toward him, her expression both wistful and glowing with anticipation. "Doesn't it excite you to live here, knowing you can find something different every day? That one day never has to be the same as the next?"

This was a surprising side to the woman who'd perfected her mothering and homemaking skills to such an extent that he'd hired her as his own resident expert. "It's not where you live, Cassie." As her eyes fastened on him, he felt an unexpected jolt. "It's who's in your life that's important."

Her mouth formed a questioning O before she glanced away, the flutter of her hands betraying her nervousness. "Home is where the heart is," she replied, the homily spilling easily from her lips, even though he sensed an underlying regret in her words.

Responding to the subtle shift in her mood, Blake impulsively headed the car in a different direction, deciding that the moment called for a quieter destination. It didn't take long to reach the outskirts of Griffith Park. Rising up from the valley flatlands, the park extended over the southern end of the Santa Monica Mountains, a green refuge amid the miles of concrete city. As the road wound upward, Cassie watched the transformation from elegant homes to sudden, unexpected open land.

Bypassing the museum, the theater and the extensive sports facilities, Blake headed directly for the observatory, parking in the uncrowded lot. Together they climbed the winding balcony that flanked the observatory. The outside terrace was uncrowded, nearly empty on the quiet weekday afternoon. When they reached the railing, Cassie paused, her gaze sweeping over the incredible view of the city.

She turned to him enthusiastically. "This is wonderful!" Then she twirled back toward the railing, pointing upward. "Look! It's the Hollywood sign! This is like having the whole city in your hand at one time!" She pivoted again to face him. Her gray eyes turned to a silver flame as the breeze lifted her heavy wheat-colored hair. "This is better than all the stores on Rodeo Drive and the rest of Beverly Hills rolled into one."

How many women would choose a public park over the famed extravagance of Beverly Hills? The simple, fresh beauty that made her stand out on Rodeo Drive suited the wild rush of deodar and Italian cypress that surrounded them.

She whirled around again, her graceful movements a pleasure to watch. "It's like being on top of the world!"

And so it was. Blake could remember sharing that identical feeling as a child. It was as though Cassie had removed his jaded blinders. The last time he had that feeling had been when, newly married, he learned he was about to become a father for the first time. His life and his world had been complete. That had been before he lost Elizabeth. And that sense of completion.

Realizing he was treading too close to those tightly sealed feelings, Blake found himself pulling back. Still enthralled with the magnificent view, Cassie didn't seem to notice.

"You were right. This city does have dozens of sides." She gestured toward the sweeping view spread out in front of them. "Back in Twin Corners, I used to think about all the places I'd never seen. But I never dreamed how different they'd be. And to think there's a whole world out there, and I expect it's all different. I mean, every big city isn't the same, is it?"

He shook his head as her words continued to tumble out in a revealing flow.

"New York, Chicago…they must all be different than L.A. And then there's the rest of the world…London, Tokyo, Paris…" Her voice softened, lingered on the last word. Then she glanced again toward the Hollywood sign, the wealth of the valleys and canyons spread out below it. "It's hard to believe the world's so big."

"This isn't the whole world," he pointed out gently.

"No. That's what I'm getting at. You said this is just one part of L.A., which is just one part of this state, this country." The excitement in her voice was contagious, if naive. "Back in Twin Corners I used to spin my globe and read off all the exotic-sounding names. But I guess I never realized just how much was hidden there under each one. On the globe they're just neatly printed words. But here…" Her arms spread wide again. "It's so magical."

Blake studied her. "I thought you spent your time raising your children and keeping body and soul together."

She flushed suddenly, then paled as her excitement dimmed. When she spoke again, her voice was quiet, subdued, yet a tremulous note crept into her tone. "I was talking about a long time ago, when I was a child. I guess all kids have foolish thoughts and dreams."

Impulsively Blake reached out to touch her arm. "I didn't say they were foolish. People need dreams." He believed that, even though he'd abandoned most of his own when he lost Elizabeth. He hadn't thought about resurrecting those dreams until he met Cassie. Somehow she made him think of new beginnings. It was that sense of discovery that she carried with her as easily as most people in the city toted designer-brand bottled water. He gentled his voice. "You just seemed too busy to have time to worry about much more than your family. We all need dreams."

Her answering smile was tight-lipped. "Maybe. And sometimes those dreams are just a road to trouble. Never mind my woolgathering. As you know, I have a tendency to run on." She laughed at herself, but not kindly. "Guess I'm just being a typical country hick. Saw so many sights, I got carried away.'' She glanced at her watch. ''We'd probably better get going.''

Blake increased the pressure on her arm, unconsciously connecting them. ''I don't know what I've said, but I think I just ruined your day.''

Her expression softened, along with her voice. ''No. I loved it all. Peeking into the Beverly Hills world, knowing it didn't suit me any more than I suited it. Seeing Hollywood, all the things I'd heard about, finding out they were more exciting than I'd imagined.'' She turned slightly toward the view of the city. ''And this. It's wonderful. And you really did take me to the top of the world.'' She met his eyes, and he wondered at the painful resignation he saw there. ''For me, this is the pinnacle. I won't be going to those other places. And if not for you, I wouldn't have seen this. So, I thank you.''

Blake tugged her arm, turning her back to him. ''I never meant to imply that you wouldn't see the rest of the world.''

''But I won't be.'' The dusky fire in her eyes simmered, as though she'd extinguished that flame, obliterating her optimistic excitement, as well. ''I'm not complaining. I've got three wonderful kids, a good job, and a new home. What more could I want?''

The entire world. He sensed it clearly, yet knew somehow he'd stumbled on something she wanted closed off. It was as though she'd posted a No Trespassing sign. He wondered why.

''Cassie, I think you can have anything in the world you set your mind to. Your children are proof of that. How many kids do you know with the same ambition as Jimmy Ray and Katherine Ann? David John will have it, too. A woman who can raise kids like that alone, with no help, can accomplish anything.''

Her smile was wise, too wise. ''My children *are* my ambition. And they will be my accomplishment.''

Despite knowing he'd pulled back himself, unwilling to delve into his own emotions, now he probed hers. ''But what about you, Cassie? Where do you fit in this picture?'' The breeze lifted her hair, teasing golden strands that danced in the sunlight. "What about the things you want?"

"It's not that easy for most of us. Like you said, I've got good kids, I've staked out a tiny part of the world I can call my own. I can't go chasing dreams. They just disappoint you, anyway."

"What hurt you, Cassie?"

Her face closed suddenly, tightly. That No Trespassing sign was back up, thrown firmly in place. He realized it was the second time since he'd known her that she'd closed up so completely. "I'm just a simple country woman. You're reading more to me than there is."

He doubted that. It was becoming increasingly clear there was nothing simple about Cassandra Hawkins. He'd been foolish to ever think so. But he also sensed it was time to back off.

"You're right. The kids will be home soon." Blake didn't want to end Cassie's day on such a downward note, and an unexpected idea struck him. "Why don't we take them somewhere for dinner?"

She glanced at him in surprise. "All of them?"

"I don't always have the time I want to spend with the boys. Why waste it?"

"Then you should take just them. My kids are used to potluck."

"I said we. Our kids live in the same house, go to the same schools. Don't you think we should do some things together? Like going to dinner?"

Something indefinable flickered across her face, then disappeared. "Sure. The kids will like that."

"And you?"

Cassie smiled—not that golden grin, yet a smile. "I'm always game."

BUT WHEN CASSIE SAW the restaurant, she reconsidered her remark. Expecting a burger or pizza joint, she was surprised when instead Blake drove them to a beautiful stucco building. A discreet sign told her that the restaurant was Moroccan. She hoped she wouldn't act like a fool—or, even worse, a country hick—in the unfamiliar surroundings.

Tall, ornate brass doors opened into a fountained courtyard, which was the centerpiece of the lofty marble entrance. Swathed in palms and pastels, it seemed regal, elegant, and utterly foreign. Glimpsing ahead as they were led into a dimly lit room, Cassie began to feel the promise of the mysterious East.

David John leaned close to her. "This is cool, Mom. Just like out of a movie."

Since it looked as though Peter Lorre might emerge from the shadows at any moment, Cassie could only nod in agreement. Was that why Blake had chosen this particular restaurant? To expose her to some of the world she'd told him she would never see?

"It beats the heck out of the Dairy Queen in Twin Corners," Jimmy Ray commented as they neared their table.

A smile hovered over Blake's lips. "So it does."

They sat at their table, all sinking into deep lounging cushions. The waiter, who looked as though he'd stepped from the pages of "Ali Baba and the Forty Thieves," brought them all bowls of warm water, kneeling at the table.

As soon as he withdrew, David John wrinkled his face in distaste. "If this is the soup, we're gonna starve."

Kevin snorted. "You dope. It's to wash your hands in."

Blake intervened tactfully. "It's a Moroccan custom. You'll see there are several more that are different from ours."

Once into the swing of things, the kids greeted each of the seven courses with enthusiasm, even the unfamiliar pigeon and rabbit dishes.

This restaurant was like a jaunt into another world. Gazing at the inlaid mother-of-pearl tables and the hand-painted tiles, listening to the gentle foreign music that surrounded them, she felt as though she'd been treated to a royal Arabian night. A glimpse into the world she'd declared she would never see.

Feeling much like her wide-eyed children, Cassie let herself be swept into this taste of another culture, relishing each moment. When the meal ended and they piled back into the van, she couldn't help feeling a bit disappointed. It was hard to leave the magic.

As Blake pulled into the traffic, Kevin let out a yelp. "Dad, there's the music store. Can we stop?"

"I don't know...."

"Please, Dad," the twins begged in unison.

With a resigned sigh, Blake changed lanes and pulled into the lot at the music store. "I can't fight all of you."

Contented after the unique dinner, Cassie smiled indulgently as Blake closed her door and locked the van. "How long can it take to stop at a music store?"

His dark brows rose. "I forgot. You don't have one in Twin Corners. I should have brought sleeping bags and survival rations. Three teenagers and three preteens—we ought to be here the rest of the night."

Cassie laughed as they walked inside, thinking he was teasing her. But nearly an hour later she saw that he was right.

"And you thought I was kidding, didn't you?" Blake asked, delighted to see the smile back on her face. "We'll be lucky if we can drag them out in another hour."

"I never thought my kids would care that much. It's not like they had any of this back home."

"Which is probably why they're so fascinated. The unknown's usually more interesting than the familiar."

Cassie gave a small shrug. "For children, perhaps."

Blake met her eyes, enjoying the contentment in her expression, the slight flush of her skin. "And adults? Don't they enjoy exploring the unknown? Discovering something or someone new?"

He was rewarded by a deepening flush, along with the disappearance of her contentment. She just shrugged and looked blindly at the next bin.

Blake purposely put his hands near hers, browsing the same section she did. When his hand grazed hers, he could feel a sudden jump in the pulse of her wrist. A change she was careful to try and disguise.

He glanced at the CDs she'd been examining. "The Beatles? Are you a fan, too?"

"Well…" Her voice wobbled, but then she firmed it. "Yes. Most everybody listened to country-western, but I was hooked on rock and roll—especially the Beatles."

"They were the best," he stated, leaving no room for argument.

Her laugh bounced between them. "As long as you're open to discussion."

"You don't like them?"

"No. I *really* do. I especially admired John Lennon."

"My favorite, too. Couldn't believe it when he was shot. That's something I've never forgotten—what I was doing when I heard he'd been killed. I was knee-deep in my fraternity initiation. I thought it was a fake report—part of my maddening initiation." He shook his head at the flashback, "Do you remember that day? What you were doing when Lennon was shot?"

She started to open her mouth, but then a wave of something grim passed over her face. Her voice was flat. "No, I don't."

"That's odd, most everybody—"

"I said I don't remember. Are you going to stand there all night cross-examining me?"

Blake sucked in a deep breath. He'd somehow stumbled on a nerve, and judging from her reaction, he'd touched a live wire to that nerve. What was it that she didn't want to discuss? Along with being defensive, she was also evasive. She must have been in high school when Lennon was assassinated. What could she possibly have to hide about her high school years?

Before he formed a reply, she pulled back from the stack of CDs. "I think we ought to round up the kids. Tomorrow's a school day. The kids don't need to waste time here and wind up falling asleep in school."

Definitely a throbbing nerve. "You're right, Cassie. Guess I forgot what time it was." But he couldn't resist one more probe. "You know how dangerous school days can be."

She lifted her head, a blaze lighting her eyes before she turned to gather her children.

He'd hit a nerve, all right. Cassie Hawkins was showing more sides than the city. And each one was proving more intriguing than the last.

AS THEY PULLED into the driveway, Blake groaned aloud, and Cassie stared first at him, then at the unfamiliar car parked in a sprawling fashion across the drive. A black Porsche carelessly blocked a good portion of the driveway, and Cassie had a sinking sensation that she knew who the car belonged to.

As the kids piled out, Blake caught her eye. "Looks like another visit from my sister-in-law."

Kevin and the twins groaned in response. "We don't hafta see her, do we, Dad?" Todd questioned.

"You can say hello," Blake responded, looking none too pleased himself.

"I hope that's all," Kevin muttered.

Blake rolled his eyes. "She's different...but she *is* your aunt."

"That's not our fault," Mark mumbled.

"It won't kill you," Blake responded.

"I'll make a fresh pot of coffee," Cassie offered.

"Daphne's more the champagne-and-caviar type," he replied with an amused laugh. "Coffee would only dampen her buzz. I'll park the van—" he glanced at the insufficient space remaining in the driveway "—somewhere. Why don't you go ahead and take the kids inside?"

Cassie was tempted to reply that her job didn't include dealing with difficult relatives. Instead, she gritted her teeth, wishing the woman hadn't chosen tonight to drop in. Once at the back door, she made herself smile as they all trooped inside.

"My, my, what an absolute *horde* of children," Daphne said by way of a greeting, her lips curling in barely concealed disapproval.

Kevin and the twins offered halfhearted hellos and gave her the expected perfunctory kisses on the cheek before disappearing. Taking their cue, Cassie's children went upstairs after politely saying hello.

"How do you do it?" Daphne asked, watching the last of

the kids sprint upstairs. "I'd have a constant migraine with that many little bodies in the house."

"That wouldn't be too good for my job, since I'm the nanny."

"True. I can't imagine why anyone would want a job like that. But then, I guess somebody has to do it, don't they?"

Cassie ignored the claw poking through Daphne's purring voice. "I'm afraid so. Otherwise the boys would have to depend on their extended family for care."

Daphne's head shot up sharply as she caught the implication in Cassie's words. Her eyes narrowed. "It's hardly your place to question my devotion to the family."

Cassie clung to her dignity. "No. I don't suppose it is. Nor yours to question mine."

Daphne shed her civilized mask. "You have a job *now,* Mary Poppins, but mess with me and you'll be out so fast you'll be breathing Texas dust again before you know what hits you."

Sucking in a gulp of reinforcing air, Cassie held on to her temper. "I don't want to argue with you, but Mr. Matthews is my employer, not you."

"And don't think I haven't seen how you're trying to make more of that relationship, either." Daphne shook back her impressive mane of hair. "But you can give up that fairy tale. Blake isn't going to get involved with a servant." Daphne's dark eyes flashed. "Especially since he's going to spend the rest of his life with me."

Chapter Eight

Cassie called a Hawkins family meeting with trepidation, the letter from her mother resting heavily in her pocket. Martha Sanders had hated to tell her, but Cassie's "perfect" tenants had abandoned the house. The rent money she'd counted on to pay the mortgage was now gone. And although her mother had put out feelers, no one had shown an interest in renting the house. As she faced her children, Cassie's heart weighed as heavily as the letter in her pocket.

"I had a letter from your grandmother," Cassie began.

"Is she okay?" Jimmy Ray asked immediately. As the oldest grandchild, he had a special connection to his grandmother. At times he felt guilty about enjoying L.A. and his computer so much, knowing they'd left their home and family behind.

"Granna's fine, but she did have some bad news. The renters moved out of our house. It's sitting empty, and the rent I planned to use to pay the mortgage won't be coming."

"Will it take most of your salary to pay the bank now?" Katherine Ann asked.

"It will take quite a bit, but I'm not sure that's what we should do." Cassie took a deep breath. "If we let the house sit empty for a year, it might take more money than we'll have to fix it up once my contract here is up."

"Don't you think Mr. Matthews will renew your contract?" Jimmy Ray asked, his young brow furrowed in concentration.

Cassie remembered Daphne's threat the week before and

wondered. If the woman did snag Blake, Cassie suspected she'd be out of a job in an instant. "I don't know. But I do know that I can't count on it. It will take a good chunk of my salary to pay the house notes, and maybe we should consider going back home while our house is still in good shape."

"No, Mama!" they all chorused, surprising and deafening her in one swift action.

Cassie tried to soothe them. "I haven't decided anything yet."

"We like it here," D.J. announced.

"We really do, Mama," Katherine Ann agreed.

"And we'd still have money problems back in Twin Corners, wouldn't we, Mama?" Jimmy Ray asked.

"Yes, we probably would, but your grandmother wants to help pay our house note, and she simply can't afford it." Their grandmother's financial situation wasn't news to the children, and the mention of it quieted them immediately. "She wants you all to be happy here. But I think we'd all have a hard time being happy, knowing she's the one making the sacrifices."

"Could you talk to Mr. Matthews?" Katherine Ann questioned. "And see if he could give you a raise?"

"That's quite a jump in logic, considering I'm not even sure I'll have a contract after this year."

"Yeah," D.J. agreed. "But we could all get jobs again, like we did back home, and help out."

"Or we may just have to move back," she suggested gently.

Jimmy Ray met her gaze evenly, his always too-grown-up, too-serious teenage face earnest. "We'll do what we have to, Mama."

Looking around the circle of cherished faces, Cassie again thanked her lucky stars for such wonderful children. Then she glanced down the hallway at Blake's study, knowing that facing him would be as difficult as facing her trio of children had been.

CASSIE PUT IT OFF as long as possible, but she ran out of excuses. Feeling much like a kid facing the school principal, she knocked on the door of Blake's study.

She interpreted the mutter she heard as assent. Cautiously she opened the door and poked her head inside, but Blake's attention was still fastened on his work. Realizing her subtle entrance would go unnoticed, Cassie braved the distance to his desk. But he still didn't look up. It occurred to her that she might need to set off a bomb to get his attention.

She had started to clear her throat when Blake surprised her by lifting his head and throwing down his pen. "Something up?"

Startled by his sudden attention, she was unnerved for a moment. "Yes, I need to talk to you."

His gaze settled on hers. "Serious?"

"I'm afraid so."

He waved her into the chair across from his desk. "Spill it."

She relaxed a fraction at his casual tone, but her mission still stuck in her gut. "I have some news...."

"I take it not good news," Blake guessed, still intently watching her.

Cassie took a deep breath. "The people who were renting my house moved out."

"And?"

"*And,* they've abandoned the house." When he didn't comment, she continued, "*And,* the rent money I counted on to pay the mortgage won't be coming in. So...I've come to ask you to release me from my employment contract."

"No."

No hesitation, no discussion. Just no.

Cassie felt a trace of panic. "My mother's trying to help pay the bank note, and I can't let her do that—she can barely afford her own home. I didn't expect my house to be abandoned when I signed the contract, and—"

"Agreed. I'll extend the terms of your contract to cover the mortgage payments on your house."

"Extend the terms?" She paused as that sank in. "Do you mean pay my mortgage?"

"Precisely." Blake picked up his pen, obviously ready to return to the stack of papers on his desk. "That and take care of any repairs and expenses you run into because the house is sitting empty.''

She stuttered. ''You can't do that!''

''Why not?''

''Well, because… You just can't, that's all.''

Blake lifted one brow. ''How can I argue with such precise logic?'' Since she was too flabbergasted to answer, he provided his own reply. ''Your employment contract's like any business agreement—there are built-in parameters, should circumstances change.'' He shrugged. ''Which they have. There's no need to cancel your contract—a simple amendment will take care of the problem.''

Cassie remembered to shut her mouth, knowing it must resemble an airplane hangar, but it was open again in seconds. ''You call that simple?''

''Why make it complicated?''

''I can't accept such generosity.''

''You just told me that you didn't calculate the renters leaving when we made our agreement. And in offering you the job, the status of your house was an important factor. So, I agree that it's part of my contractual obligation.''

''Just like that?''

''I wouldn't be an effective businessman if I couldn't make quick decisions.''

''The children *do* want to stay.…''

''And you, Cassie? What do you want?''

What did she want? She felt like a butterfly reluctant to release the cocoon. On one hand, she wanted to stay and explore L.A. and everything it had to offer. On the other, she was tempted to return to the familiar…the safe. Meeting his relentless gaze, Cassie tried to dodge the question. ''I want my family to be happy.''

Cassie could see that he wasn't fooled by her evasive tactic. He turned her statement around. ''Then you'll be staying.''

''I didn't say—''

''You want your family's happiness. They want to stay in L.A. Am I missing something?''

No, he never missed a beat. ''One thing. Why are you doing this?'' Cassie thought she saw a twitch, a quick tightening of his jaw, but his next words dispelled the notion.

''You're an excellent nanny. You've already made headway with the boys. It's in my best interests to keep you here.''

His best interests. Hardly anything personal. You're the help, Cassie. Don't forget it. ''Of course. Still, I appreciate what you're doing—and I don't say that lightly.''

One of Blake's lips curved upward. ''For all your talking, I don't think you say anything *lightly*.''

''No, I'm still small-town. From talking too much to worrying about my big old house and my kids. But you're right, my family's happiness is most important, so we'll be staying.'' Even though, in doing so, she was putting more of her emotions on the line. Emotions that apparently were not reciprocated. Not giving him time to reply, she rushed out of the study, ignoring his startled, confused expression.

Chapter Nine

Cassie looked at her bathtub's gleaming faucet in disgust, preferring to concentrate on the mundane, rather than on her tangle of emotions. Despite its architectural perfection, the stupid thing was broken. Even though Pedro performed general handyman jobs around the house, he'd scratched his head when faced with this one and repeated Blake's solution: Call the plumber.

Which sounded easy enough. Until you tried to get one to commit. She was beginning to think it would be easier to lure one of Hollywood's movie stars to the house than a licensed plumber.

And until then, she had to bathe in another bathroom. Although most of the rooms had connecting baths like hers, there was a bathroom a few doors away down the hall. Cassie just wished she didn't have to pass Blake's bedroom to get there. It was a silly thing to worry about, but she preferred it to dwelling on Daphne's words.

She hadn't forgotten Daphne's warning the other night, and still wondered whether the other woman had been telling the truth. Was that why Blake had remained so emotionless when she discussed breaking her contract? Was there more to his relationship with Daphne than Cassie had seen? Or had Daphne decided to set her claws into Blake and now hoped her words would scare away any competition?

And could she really consider herself competition? Despite

the reactions Blake could cause without any effort, Cassie knew she wasn't in his league. She must have imagined that she saw a flicker of attraction in his eyes, because from the way he'd acted last night, it was clear that his interest in her was strictly professional. And even though she disliked the calculating Daphne, Cassie had to admit the woman looked like a perfect counterbalance on Blake's arm.

Suddenly Cassie wished again for the safe familiarity of Twin Corners. It seemed the more she discovered of the world, the more she learned of its complexities. But then, back in Twin Corners there hadn't been men like Blake Matthews to confuse all the boundaries. They'd had their share of small-town hunks in Twin Corners, but none of them had been packaged like him.

The man whose bedroom she now had to pass.

Taking a deep breath, Cassie reached for a stack of clean towels and the terry robe that sat beneath them. Opening her door cautiously and looking down the hall to make sure it was empty, she darted into the bathroom. Satisfied by her quick maneuver, she deposited the towels, peeled off her clothes, then stepped into the shower. The water quickly doused her body and hair, a refreshing spray that woke up her senses and had her humming. Feeling invigorated, she climbed out of the shower and reached for her robe. But it didn't seem to be anywhere in sight.

Cassie plowed through the stack of towels a half-dozen times, then searched the rest of the counter, and the floor. All that searching merely confirmed her sinking certainty that she'd forgotten her robe.

Wrapping a bath towel around her torso, tucking the ends at chest level beneath her arms, she desperately hoped that Blake was already downstairs. Taking another fortifying gulp of air, she flung open the door, intending to race down the hall.

Instead, she ran straight into Blake, nearly toppling them both in the process. Cassie's fortified breath whooshed from her lungs as rapidly as the crimson spots that stained her cheeks appeared. Clutching the towel firmly, Cassie tried to find something, anything, to say, but for once her incredible gift of gab had run dry.

"I..." they both began, and then stopped suddenly.

"Go ahead...." they started again, in unison.

Cassie took the plunge, realizing as she spoke that she sounded completely witless. "My shower faucet is broken," she offered feebly, unable to say much more as she watched Blake's eyes darken as they roamed over her.

Blake cleared his throat, yet his words still sounded husky. "I know."

"Of course. You told me to call a plumber, but it's not easy getting a plumber. They all have waiting lists, and unless you're royalty or a movie star, they won't promise a thing. Not even an appointment, or a howdy-do. If I wanted to start a business here, it'd be plumbing. They must make a fortune—probably as much as a movie mogul. Lord, I'm babbling again, but then, I guess you could figure that out for yourself...." Cassie saw the slow smolder in Blake's eyes and heard her words trail away.

His voice, still gruff, took up where she'd stopped. "Maybe you'll have better luck today."

"With what?" she asked dumbly.

"Getting a plumber," he responded gently.

"Oh, yes. The plumber, of course. I don't know what I was thinking. Maybe I waterlogged my brain." She gestured helplessly at the long strands of wet hair. "And I forgot my shampoo. It's in my bathroom, along with my robe. Normally I don't go wandering the halls in...in just a towel."

His gaze roved over her again, and suddenly she knew she wasn't imagining the flare of attraction she saw in his eyes.

Silence fell between them, and Cassie struggled to fill it, knowing she had to turn his attention away from her. "I'd better hurry and get dressed, or the kids will eat Twinkies for breakfast."

His gaze was still roaming over her, leaving a warm path. A path that threatened to leap into a full-fledged fire.

"That doesn't sound so unappealing," Blake responded, his eyes signaling what he *did* find appealing.

Feeling the beginnings of a blush, she answered quickly, rushing her words as she inched closer to her room. "But I doubt their teachers would appreciate a sugar high…from the Twinkies, I mean. I'd better get my…"

"Robe," he finished for her.

"Uh…yes…my robe."

She turned to flee, hurrying away.

Blake wasn't sure how she managed it, but Cassie looked even sexier and more provocative in a towel than she had in that knockout swimsuit of hers. Especially with water beading over her slicked skin, creating fascinating rivulets that made him want to trace the path of each one with his lips.

It was a hell of a thing to wake up to. For a moment, he'd forgotten Cassie was his children's nanny. His sense of what category of woman she fit into seemed to be getting fuzzier all the time.

In retrospect, maybe it hadn't been such a good idea to install Cassie in the bedroom directly across from his. At the time, he'd thought the more traditional suite of rooms would be more comfortable for her and would ease the transition between their very different worlds. Children were more resilient. And they liked change, new adventures. To them the modern, high-tech house had been one of those fun new adventures. But he had suspected Cassie would be fighting homesickness.

Which was why her room was now directly across from his.

And the proximity was making him a little crazy. Looking at her closed bedroom door, he hoped from now on she planned to wear more than a towel when roaming the halls, a towel he itched to rip off. That, or she'd better take to carrying a big stick to club some sense into him.

GLANCING AT THE CLOCK, Cassie realized Blake should be home soon. She checked the hamper one more time. Everything they needed for a picnic in the park was there, except the cold drinks and fried chicken she planned to add at the last moment. She hoped Blake would go along with her impromptu picnic. In her opinion, the Matthews didn't have enough family outings.

Wrapping freshly baked rolls in foil, she glanced up in surprise as the door to the kitchen swung open. "Decide you needed a break, Jimmy Ray? I figured you'd be on your computer." She turned to the fridge, retrieving a bowl of freshly washed fruit. Offering him the fruit, she was surprised when he didn't reach for any, instead shaking his head.

"Mama, can I talk to you?"

"Sure." Seeing the troubled expression on his face, she felt a hitch of concern. "Something wrong?"

"Not exactly. Mama, do you like living here?"

She thought for a moment, considering her answer. "I like the Matthews. I like the house. I think I'm even beginning to like L.A. Any special reason for wanting to know?"

"Are we going to stay here? You didn't sound very sure the other night."

Cassie wondered what was worrying her serious-minded child, now that their scare about the mortgage notes was past. "At least for a year. I signed a contract with Mr. Matthews, which you know he won't let me break even if I want to. After that, we'll have to see." If her prayers were answered, she'd still have this one-in-a-million job—even if it meant putting all of her emotions on the line to do so. She gently ruffled his longish hair. "Are you missing Twin Corners?"

"Sort of. But I was thinking that if we're going to be staying here, maybe I ought to fit in more."

Puzzled, she cocked her head. "But you're fitting in fine."

"Not exactly. Kevin's right, Mama. I only fit in with the computer geeks."

"But I thought you loved your computer classes, and—"

"I do. It's just that I'd like to fit in other places, like I did back home. And, well…"

Sensing there was something he was reluctant to confide, she placed a hand on his shoulder. "You can tell me."

"It's my name, Mama. Nobody here goes by two names. They shorten their first names till they're almost nothing."

"And having everyone call you Jimmy Ray is an albatross."

"I didn't mean that—"

"It's okay. This *is* a different world from Twin Corners."

She bit back a stab of regret. With David John, she could dismiss his flippant new nickname, since he was only ten. But Jimmy Ray was fifteen. It was a more mature decision and, she suspected, a more lasting one. "So, what did you decide on?"

He hesitated. "What do you think of Jim?"

Very grown-up, very foreign. But she mustered a smile. "Sounds like a name that'll fit in. You couldn't get it any shorter, unless they just call you 'J.'"

"You know the one guy who's asked me to hang out—Brian—they call him 'B.' But he's *really* popular..."

"And there's no reason you won't be, too. When the season starts, you'll make more friends, being on the baseball team. And you've already been asked to join the yearbook staff."

"I know, Mama." Worry creased his adolescent brow. "But I don't want you to think I'm like David John, just wanting to be cool. And I don't want you to think I've forgotten where we come from."

"I think you're a mature young man, and that you've given a lot of thought to this decision." Her expression softened as she remembered the agonies, real and imagined, of being fifteen. "And I don't think there's much chance you'll forget your roots. We're going on a picnic for dinner." She put a shiny apple in his hand. "This will keep you till then. You can try out your new name at dinner...Jim."

He smiled, a flash of joy that turned him from somber to carefree in an instant. "Thanks, Mama."

For a moment, she saw him as he'd been as a toddler, his bright, toothy grin, shiny curls and complete innocence. All that had changed. While she wouldn't trade the wonderful young man he had become, she couldn't help longing for those simpler, more naive days. "No problem," she finally managed.

He rubbed the apple against his sleeve. "I can help you with supper."

Although always helpful, he'd been inseparable from the computer unless he was at school or asleep. Touched, she realized there were advantages to his years, such as thoughtfulness. He was sensitive enough to realize that she might be upset or nostalgic about the name change.

"Dinner's under control, but I could use your help loading the van. If Mr. Matthews agrees, I plan on a picnic, and we'll need the tablecloth, blankets, cooler..."

Her voice trailed off when she saw Jimmy Ray's grin. She smiled reluctantly in return. "I guess if you're old enough to shorten your name, you're old enough to figure out what we need on a picnic. Would you mind checking on David John and the twins? They're in the pool and it's about time for them to get out and get dressed."

"Yes, ma'am." He pulled open the back door, then paused and turned back around. "You're the best, Mama."

As he disappeared, Cassie felt a lump of gratitude thicken in her throat. She might not have the world, but she had the best kids in that world.

In a few minutes, the door opened again. Expecting Jimmy Ray, Cassie didn't turn around. "You'd probably better put a few folding chairs in the van, too. The Matthews might not be used to sitting on the grass like we are."

"I don't know. I've sat on my share of grass." Blake's deep voice washed over her, and Cassie whirled in startled surprise.

"I thought you were Jimmy Ray." As she felt the heat of embarrassment bloom in her cheeks, it was all Cassie could do not to throw her hands over her face to hide the telltale color.

But Blake was grinning. "I guessed as much. So where are we going that we'll be sitting on the grass?"

"A picnic," she blurted out. "That is...if you're in agreement. I made fried chicken, potato salad and coleslaw. And I baked fresh rolls. Oh, and there's a yellow cake with chocolate and Heath chip frosting. And fruit, too, so you won't have a cholesterol attack. I know that's important to you. That's why the cake doesn't have any eggs, the potato salad, either, and..." She saw the amusement twinkling in his eyes. "I guess I'm talking too much again."

"I doubt you're ever at a loss for words, Cassie, but that doesn't mean you talk too much. Why the picnic?"

"It doesn't seem like you have many family outings. I thought this might be a good opportunity to spend time together—no pressure, just a simple picnic."

He shrugged. "If it doesn't take too long. I've got work to do tonight."

"I doubt you'll ever be at a loss for having work to do," she replied, mimicking his words, although not unkindly.

He smiled again. "Got my number, haven't you?"

"I know your business is important to you, Mr. Matthews."

He made a sound of distinct displeasure.

Worried, she bit her lip. "Did I say something I shouldn't have?"

"Yes, Cassie, you did. Don't you think it's a little ridiculous to keep calling me Mr. Matthews?"

"You're my employer, and—"

"That's right. I am. And we're not at the boardinghouse anymore, where you set the rules. Since theoretically I'm in charge, I want you to call me Blake."

"But it's not necessary—"

"Yes. It is."

His eyes held hers, and Cassie felt a new emotion thickening her throat, along with a sizzle that had nothing to do with the sun blazing through the oversize windows. "Whatever you say…Blake." Seeing his eyes darken, she scrabbled for something to fill the throbbing silence, something to divert the sudden turn in their conversation. She couldn't jeopardize her job by letting herself believe there could be anything more than an employer-employee relationship. Too much was at stake that could be lost. "It seems that this is a day for name changes. Jimmy Ray decided he wants to be called Jim, so he'll fit in at school. Seems the kids are all abbreviating their names…" She tried to look anywhere but at him. "And now you want me to call you…"

"Blake," he supplied.

She found it was difficult to answer when he spoke in such a dangerously soft voice. Swallowing, she struggled for normality.

The back door banged open suddenly, and a swimsuit-clad D.J. burst inside. "Jimmy Ray said we had to come in and get dressed," he complained. "How come, Mama? It's not suppertime yet."

The twins followed, dragging their feet, both quieter than usual.

"Because we're going on a picnic," Blake answered for her. "You guys better hustle, or I'm eating your fried chicken…and potato salad…and maybe your cake."

Squalls of protest filled the air as D.J. ran upstairs, not wanting to miss out on his favorites. The twins trailed him, obviously less concerned about their father's threats.

Still, the noise rousted Kevin, who strolled into the kitchen. "Who's torturing the twins?"

"Your father and I take turns," Cassie replied.

"So, what's up?"

"We're going on a picnic," she answered, offering him the bowl of fruit.

He ignored the outstretched bowl. "I don't have time for junk like that."

"I think you can take time out of your busy schedule," Blake replied dryly.

"What *is* this? Now we're supposed to be doing some sort of 'Brady Bunch' garbage?"

"Would you rather be 'The Addams Family'?" Blake questioned, reaching for a nectarine.

Kevin rolled his eyes. "This is so dumb. Before she came here, we never had to do this hick stuff."

Blake saw that Cassie was trying not to let Kevin's comment affect her, but it was difficult to miss the tightened lips, the quick flash of hurt. He sensed that she'd been working hard to erase the signs of her rural background—from her clothing to her way of speaking. "Just because we're not used to going on picnics doesn't make them hick stuff." Blake draped his arm over Kevin's shoulders. "Come on, champ. Let's change, and you can help me load the cooler." Blake led his grumbling son away, the door to the kitchen swinging shut behind them.

"Dad, how come you couldn't hire someone from L.A.?"

"Why do you think I had to go all the way to Texas to find a nanny? Everybody in L.A. knows about you three."

Kevin grinned unexpectedly. "Yeah, I guess we're famous."

"I think that's *notorious,*" Blake replied dryly.

"Think Cassie knows why?"

Blake felt a sudden spurt of misgiving. "I don't know. But don't plan on anything that'll get you more P.R."

Kevin grinned again. "Sure, Dad."

Darting a glance at his son, Blake wondered what was going through his ingenious mind, then, just as quickly, decided he didn't want to know. Besides, after a few more great family outings, they'd all be singing a different tune.

THE TUNE, as they trooped back into the house a few hours later, was a cross between "Raindrops Are Falling on My Head" and "How Wet I Am."

Clouds had scuttled across the sky as they arrived at the park, dimming the previously bright sunshine, along with a great deal of Cassie's enthusiasm.

After D.J. and the twins dropped the hamper upside down, spilling all the food into the grass, Blake had heartily insisted the meal was still fine. While everyone was picking blades of grass from the potato salad and between their teeth, a huge wind had come up, sending the tablecloth, the quilts and the paper plates, cups and napkins flying. While everyone tried to catch the scattered debris, Gulliver had chased a nearby cat that turned on the dog, scratched his nose and then chased him through the adjoining picnic sites. Before the kids could corral him, Gulliver had made an even bigger mess of their upturned hamper and debris, not to mention the picnic supplies of several angry strangers.

As they struggled to gather their things, rain had poured suddenly and insistently, soaking them all as they battled the wind to retrieve the runaway quilts and paper goods.

An accusing silence had filled the van as they rode home, everyone shivering in the chill of sodden clothes. Now, as they trooped inside one by one, the Matthews children divided their glares between Cassie and Blake.

"I told you this was a dumb idea," Kevin threw back over his shoulder before pounding up the stairs.

"Yeah," the twins chimed, following their brother.

Jimmy Ray headed into the laundry room with the sodden

quilts and tablecloth, sending his mother a comforting glance. "You can't control the weather."

Blake put the destroyed hamper on the counter. "You're right about that, Jim."

Looking pleased that Blake used the shortened version of his name casually, Jimmy Ray came back into the kitchen, taking some fruit from the fridge. "I've got a project due next week I'd better work on."

Smiling wearily, Cassie tapped his arm. "That's fine Jim—" She stopped before calling him Jimmy Ray. Barely.

Katherine Ann and D.J. trailed in the back door, with a sad-looking Gulliver.

"I think he's okay, Mama," Katherine Ann announced. "That cat hurt his pride more than his nose."

"But I think I'd better take him upstairs with me," D.J. added.

"Hold on—" Cassie began.

Blake intervened, sensing that Cassie was close to the end of her patience. "Sounds like a good idea. He'll settle down after he dries out."

Cassie tried again. "But the wooden floor—"

"I'll put down lots of towels," D.J. pleaded. "And he'll be good."

Blake waved D.J. and Gulliver toward the back staircase.

"Try not to use the best towels," Cassie relented, before muttering under her breath, "although all of your towels are good ones."

"That can be washed," Blake pointed out.

Cassie leaned back against the island in the middle of the kitchen. "Well, I guess that wasn't exactly a smashing success."

"As your son pointed out, you couldn't control the weather."

Earnestly Cassie glanced up at him. "But I wanted it to be a good experience, one to build on, so your boys would want to spend time with you as a family. But after today, they'll all probably run shrieking the next time I suggest something."

"I don't know...." he mused. "I doubt you could top yourself—unless, of course, you can whip up an earthquake or tornado.''

She smiled finally—a flash of sunshine amid the storm—and he couldn't take his eyes off her. He'd have expected her to either rage, sulk or whine, but instead it seemed she was finding a renewed burst of good humor, despite her drenched clothing. He allowed his gaze to drift downward, something he'd restrained himself from doing until now.

The rain had plastered her T-shirt and shorts to her form, leaving only a few flimsy barriers between her body and his gaze. And the more he looked, the more he wanted to continue looking.

She pushed suddenly at the heavy sheet of her wet hair. "I'd probably better go take a shower."

Their eyes met at her unfortunate choice of words, their meeting that morning in the hallway flashing between them.

Blake couldn't understand the strong effect she was having on him, the pull he felt. Although he'd dated since Elizabeth's death, none of the casual dates had involved any emotional connection. And that was what he was feeling now. He had a strong urge to peel away the layers, to learn more about this so-surprising woman. He wondered at the secrets she kept hidden, the many sides of her personality that continued to startle him.

And the undeniable attraction that ricocheted between them.

Unable to resist, Blake reached out one hand, seeing the sudden trembling of her lips, the darkening of her silver eyes.

Footsteps sounded on the back stairs as the twins came into the room.

"We're hungry," Mark announced.

Blake tore his gaze from Cassie, knowing they'd interrupted a hunger of his own, a far different hunger.

"And we don't want anything with grass in it," Todd added, his tone far nastier than usual.

"That's enough, Todd," Blake warned.

The boy stuck out his lip belligerently. Still, it trembled slightly. "Fine. I don't want anything, anyway." He ran back up the stairs before Blake could reply.

Mark filled his arms with a loaf of bread, peanut butter, jelly, grapes, and at least a dozen cookies. He sent Cassie a challenging look, but she didn't question his choices. As he retreated up the stairs, no doubt to share his loot with Todd, Blake shook his head.

"I don't know what's gotten into them. I'm sorry, Cassie. They shouldn't speak to you in that tone."

But she wasn't looking at him. Instead, she gazed after Mark with a worried expression. "Something's wrong with them."

"They're probably just cranky because they're hungry."

"No. They've been quiet the last few days, too quiet. I thought maybe they were coming down with colds or the flu, but I don't think that's it."

"Don't worry so much, Cassie. Kids act up, they get over it."

She raised her gaze to him. "Much like adults?"

"What do you mean?"

"That adults sometimes think they can start something, then walk away. It's not always that easy."

Feeling as though his hand had been slapped…simply for his thoughts…Blake drew his brows together. "Meaning?"

"That I need to be concentrating on my job…your children rather than being distracted."

"Am I distracting you?" He studied her face, wondering whether she would admit that she was equally affected.

"Maybe I'm simply distracting myself," she replied, not answering his question.

He saw her resolve assert itself, saw the strength he knew she possessed chase away the softness. Perhaps she was right. He'd hired her to work with his kids, not to work him into a frenzy. So she wanted distance. That shouldn't be too difficult. But he planned to find a plumber tomorrow, if he had to pay a king's ransom. Any more towel-draped encounters, and the only distance she'd find would be on the path to his bedroom.

The doorbell rang suddenly and insistently. Cursing beneath his breath, Blake turned just as Maria entered the kitchen, the sound of impatient high heels tapping behind her. "Mrs. Kerara is here,'' Maria announced unnecessarily as Daphne walked past her, eclipsing the need for a reply.

Blake saw the unguarded look on Cassie's face before she fixed a resolute expression in place. Sighing inwardly, Blake wondered why his sister-in-law had chosen to make more appearances in the past month than she had in the past year. True, she asked for investment advice, but most of her questions could have been answered by phone or fax. "Slumming again, Daphne?"

She presented her flawless cheek for a kiss. "Hardly, darling." Then her gaze settled on Cassie's bedraggled appearance, and her lips curved in wicked pleasure. "Although I can see why you asked."

Blake winced on Cassie's behalf. He knew no woman enjoyed being caught looking her worst. Purposely, he glanced down ruefully at his drenched shirt and jeans. "I've never looked my best wearing wet clothes," he replied, hoping to direct Daphne's unkind comment away from Cassie.

Daphne's gaze traveled slowly over his form. "Oh, I don't know. You could start a trend." Then her gaze settled deliberately on Cassie. "What do you think, Cassie?"

Hesitating only slightly, Cassie was proud that her voice emerged strong and steady. "I've never been much for trends myself."

"How fortunate for you. After all, I don't imagine living in Outer Mongolia would make it easy to follow trends."

"I don't live in Twin Corners anymore," Cassie reminded her in a deceptively mild tone.

"So you don't. Still, trends aren't really your style, are they?"

Cassie glanced between the two beautiful people dominating the room, knowing with a sinking feeling that Daphne was right. Only one person in their tableau seemed out of place. And it wasn't the golden couple she was staring at. They belonged. She was the outsider.

Chapter Ten

After watching and listening to the twins for a few more days, Cassie still didn't know what was bothering them, only that something was wrong. Deciding she couldn't learn what it was without help, and since Blake had left the country again on another business trip, she approached D.J.

Her son's room, decorated in his new idea of cool, was still somewhat of a shock to her. Posters had replaced cartoons, CDs had taken the place of airplane models, and a stack of teen magazines had shoved aside his forgotten rock collection. Bending over, she automatically picked up a T-shirt emblazoned with an indecipherable slogan. Part of D.J.'s new wardrobe and identity.

"Hey, Mama."

"Hey, yourself. Working on your homework?"

"Yes, ma'am." He twisted around in his chair, grinning up at her. "I got a great idea for making some more money. Kids here are willing to *pay* to have their homework done."

Cassie kept from choking, with an effort. Ah, her little entrepreneur. "But you can't do it for them. That's cheating."

"But it's not a test, Mama."

"No. But it's the same thing. It's simply dishonest. Not to mention, if these kids don't do their own homework, they won't be able to pass their tests, because they won't have learned their assignments."

D.J. bent his head over his desk for a moment, frowning at

the page of numbers he'd been scribbling on. "It's really cheating?"

"Absolutely."

He sighed, then reached for the paper, crumpling it up. "Guess I'll have to find another way to pay for my Porsche."

Cassie hid her smile. "Guess so. Listen, champ, do you know if anything's bothering the twins?"

He shrugged. "What do you mean?"

"They've been awfully quiet lately."

"Oh… Yeah, well, it's 'cause of the other kids and stuff."

"Aren't they pretty popular in school?"

"Sure, but the other kids have been giving them the business 'cause they haven't got a mother to bring to their class."

Cassie wrinkled her brow. "I don't understand."

"Their grade is having teacher appreciation week. The other kids' mothers are bringing treats and stuff. Even the kids with stepmothers are getting them to come. And the ones that work are coming before school or during lunch. So Mark and Todd said they didn't have to do dumb stuff like that 'cause they don't appreciate the teacher. She got mad and made them clean the room, and the kids started picking on 'em and saying they just said that 'cause they don't have a mother."

The sudden constriction in her throat made Cassie pause. For all their toughness, Mark and Todd were still motherless little boys. "Would it be okay if their dad came instead?"

D.J. shrugged. "Nobody else had their fathers come…. It might make 'em feel even dumber."

Cassie took another stab at an unlikely alternative. "How about their aunt?"

D.J. looked at her as though she'd suggested sending Godzilla. *"Daphne?"*

"Okay. Bad idea. Can you say anything to help them at school?"

"Gee, Mama, I'm the new kid. Nobody listens to me."

She reached out to ruffle his hair. "Let's keep this talk just between us, okay?"

"Sure, Mama. You got any ideas so I can make money?"

Smiling, she walked to the doorway. "Yes. Study hard so you can get into a good college."

THE PHONE RANG, and Cassie glanced automatically at the clock on her bedside table. It was late for someone to be calling. She hoped nothing was wrong with her mother. Unexpectedly nervous, she grabbed for the phone, and her voice was breathy with concern as she answered.

"Cassie?"

"Yes?"

"It's Blake."

She nearly sighed aloud with relief, then glanced again at the clock. "What's wrong?"

"Nothing. Why'd you think something was wrong?"

She remembered his last two trips, the solitary phone call during each one to check on his children. So far, he'd called every other day on this trip. "No reason. The phone ringing at night after I go to bed always startles me."

"Did I wake you?"

"No."

"But you *are* in bed?" he asked, a different note in his voice.

She blushed, even though she knew he couldn't see her. The skimpy nightgown she wore was in deference to the unexpectedly warm temperature. "Uh…yes," she answered, reaching out to pull the light cotton blanket over her legs. "But I guess you're up and about." Even with her legs covered, she broke into a nervous babble. "With the time difference and all, it can't be bedtime there. You must have already had your breakfast. Kippers. I'm not sure about eggs, though. They have kippers for breakfast, don't they? And…"

Amusement flared in his soft chuckle. "And I thought you might be too tired to talk."

A flush of tidal-wave-size embarrassment washed over her. "It must be costing a fortune to call from across the world. I guess you want to talk to the boys, and—"

"Wait! I'll talk to them in a minute. And, yes, they do have kippers in England, but I'm in Paris now. And I had fresh croissants for breakfast. Don't tell my London office, but the food here's much better.''

"Can you see the Eiffel Tower?" Cassie asked, a sigh of dreamy envy permeating her voice.

"Not from my hotel room, but I'm sure it's still here."

"Then you are at your hotel?"

"Yes, but I'm not lucky enough to be tucked in bed."

Awareness flared again. Despite her enchantment with the city she'd often dreamed about, Cassie couldn't get past the image of them talking while in bed, linked by a telephone, separated by an ocean. "But you have all of Paris at your feet."

"Sometimes a man wants more than a city at the end of a day."

It was ridiculous, she told herself, to have her heart threatening to jump from her chest simply at his words. Words spoken on a telephone. Two continents away.

Cassie cleared her throat, scrabbling for normality, wishing at the same time that she could fling responsibility away and dive into the warmth she heard in his voice. "Paris isn't just a city. It's light and dark…and art and couture, and the Left Bank, and the Louvre and—"

"And the Champs Élysées," he added. "But that's not a street you want to stroll on alone."

No, in her dreams she'd always walked hand in hand with a handsome stranger down the famous boulevard. "Surely you have contacts there."

She could almost hear the shrug she knew he was making. "That's not quite the same thing."

Regretfully, Cassie knew it was time to change the subject, to skirt this dangerous one. "Daphne came by again today. She wanted to know when you'd be home. I told her it would depend on how your business goes."

"You could have told her I was taking a sabbatical."

And Daphne would have followed him across the world, Cassie concluded silently. "She wanted to check on the boys."

"Cassie?"

"Yes?"

"I didn't call to talk about Daphne."

A strident knocking on her bedroom door startled Cassie. Recovering, she spoke above the receiver. "Come in."

Kevin stood at the doorway, obviously unwilling to enter her room, equally obviously wanting something. She smiled at him. "Your dad's on the phone. He called to talk to you and your brothers."

Kevin looked skeptical at best. "Yeah?"

"Yeah." Then she spoke into the receiver. "Stroke of luck. Kevin's right here. I'll go collect the twins while you two talk."

Cassie heard a brief, aborted snort of exasperation before he spoke in a resigned tone. "I'm not sure how you managed that, but you can put Kevin on in a minute. First, how are the twins?"

She stalled. "Why don't you see for yourself when you get home?"

"There's not anything you're not telling me?"

Two of her fingers slid together behind her back. "Of course not. Except for one thing. The boys and I are glad you're calling. Here's Kevin."

Not waiting to hear any more questions, Cassie thrust the phone at Kevin and disappeared, not sure whether she was more uncomfortable from avoiding talking about the twins...or from simply avoiding hearing what else Blake might have said, had Kevin not interrupted. Deciding it might not be safe to dwell on that answer, she sped toward the twins' room and away from any more questions, guessing she'd spend the night dreaming of strolling down the Champs Élysées. But this time the handsome man would no longer be a stranger.

CASSIE GLANCED at the peasant skirt she wore, hoping the outfit wasn't too much. Gripping the platter in her hands, she fixed a smile on her face and walked through the open door, into the classroom.

Mrs. Roman, the twins' teacher, greeted her with a big smile. Since Cassie'd had a heart-to-heart with the teacher, Mrs. Roman now understood the pain behind the twins' inappropriate comments, and was more than willing to help Cassie with her stand-in-mother plan for providing the class lunch.

"Children, we are lucky to have treats provided today by Mark and Todd Matthews." Mrs. Roman gestured toward the surprised-looking twins. "Come up front and help serve."

As planned, sturdy paper plates were stacked on the table beside Mrs. Roman's desk. The still-startled twins stared at Cassie for a moment, then at the huge platter of nachos she held out to Mark. It was a far cry from the ordinary cupcakes and cookies the other mothers had brought. Mrs. Roman filled Todd's hands with plates. Then the teacher called up a few other kids to help, having them dispense mock margaritas from the huge drink cooler into stemmed plastic cocktail glasses already sitting on the table.

"Cool!"

"Hey, it's not Kool-Aid."

Those and other assorted comments filled the air as the kids eagerly scooped nachos onto their plates and tasted the delicious, grown-up-appearing drinks.

As she'd worked out beforehand with Mrs. Roman, while the kids were eating their nachos, Cassie, with Maria's help, removed her casseroles of homemade enchiladas from the school's oven. The twins' eyes widened as they saw the steaming casseroles.

Amid the curious, excited chatter of the children, Mrs. Roman recaptured their attention. "Mark and Todd have a surprise for us. For teacher appreciation week, their family has brought lunch for us today. No cafeteria food."

Cheers greeted her words. Together, Cassie and Mrs. Roman served the enchiladas, with plenty of eager volunteers willing to pass the plates. Cassie glanced at her watch. As they'd prearranged, Maria had disappeared as soon as she brought in the casserole dishes, heading for the kitchen. Cassie hadn't wanted it to look as though the Matthewses' staff were preparing lunch, and after a tactful discussion with Maria, they'd agreed that she would keep a low profile. With only Cassie's presence, she hoped it would seem more as if a mother figure were providing lunch.

And now Maria was busy with dessert. The understanding Mrs. Roman had coaxed the school's dietitian into allowing them to use the huge deep fryer. Seeing that the children were busy digging into the enchiladas, Cassie slipped out, meeting Maria in the kitchen. Like a well-oiled assembly line, they formed the sopapillas, put them in frying baskets, set the timer and then dusted the fragrant drained triangles of golden fried dough with a generous amount of powdered sugar.

When she had a full platter, Cassie left Maria to busily cook more as she took in the initial batch. The kids, now fully into party mode, greeted the still-warm sopapillas with enthusiasm. While they were eating the popular dessert, Cassie ducked back into the kitchen, saw that Maria had just finished the last of the sopapillas, then dashed back to the classroom with the newly filled platter. As the children finished eating, she then retrieved the pièce de résistance.

Cassie took her last surprise into the large, empty room that was used for everything from indoor rec on bad-weather days to parent-teacher conferences.

Hurrying, she made sure the chairs were all folded and stacked against the wall, so that they wouldn't get in the way. She picked up one to stand on, removing a potted fern from a hook on the ceiling. As she took the plant down, she couldn't stop a shake of her head. Only in the big city could schools afford to decorate. Still, she was glad the hook was secured to the ceiling. Especially as she tied her surprise in place.

A piñata.

For a moment, she hesitated, wondering whether this was too much. She hoped the sophisticated city kids wouldn't think it was stupid. But then, she'd been worried about how they would accept the entire concept, and so far, so good.

Crossing her fingers, Cassie placed the baseball bat she'd brought on the small stage and dashed back to the classroom. As she walked inside, Mrs. Roman was instructing the kids to put their lunch things in the trash can at the front of the room. Seeing Cassie, she sent her a conspiratorial smile.

"And after you put your plates, forks and cups into the trash can, I want you to line up at the door. We're going—quietly—

to the all-purpose room for the remainder of Todd and Mark's presentation.''

As the children chattered, then whispered among themselves, Cassie spotted Todd and Mark, who were both staring at her in trepidation. They were probably wondering whether she planned to present something à la "The Beverly Hillbillies" that would embarrass them.

She sent them a reassuring smile, hoping she'd guessed right. Recrossing her fingers for luck, Cassie accompanied the line of curious children.

When Mrs. Roman opened the door and shepherded them inside, it was immediately clear that the piñata was a success. Laughing and chattering, the kids jockeyed for places in line as Cassie retrieved the baseball bat. She tried to hand it to the teacher, but Mrs. Roman waved her away with a smile. "This is your show. Go ahead."

Having enlisted Maria's help in its creation, Cassie knew the piñata was of exceptional quality, lasting through each child's attempt to break it open, which just upped the excitement. Whacking it with all their might, each kid was determined to be the one to bust the piñata. Mark picked up the bat when it was his second turn. Swinging at the colorful crepe-paper-covered donkey, he screwed his face into a mask of concentration and let go. With a huge crack, the piñata burst, spilling candy and prizes to scatter over the floor. As it broke, Mark sent Cassie a dazzling grin.

Abandoning their line, the kids dived for the contents, acting as though they were scrabbling for expensive items, rather than trinkets. As the other kids excitedly battled over the loot, Mark and Todd glanced at one another, and finally turned to Cassie. And then they smiled, sweet nine-year-old genuine little-boy smiles, causing another hitch in her heart.

CASSIE HUMMED as she filled the rattan tray with condiments, checking to make sure she had everything. Since Blake was returning today, she wanted to serve an all-American meal. And she wanted it in a more special setting—something that didn't scream, "Eat fast and then escape to a briefcase full of work!'' Seeing that she needed to add pickles, she turned to the refrigerator, just as Kevin ambled into the kitchen.

"What's this stuff for?" he asked, looking suspiciously at the tray that held mustard, ketchup, and other picniclike items. "You're not planning another fun family outing, are you?"

Cassie steeled herself to not react to the sarcasm in his voice as she turned from the refrigerator. "We're having hamburgers outside on the grill."

"Then what?"

She lifted one shoulder in a casual shrug. "Then, if you've finished your homework, you've got a free evening."

Kevin mumbled something under his breath as he turned to leave.

"Kevin, would you grab the fire extinguisher and take it outside, please?"

"What for?"

She called on her patience. "So we're prepared. Probably won't need it, but it's better to have it close by."

Rolling his eyes, Kevin retrieved the fire extinguisher from the rack inside the pantry and headed outside, muttering again, just low enough that she couldn't make out the words.

He was the difficult one. But Cassie couldn't find it in herself to be angry about his attitude. Being the oldest, he'd had the most years with their mother, and no doubt he missed her terribly. And because Kevin was a "cool" teenager, he tried to act tough. Her attempts at reaching him had been unsuccessful so far. The only one who really seemed to relate to him was Katherine Ann, which was unexpected, since she was more interested in intellectual pursuits than in the latest rock icons, as Kevin was.

The door opened again, and Cassie was surprised to see Blake. After his trip, she'd expected him to be late. Instantly she remembered their phone conversations—the overtones in his last call. She fought the fluttering in her stomach as she tried to sound casual. "Hey, you're early."

"The plane got in before schedule. We had a good tail-wind." Blake scanned the tray. "You up for another try on the family picnic?'' He unsuccessfully tried to hide his grin. ''I'm not sure you can whip up an earthquake this fast.''

She quirked her brow as she lifted one side of her mouth in a mocking half smile. ''We're just cooking burgers outside, to keep things simple.''

''Don't think we'll blow up the grill?'' he teased.

Before she could answer, the twins pounded down the stairs and burst into the kitchen. ''Hey, Dad!'' they chorused.

''Can we have something to eat?'' Todd asked.

''Yeah, we're starving,'' Mark added as they converged on Cassie and the refrigerator.

She held up her hands. ''Whoa! We're having hamburgers outside. You help carry everything outside, and we'll eat sooner.''

''Cool!'' Mark whooped, grabbing the rattan tray as Todd reached for the package of buns.

As they disappeared, Blake gave her a smug, pointed look. ''See, they're already back to normal. I told you there was nothing to worry about.''

Cassie hid her smile as she retrieved the hamburger, using the refrigerator as a shield for her disbelieving expression. ''I guess you're right.''

''Well, I *have* known them a little longer.''

Cassie smiled to herself as she formed the patties. ''Yes, you have.''

''My boys are tough.''

''Hmm. Well, as you said, you know them best.'' She picked up a tray heaped with hamburger patties. ''I'll check the grill.''

''And I'll go change,'' Blake replied, loosening his tie.

She nodded, then headed outside as the twins flanked him.

''How was the trip, Dad?'' Mark asked.

''Yeah, did you bring us anything cool?'' Todd chimed in.

''Nope, just me,'' Blake replied, glad to see the positive change in them.

''That's okay. It's better having you home, anyway,'' Todd told him, offering Blake some of his chips.

Automatically Blake took a few as he looked in surprise at

his son. It wasn't a typical comment for him to make. "How did things go while I was gone? Anything special?"

"Gosh, Dad. You should have seen what Cassie did!" Todd announced.

"Yeah, Dad," Mark added. "It was way cool."

"Fill me in," Blake urged, watching their happy faces.

They eagerly gave him a detailed description, not hiding any of their enthusiasm. He was stunned by the amount of trouble Cassie had gone to. She could have simply baked cupcakes or cookies, but she'd gone beyond the expected, to make sure that the twins felt special—that they didn't lack what the other kids had.

It was clear that Cassie had transformed them from sullen, dejected kids to happy ones by showing them how much she cared for them. Yet she hadn't let on to him for a second.

Blake cringed inwardly, remembering his flippant remark. She had remarkable control, not to have given him a big "I told you so." Impulsively he reached out to hug his sons, and was rewarded with answering hugs.

"We're glad you're home, Dad," Mark spoke first.

"Yeah."

Blake glanced outside, toward the patio. "Me too, guys. Me too."

OUTSIDE AT THE GRILL, Cassie shook her head, remembering Blake's simple male logic concerning his children. But all that mattered was that the boys were happy—she didn't need any other praise. Their smiles were her accolades.

Cassie checked the patties, turning them. One burger stuck to the grill, and she wrestled with it, not wanting it to tear apart and fall through the grid. Abandoning the spatula, she reached with her fingers to unstick the stubborn meat. Miscalculating, she grabbed part of the grill, as well.

"Yow!" she yelped, holding her stinging finger, looking around for water or ice, then remembering she hadn't brought out the drinks yet.

"What'd you do?" Kevin asked.

"Burned myself. I'd better put something on it."

When she spun around, Kevin stood directly in front of her, pointing the fire extinguisher at her. Before she could protest, Kevin squirted the fast-flowing foam over her hands, legs, torso and face.

Spluttering, she wiped layers of foam from her face.

"Kevin!" Blake's voice thundered across the patio.

"Uh-oh," Kevin muttered, hearing the anger in his father's voice.

"What do you think you're doing?" Blake demanded.

"She burned herself, Dad."

Blake whirled around, reaching out to grab her arms. "Are you all right, Cassie? Do you need to go to the emergency room?"

Reluctantly she held up her burned finger. "I think I'll live."

Blake turned again to Kevin. "You did all this because of a burned finger?"

Kevin gulped. "I wasn't sure exactly what she'd burned."

Seeing that Blake was about to explode, Cassie spoke up. "I don't think I said exactly what I'd burned."

"That's generous of you, Cassie, but I think this is more than overkill."

"Why don't you have Kevin finish cooking dinner and bring everything else outside that we need? I can change, and we'll eat."

Blake glanced between his stricken but hopeful-looking son and his drenched nanny. He wasn't sure why Cassie wanted to let Kevin off the hook, but she was the one who'd been doused with foam. "Since Cassie's in charge of you guys, I'll let her make the call. But don't let me catch you doing anything like this again."

"Okay." Kevin took the reprieve and ran, scooting inside before his father could change his mind.

Blake turned to Cassie, instinctively reaching out to wipe away some of the remaining foam on her face. His fingers lingered on her cheek, and he realized her skin was like warm velvet. Her eyes, seeming larger as the wet hair framed her face, focused on his.

Abruptly he withdrew his hand. "I guess you'd better get

changed. That goop must feel pretty miserable.'' His gaze
drifted over her once again. Then, turning on his heel, he left,
but he headed away from the house, down toward the gardens.

Cassie stared after him for a moment as she reached to touch
the spot where his fingers had lingered. The warmth remained,
as did the flutter of awareness he'd caused.

Chapter Eleven

Cassie handed Mark's vocabulary page back to him. "I think you've got them down now."

"Yeah. Uh, thanks."

"Sure, Mark. Now you guys can go to your Cub Scout meeting and not have to worry about homework when you get back."

"We better go put our uniforms on," D.J. added.

As they cleared out of the breakfast room, Kevin, Jimmy Ray and Katherine Ann came in from school. "Snacks are on the counter. How'd the college prep testing go, Katherine Ann?"

"A cinch. You'd have to have butter beans for brains not to ace the test."

Cassie watched a flash of hurt pass over Kevin's face.

"I'm glad you did well. How about you guys? How'd your day go?"

Jim shrugged. "Computer network was down. It was kind of boring."

Kevin remained conspicuously quiet. Since he'd had an English test that day, she didn't press, not wanting him to have to reveal how he'd fared in front of the others.

Katherine Ann took a cup of yogurt and one of the miniature veggie pizzas Cassie had prepared. "I'm going to take this outside, if it's okay, Mama. Then I'll swim for a while. No homework, since the test took all day."

Cassie knew she didn't have to worry about her daughter blowing off homework. Katherine Ann loved the accelerated classes she'd been placed in, and she was excelling in them. "Sure. Don't get too much sun."

"You put enough sunblock in the cabana for the whole neighborhood."

"Then use it," Cassie replied with a smile.

Katherine took her snack and headed outside.

"I want to go to the computer lab at the library, Mama," Jim added. "Albert said he wouldn't mind taking me."

She glanced between the boys. "Maybe Kevin would like to go with you."

Kevin rolled his eyes, and Jim looked pained.

Cassie took the hint. "Of course, Kevin might have plans of his own."

Relieved, Jim picked up an apple. "I won't be late, Mama."

As he left, Cassie smiled at Kevin. "Looks like you've got the house to yourself. The twins and D.J. are headed for Scouts. Guess you can do what you want."

"I've been thinking about yesterday—the fire extinguisher— and I thought I ought to do something to make it up to you."

"That's not necessary."

"Yeah…well, I was thinking we could fix the faucet in your bathroom. I know you've been trying to get a plumber."

Cassie blinked. "I didn't realize you knew how to work on plumbing."

He shrugged. "Doesn't take a genius."

Remembering his pain at Katherine Ann's casual remark, she softened. Even if he wasn't an expert at plumbing, what could it hurt? Perhaps he needed this chance to shine. Still, she hesitated. "Are you sure you can handle this?"

"I might need you to help."

"That wouldn't be a problem. Sure, I'd love to have the faucet fixed. We'll have to round up the tools—"

"Why don't you let me do that? I'll get everything and meet you upstairs."

She glanced at the kitchen counter. "I should put things away—"

"Good… I mean, okay. I'll have everything in the bathroom by the time you're done. Just ring me on the intercom when you're ready to come up."

Still surprised, Cassie straightened up the kitchen, clearing the table and counters. Pleased that Kevin was taking a step in her direction, she realized it would be worth an afternoon wrestling with the plumbing.

Upstairs, she saw that Kevin had gathered the tools, an impressive display. She hoped he knew which ones to use. "I'm ready if you are."

"Looks like I'll need your help. If you could hold the faucet while I loosen it.…"

Obligingly Cassie walked over to the tub, then reached for the faucet. Gripping her hands around the smooth metal surface, she held on as Kevin slowly maneuvered the wrench.

"This is a little harder than I thought," Kevin remarked as the wrench barely moved.

"I could help do that part—" Cassie offered, starting to release her grip on the faucet.

"No! You need to hang on to the faucet, or we'll mess it up. It's better if it comes off slow anyway."

And it was extremely slow. Cassie shifted, trying not to appear restless. After all, this was Kevin's project. Since she couldn't use the tub, anyway, if his repair didn't work, they wouldn't have lost anything. "Pedro said he thought it was the pipes, not just the faucet."

"That's 'cause he didn't want to fix it," Kevin replied.

Cassie digested this. He *might* be right, but Pedro always seemed like a hard worker. "Maybe it was a little too complicated for him."

Kevin shrugged. "Maybe." Slowly he turned the wrench again.

At this rate, Cassie figured, they'd have the faucet loosened by dinnertime. But sometimes it took patience with kids.

Nearly half an hour later, Cassie found herself wishing she could trade patience for a little speed. "Kevin, maybe I should help you. We could trade positions."

He smiled. "That might be kinda hard."

"No, it shouldn't be…" Releasing her grip, she tried to pull her hands away and found they wouldn't move. Struggling, she tugged harder, but her hands didn't budge. "What in the world?"

Kevin backed away, putting the wrench in the toolbox, a smirk covering his face.

"Kevin. What did you put on this faucet?"

He picked up the toolbox. "I better put this stuff away."

"Very funny. Now help me get unstuck."

"I think I'll go take a swim."

"Kevin!"

"You said I could do what I want."

"But that's not—"

Kevin disappeared.

"…what I meant," she finished in exasperation.

By her reckoning, the house would be empty for hours. The rest of the staff had finished their work earlier, while D.J. and the twins were doing homework. It was unlikely one of them would happen by the far end of this hall. Between the Scout meeting, the library and the pool, none of the kids would be looking for her. But by dinnertime, hopefully, someone would miss her. Shifting to keep the kink in her back from stiffening, she settled in for the wait.

BLAKE PUSHED OPEN the back door, then dropped his briefcase on one of the bar stools. Glancing around, he had a sense that something was wrong. The kitchen was both quiet and immaculate. And it penetrated his fatigue-clouded mind that that was what was wrong. Normally the kitchen generated an array of tantalizing smells, and Cassie's bustle kept it from being quiet. And by now the table was normally set, and the counters were filled with intriguing dishes. Now, by contrast, it seemed sterile, neglected.

And none of the kids were around. Had something happened? Fearing the worst, he pressed the intercom. Maria answered, assuring him that no one had been in an accident. Thanking her, Blake glanced around the kitchen, still feeling uneasy.

Then he realized that Cassie must have come up with another unique dinner idea. He wondered if they were going to try picnicking again. One thing he had to say for her, she never said die.

Whistling, he climbed the staircase, needing to fill the too-quiet house with sound. He headed down the hall toward his room, ready to change into something casual. But as he followed the curve of the hall, he noticed a light shining from Cassie's bedroom. He started to ignore the light, then wondered again if everything was all right. But his knock didn't produce the answer he expected.

"Thank God."

Hearing Cassie's weary, weak-sounding voice, he disregarded thoughts of privacy and rushed inside. But he didn't see her in the bedroom or the sitting room.

"Cassie?"

"In here."

As he headed toward the bathroom, he realized why her voice had sounded so weak from the hallway. He was lucky to have heard her at all from this distance. Entering the bathroom at a near run, he saw Cassie sitting on the side of the tub, latching on to the faucet. "Cassie?"

"I wondered when the cavalry would get here."

Blake tried to adjust gears from near panic to just plain confusion. "What are you doing?"

"Having loads of fun. You want to help me?"

Moving closer, he glanced cautiously at the tub. "Help you what?"

"Get unstuck."

"Just let go."

She sighed. "It's not quite that easy."

"Why not?"

"I've been superglued to the faucet."

Blake wondered if she'd lost her senses. "Did you try to fix it yourself instead of calling the plumber?"

She stared at him. "Right. I thought I'd just glue the leaks shut. Back in Podunk, that's what everybody does."

Hearing a note of anger mixed with her weariness, he

paused, suspecting he was treading on uncertain ground. "So, how'd you get yourself glued to the faucet?"

"Let's just say it wasn't a solo project."

"If those twins—"

"It wasn't the twins."

Blake pulled his brows together. "Kevin? After what he pulled last night? Wait till he—"

"Blake? Do you think you could get me unstuck before you put Kevin in the torture chamber?"

"Sure." He turned and headed toward the doorway. Stopping suddenly, he looked back at her. "Any idea how to do that?"

"Call around, find out who carries the antidote."

He looked at her blankly.

"You know. The stuff that makes superglue let go."

"Right. Will you be okay till I get back?"

Cassie sighed as she shifted position. "I've been fine for the last three and a half hours. I'll probably make it through a few phone calls."

Blake was torn between murdering his firstborn and finding the fastest way to locate the unsticking solution. After a few fruitless phone calls, inspiration struck. Blake talked to a technician at the local emergency room, then called the hardware store he suggested. Finding out he had barely half an hour before the store closed, Blake rushed upstairs, filled Cassie in, then sped away.

With the antidote in hand, he returned just as quickly.

Reentering her suite, Blake was struck by her quiet patience, the incongruity of her soft yet steely strength. Most women would be screeching endlessly, cursing him and his children. Instead, she'd seemed reluctant to name the culprit. It was the contradictions, he realized, that drew him. The steadiest woman he'd ever known, she was at the same time unpredictable.

"Got it," he told her, stripping off his jacket as he approached the tub. A devilish glint matched his sudden grin. "Any incentives for rescuing you?"

"Sure. I don't quit and leave the boys to glue you to the next nanny," she retorted.

Blake moved closer. "I don't know. I could think of worse punishments. Of course, I'm not sure the next nanny will look like you." He angled his face closer. "Or smell like you."

Panic struck, and it showed in the nervous clearing of her throat. "We could banter all night, but I *am* stuck to the faucet, remember?"

"Vividly. You can't run away."

Cassie remembered a time when all she could do was run. Forcing herself to ignore the appeal of his smile, she shrugged her shoulders. "You don't have to tell me. I've been stuck here for hours."

The words galvanized him. "Right. And when I get my hands on Kevin—"

"The antidote," she reminded him gently.

Blake tried to reach between her shoulder and the tub wall, but she was positioned so that it was impossible to reach the faucet from that angle. Slipping behind her, he straddled the outside wall of the tub, spooning his chest to her back. He heard a sudden, unexpected whooshing sound of nerves before Cassie stiffened.

"*What* are you doing?"

"Ungluing you," he replied.

"Do you have to be so...so *close?*"

"Afraid so."

She craned her head backward, meeting his eyes. The sudden heat in his gut had nothing and everything to do with the way they were sandwiched together. Seeing her eyes darken, the sudden melting of gray into pewter, he recognized that she felt the same impact. He sensed that she wanted to pull her gaze away, but, like him, was paralyzed by the intensity of the attraction.

"Cassie—"

Her voice was a mere croak. "Please..."

Please what? Continue? Stop? Erase what they both knew was pulsing between them? "Yes?"

"Use that stuff," she answered, a desperate note coloring her tone. "And get me loose."

For a moment, one that stretched out infinitely, he paused,

wondering why she wanted to run...wondering what or who she was running from. Then, giving in to the pleading in her eyes, he quickly applied the antidote, seeing her relief when her hands slid free. Unable to resist, he reached out and touched those hands, reddened by the pressure and the glue. Still, they were soft. He wondered if there was a matching softness in her. Resisting the urge to find out, instead he pulled her up as he stood, studying her hands.

"We need to get these checked out."

"Checked out?" she echoed.

"At the hospital."

"But there's no need. I'm fine now. No sense wasting money to have them tell me the same thing."

"The technician told me to take you in so they can make sure there isn't any serious injury from the contact, since it covered quite a bit of skin." His expression tightened as the anger at what Kevin had pulled resurfaced. "And since my darling son was responsible..." Her mouth opened again, and he laid a gentle finger across her lips, effectively silencing her. "Humor me. Pretend I'm in charge around here."

Either his words or his touch did the trick, because she gave up the argument, remaining uncharacteristically quiet as they drove to the hospital. The examination didn't take long. Luckily she hadn't suffered anything more serious than a mild skin irritation and a few kinks in her back. As they left the emergency room, Blake issued a muffled curse as he thought of the mean trick Kevin had played on her. And he'd been sure the boy was remorseful, that he'd made a connection with his son. Instead, it was clear that they were even more out of touch than he'd imagined.

"I hope you don't plan to heap that on Kevin's head," Cassie commented as she reclined back against the seat, looking exhausted.

"I'd have thought you would want to be part of the lynching party."

"Surely you can see that he's doing these things to push the boundaries? You know I don't believe in letting kids get away with murder, that I think they need as much discipline as love, but this is different. Trust me, I'm no saint, and I wasn't crazy about being glued to a faucet for hours, but these are just symptoms.''

Frustrated, Blake tapped the steering wheel, a fraction too hard. ''Of what, I hate to ask?''

''Kevin wants to make sure he has your attention. And that the main focus of the family hasn't changed since the kids and I came here. Before we moved in, you used to put him in charge pretty often—when housekeepers wouldn't stay with the twins and baby-sitters didn't show up. But now, that's all been taken away from him. And he wants to make sure you're not taking away your love, as well.''

Blake couldn't resist an impatient snort. ''He knows I love him.''

''Deep down. But he needs a reminder. He needs to know he's an important part of your family and that that won't ever change.''

''And I'm just supposed to let him off the hook for nearly drowning you with a fire extinguisher, then gluing you to a faucet?''

''No. He needs to know that you care enough to discipline him, too. But that will have to come from you. I don't mind taking the heat for punishing him, but he has to know that you are always aware of him, and that he matters enough for you to notice what he's done.''

Blake glanced over at her. For a moment, he was floored by the realization that without her guidance he might have sent a destructive message to his son. ''Any suggestions on the punishment?''

''It can't be just a slap on the wrist, or too severe. It's important for him to see his friends, so if you take away that privilege, it'll have impact. I'd ground him for two weeks, but I'd give him the option of working for free time. Tell him that if he's willing to do chores, he can accumulate time off his grounding. And it would be a pretty good idea if you could be home a lot during that time. Let Kevin know that if he's got to be housebound, you don't mind being there with him.''

''How'd you get so wise, Cassie?''

She stared into the darkness for a moment. "Experience. I've been at this single-parent thing longer than you have. You only lost your wife three years ago. I'm been on my own since David John was a baby. And I've been able to spend more of that time with my kids."

Realizing a fraction of her loneliness, he kept his voice gentle. "I don't know that being alone longer makes it easier. In fact, I think it would just get harder with time."

AS THEY BRACED THEMSELVES and entered the kitchen, Blake and Cassie were greeted by the aroma of roasting chicken.

Katherine Ann turned from the stove, her face flushed with effort, a voluminous apron enveloping her body. "Hi! Maria said you guys had to go on an errand, so I figured I'd better make some dinner. I let D.J. and the twins eat already—they were starving. Jim's still on his computer, and Kevin said he wasn't hungry."

"It smells wonderful, Katherine Ann," Cassie answered. "And I'm glad you let the younger guys eat. Otherwise they'd have filled up on junk food by now."

"Sure." She glanced from her mother to Blake. "Everything okay?"

"It's fine," Blake replied. "What smells so wonderful?"

"Rosemary chicken. I hope I did it like Mama's. The boys said it was good, but—"

Cassie gently broke the flow of words. "I'm sure they're right, and we're starving. Why don't you run upstairs and tell Jim to get washed up?"

"Yes, ma'am."

As Katherine left, Cassie turned to Blake, quirking her mouth.

"Do you want to talk to Kevin before dinner, or—"

"Definitely before. I don't want to be the only one choking on the rosemary chicken."

Katherine Ann skipped down the last few stairs. "Jim said he'd be down in a few minutes—he has something processing that'll be finished then. That'll give us time to toss the salad and make some fresh tea.'' She paused, glancing at Blake's sternly set face. ''That is, if you're really hungry.''

Blake forced his thoughts away from the looming talk with Kevin. ''Famished. And I want to try your cooking, Katherine Ann. I'll be ready to eat in a few minutes. And I'll let Kevin know that dinner's ready.''

''Thanks, Mr. Matthews.''

''Blake,'' he corrected in an absentminded tone, already heading out of the kitchen.

''Mama, is something wrong?''

Cassie smiled at her daughter. ''I think Blake's taking a crash course in parenting. But they'll both survive it—probably.''

Katherine Ann gave her one of those tolerant teenage looks that implied that Cassie had gone into one of her alien-world-parent dialogues.

''Don't worry, Katherine Ann. When you're a little older, I won't seem so strange. Or if I still do, you'll understand why.''

''Mama? Can I talk to you about something? I mean, if it's not a good time, I can wait.''

Cassie withheld her sigh. ''I suppose you want me to start calling you Kathy?''

''No. There are a ton of Kathys. It's kind of cool to have a name no one else does.''

Different children, different perspectives. ''So, what is it?''

''Well, back in Twin Corners I wouldn't have even asked…and I probably shouldn't now…''

Cassie prayed her most adventurous child wasn't about to request something she would not only deny but wish Katherine Ann hadn't asked about. Visions of boys and birth control danced menacingly in her thoughts.

Katherine Ann took a deep breath. ''It's just that the Russian Club is going to take a trip…and I wondered if maybe I could go.''

Field trip. What a relief. ''If the time and hours are reasonable, I think it sounds all right.''

''But, Mama, it's so expensive! I'd work—baby-sitting, anything I can to earn extra money, but…''

"Katherine Ann, how much can a field trip cost?"

Her daughter blinked. "Mama. They're going to St. Petersburg." She paused. "Russia."

Cassie gulped. "What?"

"That's why it's so expensive. I knew I shouldn't have asked. I just thought maybe now that things are better…and if I earned and saved a lot… I've got all the allowance you started giving me, except seven dollars, and I spent that on a book… and some nail polish."

Cassie had just begun giving her children an allowance since they moved to the city. "Katherine Ann, I'll have to think about all this. I know it sounds like a wonderful opportunity. Why don't you bring home the brochure, and we'll look through it?"

Katherine Ann dug into the deep apron pocket. "They gave them to us last week. I didn't think I ought to ask, but then… It's okay, Mama. Guess I was just dreaming again."

Cassie's throat thickened suddenly, as she remembered her own junior year, and the trip to California the band and drill team had taken. They'd washed cars until they were waterlogged, sold candy and magazines until the residents of Twin Corners were ready to flee at the sight of another determined teenager. But that had been before…before her life changed. And she hadn't been able to take the trip. It was something she'd never forgotten, something she'd always regretted. Gently she reached out and took the brochure from Katherine Ann. "I'll look at this. I'm not making any promises, because I don't want to disappoint you."

"Thanks, Mama. And, really, it's okay if we can't afford it."

"Afford what?" Blake asked as he reentered the kitchen, a reluctant Kevin trailing behind him.

"Nothing," Cassie said dismissively, purposely folding the brochure and sliding it into the towel drawer. "If you guys are hungry, we're about ready. If not, I'll probably eat the whole chicken by myself."

"D.J. and the twins already had a head start," Katherine Ann reminded her. "There's not a whole chicken left."

Jim ran down the stairs. "Sorry I'm late. I didn't think it would take the routine so long to finish."

"It's okay. We're just getting started. Jim, why don't you grab the jar of sun tea from the patio?" Cassie glanced at Katherine Ann for confirmation, and her daughter nodded, indicating that the tea was outside. "Your sister's made dinner. The younger guys have already eaten."

"I didn't hear any of them moaning from food poisoning," Jim remarked, grinning at his sister. "I'll get the tea."

Cassie glanced between Blake and Kevin. "Katherine Ann, why don't you show him where you put the jar?"

"Anybody could…" Katherine Ann glanced at her mother's face, saw her no-nonsense expression and amended her words. "Sure. I'll check on Gulliver while I'm out there."

"Perceptive child," Blake commented as the door closed behind Jim and Katherine Ann.

"At times."

"I think Kevin has something he'd like to say to you."

"Uh, yeah. I'm sorry I glued you to the faucet and sprayed you with the extinguisher." Kevin glanced upward at his father, whose expression urged him to continue. "And I won't be pulling any more dumb tricks."

"Glad to hear it, Kevin. I wasn't looking forward to finding my bed short-sheeted or filled with shaving cream."

From the expression that flashed across Kevin's face, it was all too clear to both adults that he regretted not having thought of these delights as well. "Yeah, well…"

"Tell you what—if you're washed up, why don't you grab the casserole dish from the oven, and we'll have dinner?"

Kevin glanced at her suspiciously, obviously waiting for the other shoe to fall. "That's it?"

"I don't usually suggest tar-and-feathering until the third offense, and you *don't* want to know what I recommend on the fourth. There's an oven mitt next to the trivet."

As she continued her calm, casual behavior with Kevin, Blake could only watch with nothing short of amazement. While she hadn't dismissed Kevin's actions, she also hadn't made him feel awkward and uncomfortable.

It was more than just a touch with kids. It hit him that she actually cared for them. Despite the sarcasm, taunts, pranks and other grief they'd given her, Cassie worried about them, celebrated their triumphs and helped them with their weaknesses. He thought of how she'd turned the twins' attitudes around.

Watching her, Blake wondered just how many other changes she would be making in their lives.

Chapter Twelve

Katherine Ann peeled a potato, then shoved it down the garbage disposal. Since it was the second one she'd destroyed, Cassie guessed there was something on her daughter's mind.

"School going okay? You've got quite a load this semester."

Katherine Ann shrugged. "Sure, but the work doesn't bother me."

"You're lucky that way. Things come easy to you."

Katherine Ann deposited a big clump of peelings into the casserole dish that held the potatoes. "Some things."

Ah, there was a problem. "Something that doesn't come so easily?"

"Mama, do you think if I go to the dance, that anyone will ask me to dance?"

Cassie's throat thickened, remembering her own slew of insecurities at that age. "Of course I do. You're a very pretty girl."

Katherine Ann studied the tile floor. "You have to say that. You're my mother."

"Actually, I *don't* have to. I said it because it's true."

Her daughter's gaze lifted to meet Cassie's, her young face screwed into earnest concentration. "Mama, there's this one boy. His name is Chad. You've seen him—he's on the debate team, too. He's got blond hair—the only cute guy on the team. I really like him, but…"

"But what?"

"He probably won't like me. He likes cool girls…city girls."

Cassie reached out to smooth her daughter's silky hair. "Just be yourself, and he can't help but like you. You're a very special person, Katherine Ann, and it shows."

A ray of hope shone in her daughter's eyes. "Then you think I ought to go to the dance?"

"Definitely. And I'll do everything I can to make things easier—you know I already volunteered to help out."

"Can we get a new dress, Mama?" She rushed the next words, as though anticipating a protest. "I know you already bought me a lot of nice stuff, but I thought, maybe something special? You know, that might make Chad notice me."

Cassie drew her into a hug. "I think sometimes every girl deserves a magical dress for a magical evening. The dance is in three days, so we'd better hurry." She drew off her apron and eyed the messy potato casserole ruefully. "Let's get a head start on the traffic."

"But what about dinner? I thought you wanted to make it ahead."

"I think it might be a good night for pizza or burgers. Kevin and the twins are probably having withdrawal from not getting enough take-out food, anyway."

Katherine Ann gladly abandoned her task. "I wasn't in the mood for scalloped potatoes anyway."

Cassie took one last look at the mangled potatoes and muttered, "Good thing."

BLAKE PULLED into the driveway, pleased that he'd gotten home on schedule. It had been difficult to pull off—he'd crammed eighteen hours of work into thirteen. But it was worth it.

Kevin was slowly coming around, having volunteered for household jobs that amazed Blake, even though he knew his son was motivated strictly by the desire to earn time off from his grounding. Kevin had managed to reduce his grounding by nearly a full week. The minute he came home from school, he started on the work list Cassie had drawn up for him, and he didn't quit until bedtime, hustling as Blake had never seen him do.

Blake was proud of him, and he wanted to show Kevin just how much. He could hardly wait till Kevin found out what he'd planned. Never having had time to involve himself in any of Kevin's school activities, Blake had decided to change that. Tonight was the school dance. Having heard Cassie and Katherine Ann discuss little else for the past three days had given him a great idea.

Blake had called the school counselor and offered to chaperon. It wasn't normally his sort of thing, and he hoped Kevin would see it as a move on his part toward the bonding he'd told his son he wanted. And since the school was woefully short of chaperons, his offer had been eagerly accepted.

Despite a hectic day, he'd managed to eliminate the biggest obstacle—five more hours of work.

Whistling, Blake strode inside, nearly as eager to surprise Cassie with his news as he was Kevin. He sensed she'd be startled—and pleased. She'd told him often enough that he had to be the one to take the steps to ensure that he and his sons stayed close...actually, she'd said to *grow* close. But he considered it repair work. He knew he'd spent more time working in the past three years, since Elizabeth's death, but his business had filled a huge void in his life.

Shaking away the memories, Blake concentrated on the present. Glancing at his watch, he realized there was less than half an hour to shower and change. Not seeing Cassie or Kevin, he hurried upstairs to wash away thirteen hours of work and tension. Sprinting down the stairs with five minutes to spare, Blake headed for the kitchen. Finding it empty, he turned toward the living room. At the doorway, however, he paused.

Standing silhouetted by the late-setting sun, Cassie was a vision in a simple sheath of a dress. She looked incredible. The scoop neck of the black silk accented her delicate collarbones, while the cap sleeves revealed her toned arms. His eyes slid to the abbreviated hemline—while a popular length, it was shorter than anything he'd seen her wear before. Simple black heels accentuated her long legs.

She'd left her hair loose, hair he'd once thought frumpy because it wasn't tamed into a sleek, sophisticated cap. It was the color of burnished wheat, long and thick—a stylist's dream. As she stood there, tall, slim, utterly unselfconscious, her fresh beauty was stunning.

Then she stepped closer. And took his breath away. Eyes of smoke—pure gray, with no hint of blue or green—focused on him. Had he once thought she needed more makeup? She was perfect just as she was.

Cassie gestured nervously toward the dress with her hands. "It's too short. I know it is. I didn't mean to shorten it this much. I was redoing my old dress…Katherine calls it my funeral dress…fixing the neckline and sleeves and all…and I guess I was a little nervous. Anyhow, I wound up taking off more material than I meant to. I know people are wearing them like this, but it's not really me. At least, I guess it's not." She met his gaze. "What do you think?"

Magnificent sprang to mind. "It looks good, Cassie." He cleared his throat. "Real good."

She smiled finally, a bit of her nerves fading. "I thought you were going to be a lot later." Then her gaze took in his damp hair. "Well, look at you. You're all showered and changed. You going somewhere special?"

"I should ask you the same thing."

"Mama, Mr. Matthews, you look great."

Cassie gazed past him into the hall. "Thanks, Katherine Ann. You guys about ready?"

"Yes, Mama."

Blake turned, seeing Kevin. "Not so fast."

"But, Dad, my grounding was up yesterday, and—"

"I know. But before you leave, I have a little surprise for you."

Kevin looked suddenly wary. "What?"

Blake smiled. "I volunteered to chaperon your dance tonight."

"What?" But the startled question came from more than just Kevin. Cassie's voice was chiming in, as well.

He spun around. "I knew you'd be pleased."

She stared at him. "I volunteered, too."

"Great." Kevin threw his hands upward. "Could this *get* any more embarrassing?"

Blake looked in surprised dismay at his son. "What's so embarrassing about it?"

Kevin wore the look of perpetual teenage disgust. "Well, if you can't figure it out…"

"I know that acknowledging you have parents at your age is an embarrassment in itself, but somebody's parents have to be the chaperons or there's no dance."

"But why'd it have to be you two?"

Blake glanced at Cassie long enough to see her register the insult.

But she quickly camouflaged her feelings. "Katherine Ann knew that I'd volunteered, and I don't plan to cancel. Actually, neither of us can cancel or, as your dad pointed out, there'll be no dance."

"I killed myself for a week so I could take Jenny to this dance, and now you guys…" Kevin sank onto the ottoman. "Got any more wonderful surprises?"

"Actually, I do," Blake answered, disappointed by Kevin's reaction. "Keep up this attitude, and after the dance you can look forward to another week of grounding."

Obviously startled, Cassie looked at Blake with growing admiration. "Well, we'd better get going."

"Can't Albert drive us?" Kevin asked. "I mean, Katherine Ann and Jenny and me? Please?"

"What about Jim?" Blake asked, not sure he should accede to Kevin's wishes.

"He doesn't have a date. He's going to watch D.J. and the twins. Please, Dad?"

Remembering the embarrassment of being chauffeured by his father at that age, Blake wavered. "I guess that would be all right. Cassie and I will see you at the dance."

"Great," Kevin mumbled.

"What?"

"Nothing. I mean, thanks, Dad."

As Katherine Ann and Kevin started to leave, Blake called out. "Katherine Ann?"

She paused. "Yes?"

"You look really pretty tonight."

She blushed, looking much the way her mother did when pleased. "Thanks. It's a new dress."

He smiled. "The dress is nice, too."

Flushing under his praise, Katherine Ann literally shone. "Thank you." Her gaze skipped toward her mother, her eyes telegraphing her gratitude, both for the guidance and for the new dress.

Noticing the glance, Blake realized that Cassie looked as touched as her daughter. He doubted Cassie would have been any more pleased if the compliment was directed at her.

Katherine Ann turned to leave just as Kevin returned.

"Dad, you're not going to…you know…hang out with us at the dance, are you? Not that it wouldn't be…uh, cool, but Jenny doesn't know you're coming, and…"

Blake let him off the hook. "Don't worry. We'll remain anonymous. And I imagine we can find something to do other than hang out with you two. Even though that would be 'cool.'"

Kevin looked as though he'd just been rescued from death row. "Okay, see ya."

As he and Katherine Ann disappeared, Blake turned to Cassie with a wry smile. "We haven't even gone to the ball yet, and one of the coaches has turned into a pumpkin."

"A chauffeur-driven pumpkin," she reminded him, a smile tilting her lips.

Blake shook his head. "Prince Charming better work on the charming part before they pick up Jenny, or she's not going to let him anywhere near her glass slippers."

Cassie laughed—a warm, throaty, exuberant laugh. It was a sound that reached down and snagged him, making him think of cool evenings, a brightly burning fireplace, and lights turned down very low.

She stepped forward, picking up a small purse. "With an example like you, how can he miss?"

The doorbell rang suddenly, breaking the moment. Cursing under his breath, Blake didn't wait for Maria to answer the door, instead striding over and yanking it open himself. Daphne was poured across the door frame, as though her voluptuous body had been molded for just that purpose. Blake bit back a second curse. "This is a surprise, Daphne."

Well tended, perfectly shaped brows rose. "Really? You look all dressed and ready for me."

He glanced at her form-fitting evening gown. "Afraid not. You're not outfitted for a night at the high school gym."

She made a moue of disapproval as she slinked inside. "And why would anybody want to be?"

Blake chuckled, knowing Daphne's tastes didn't run to anything so mundane. "To chaperon a school dance."

"Surely they have people to do that sort of thing."

"Yeah. They're called parents."

She give a small shiver of distaste. "How dreadful for you. How'd you get roped into this?"

"I volunteered."

"Oh, darling. You're just getting entirely too serious about this parent business."

Blake tried to remember that she didn't know anything about the "parent business" she so casually dismissed. Before he could respond, Daphne had entered the living room and spotted Cassie.

"Well, if it isn't Cinderella," cooed Daphne. "Traded in your Mary Poppins persona?"

"Cassie volunteered to chaperon as well," Blake offered.

"How very convenient. Aren't you lucky to have someone right here in the house to help with all these parent chores?"

Blake studied Daphne warily. It wasn't like her to be kind, especially to Cassie. "Yes, I am."

"Would you be a dear and get me something to drink, Blake? I'm about to perish."

Blake turned automatically toward the bar.

"Do you have some tea or juice? I'm really not in the mood for anything stronger."

This *was* a different side to his sister-in-law. "Sure. I'll see what I can find in the kitchen."

"I COULD GO—" Cassie started to offer, as Blake left the room. Waiting on Daphne was definitely preferable to being left alone with her.

"When a man offers, take advantage of it," Daphne said, interrupting her. "It's not like it happens all that often."

Cassie nodded, also suspicious.

As Blake disappeared, Daphne turned toward her, and Cassie knew she had good reason to remain wary. But Daphne's words threw her.

"You look very nice, Cassie."

Cassie glanced down, still self-conscious about her converted dress. Especially since the other woman was expensively gowned in what was no doubt a designer original. "Thank you."

"So you're accompanying Blake to the school dance?"

Cassie nodded. "Well, we're both chaperons."

"But to all appearances, he'll be escorting you."

"I suppose so."

Daphne's smile was offset by a look of deep concern. "Do you think that's wise?"

"I'm not sure I know what you mean."

Daphne waved her hands, gesturing around the expensively furnished room. "Blake has a certain…image to maintain. Most especially for his business contacts. As you no doubt have learned, his business is very important to him. I wonder what the men he deals with would think of him escorting his children's nanny."

"I suppose you think you'd be a better choice?" countered Cassie.

Daphne shrugged one of her perfect shoulders. "I didn't say that. But how does it look with you on his arm? And trust me, in L.A., you will be seen, whether you're at the local school or in the Polo Lounge."

"I think you're exaggerating," Cassie replied, adding silently, *or just making trouble.*

Daphne's eyes narrowed as she sighed. "I know you've done your best, but you and I both know that little dress you're wearing isn't quite up to the standards of Blake's circle. While I'm sure it was fine back in Oklahoma—"

"Texas," Cassie corrected.

"Of course."

"There's some fresh sun tea," Blake announced, coming back into the living room. "Cassie makes some every day."

Daphne accepted the tea, curling her manicured nails around the glass. "Then I'm sure it must be wonderful."

Blake draped a casual arm around his sister-in-law's shoulders. "Daphne, you don't mind being on your own, do you? We'd better leave, if we're going to be on time."

"Maybe Daphne would like to go with you," Cassie said challengingly.

Blake laughed. "I don't think so. Daphne would rather go without a manicure than be dragged to a high school gymnasium. Come on, Cassie."

Blake steered her toward the door. Glancing backward, Cassie saw a mixture of sympathy and frustration etched across Daphne's face. And she wondered suddenly whether the other woman was right.

HIGH SCHOOL GYMNASIUMS hadn't changed that much, Blake noted. Like his sons, Blake had attended public school, at his father's insistence. While his mother had preferred a well-known prep school, his father had said that would turn him into a wuss. And his father had prevailed—as usual.

Blake reached for Cassie's elbow as they strolled farther inside, and was surprised when she first jumped, then sent him a nervous smile. Glancing around, he saw that none of the kids were really paying any attention to them. Despite Kevin's apprehension, Blake suspected most of the kids were more concerned with their dates and friends than with the chaperons.

"You don't have to act like I'm going to bite," Blake tried to joke, wondering at the strained look in Cassie's eyes.

"Of course not. But some of your influential friends or associates might see you here."

"In the high school gym?" Incredulous, he stared at her. When had she started to care about seeing and being seen?

"I thought in L.A. you could be seen anywhere."

"I hardly think that includes the public high school gym. But even if it did, why should I care?"

"You have an image to maintain…one that doesn't include being seen with your nanny."

"You're the children's nanny, not mine," he pointed out, hoping to erase the frown between her eyes. "Although I'm not averse to a little nurturing."

"You're not taking this seriously."

"Of course not. Sounds like you swallowed a book on snobbery. And trust me, all that will get you is indigestion."

Her lips twitched. "Then you don't mind being seen with an employee?"

His eyes traveled over her appreciatively. "I don't know. Maybe it would be better for my *image* if everyone thought you just couldn't resist me."

That twitching was turning into a full smile. "Don't think much of my powers of resistance?"

"Actually, I think they're way too high. But we can work on that."

Cassie avoided his gaze and spotted someone headed in their direction. Tugging on Blake's hand, she leaned toward him. "There's Mr. Eldon."

"Who?"

"The principal," she explained, a touch of exasperation on her face. How could he not know who his son's principal was? "We'd better go speak to him."

As Cassie greeted him, Blake saw the principal's obvious surprise and admiration as he took in Cassie's transformation. When the man continued staring, Blake felt his jaw twitch.

"Mrs. Hawkins, delighted to see you." The principal's eyes signaled approval. "Just delighted."

"Nice to see you too, Mr. Eldon. I'd like you to meet Mr. Matthews—Kevin's father."

Mr. Eldon dragged his gaze from Cassie, slipping back into his official principal role. "Pleased to meet you, Mr. Matthews. We always appreciate parents who care enough to donate their time."

Blake tried to put on his best fatherly persona, remembering how much he'd disliked the principal when he was a student, also trying to remember that he was here voluntarily, that Mr. Eldon hadn't summoned him into his office to discuss one of his many high school pranks. "Our kids are worth it."

Cassie smiled—one of those sunshine bursts. And Blake realized his words had impressed her more than Rodeo Drive and Hollywood put together.

"Very good." The principal harrumphed. "I'd better go patrol the parking lot. Some of our kids tend to forget the dance is *inside.*" After raising his eyebrows to make sure his meaning was understood, Mr. Eldon left.

Blake stared at the principal's retreating back. "Let's liberate the kids...maybe lock the door so Eldon can't get back in."

Cassie shot him a stern glance, but then her lips quivered as they pushed upward in a grin. "He is a pompous old thing, isn't he? But I guess he got that way from dealing with thousands of teenagers."

"Thousands... On second thought, he probably needs a vacation and lots of sympathy. I doubt I'll be able to manage my own, much less thousands."

Cassie's smile softened. "You'll do fine. You just had to get back into practice."

Blake studied her face again, her entire appearance. He wondered if he'd been in some sort of blind, comatose state when he first met her. Or had Cassie changed so much? Besides oozing sex appeal, she'd obviously acquired a sense of style. Just by altering an old dress, she'd made it distinctive, fashionable. He guessed it was a combination of both. She possessed a natural beauty, yet she'd changed, too. It was as though removing her from Twin Corners had allowed her to blossom, to remember that she was a desirable woman.

The music slowed, and it was a recognizable tune. Suddenly,

Blake wanted nothing more than to hold her in his arms. He stretched out one hand. "Dance?"

"Ah, well, I guess that would be okay. I mean, we are the chaperons and all, but—"

He placed two fingers lightly against her mouth. "Let's don't make this a brain buster. I think we're allowed to dance."

Nodding, she accepted his hand. The music softened even more as the lights dimmed. Blake swept her into his arms, startled at Cassie's unexpected trembling.

Drawing his brows together, it hit him that she was nervous about being either in any man's arms...or specifically in his. He had a growing need to know which it was.

She seemed delicate within his embrace, something else he hadn't expected. The softness had been a shock. Now the delicacy was, as well. Although most of the teenagers were fitted against one another as though they'd been poured from twin molds, Blake held Cassie a respectable distance away from him. Then the lights dimmed a bit more.

"To hell with respectability," he muttered beneath his breath, pulling Cassie closer.

Although she didn't resist, he could feel a new quiver of awareness—along with the press of her full breasts against his chest, the wisp of her waist that his hands easily spanned. It was hard to believe she had three half-grown children. Having seen her attired in both a towel and a bathing suit, he knew her spectacular figure wasn't the result of carefully chosen clothing. Amazingly, she didn't seem to be aware of her impact. Instead, she seemed as nervous as though this was her own high school dance.

Cassie glanced up at Blake, trying to still some of those nerves. How long had it been since she was in a man's arms? Longer than she wanted to think. Far too long.

And she was enjoying it far too much.

Reality needed to make a quick appearance, but for the moment, she savored the sensation, enjoyed the feel of the hard lines of his body, the strength in muscles she'd seen firsthand. In another time, another place... She wondered if they could have bridged the wealth of differences between them, the separate worlds they came from. But there wasn't another time for her. She'd wasted all her chances long before she met Blake.

And she couldn't waste this opportunity for her children's chances. Giving in to the thoughts she was having about Blake could only spell disaster. If he reciprocated in any way, and things turned out badly, she and her children would be turned out. No man would keep a woman from a soured relationship around to raise his children. She had to remember that—and not give in to the tug of emotions that pulled at her.

Then the rush of his breath tickled her neck, making her want to throw her head back and allow him access to the sensitive areas of her throat, to allow him to explore further....

Kevin danced by with his date, Jenny. Glancing at them, Cassie stepped back a bit, just as Blake did, obviously having spotted the young couple at the same time. Still, Cassie was vibrantly aware of Blake and his hold on her.

Blake was no less aware of Cassie. Realizing that this wasn't the place to push any further, he tried to instill a degree of normality into his voice. "Do you remember your high school days? All those nervous, sweaty dances?"

He felt her stiffen within his embrace, yet her voice was steady. "Sure."

Blake wondered why she was holding herself so rigidly. "Who'd have thought we'd ever look back on them as our best times?"

"Not me," she replied, sounding a bit strangled.

"We had it good then, didn't we? No responsibilities, no kids to worry about, no deadlines breathing down our necks." He relaxed, remembering those carefree days. "But I guess everybody slides through high school, not realizing how lucky they are."

"I guess so," she replied shortly.

He wondered why she'd suddenly gone nearly mute. It wasn't like her. Usually, he couldn't get her to stop talking. "It probably doesn't matter if you live in Twin Corners or the big city, it was an easy time."

Cassie didn't reply, but now she was even more noticeably tense—far more than her initial stiffness. It was as though something about her high school years upset her. He wondered what could be bothering her. Suddenly he remembered how she'd clammed up in the music store when he asked about John Lennon's assassination, something that had taken place during her high school years. What was it about that time that upset her so?

Come to think of it, he knew very little about her past. She'd been evasive about her swimming and diving skills, as well. It was as though that part of her life were strictly hands-off. Again, he wondered why. And wondered more at his need to know all about her. If she weren't so open and talkative about everything else, it wouldn't seem so out of character.

She finally glanced up at him. "I prefer to live in the present."

"You're right. The past always looks better because we've left it behind." He knew it was time to put the conversation behind them, too. "Besides, I'm having a pretty good time right now. I don't think I ever enjoyed being in a school gym this much before."

It took her a moment to reply, and she didn't meet his eyes as she spoke. "You like being a chaperon?"

"The chaperon part doesn't have anything to do with it. It's strictly the company."

Amazingly, he saw a blush build, warming her cheeks with delicate shading. Women didn't blush anymore, did they? The song ended, and Cassie stepped out of his arms.

"I think we should get back to our chaperon duties," she suggested, her voice a little more high-pitched than usual. "I wonder if Katherine Ann's having a good time. I haven't seen her dancing."

Blake gently turned her around toward the refreshment table, where Katherine Ann stood next to a boy—no doubt the infamous Chad—engrossed in conversation.

Cassie kept her gaze on the young couple, then released a sigh. "She's so serious, I was afraid she might not fit in. But this looks like it could be a 'Dear Diary' moment."

"Katherine Ann's doing fine, just like D.J. and Jim. They're doing more than just fitting in. They've taken L.A. in stride."

As Blake spoke, he realized that Cassie had deliberately turned the conversation away from herself. He would let it go for now, but he planned to pursue it again, without a gymful of teenagers for an audience.

"Kevin looks like he's having a great time." She smiled in his direction.

"Guess he likes this girl," Blake replied, following her glance.

"More like an impossible crush, but she's a "brain," and he was afraid she wouldn't like him. But she's a really sweet girl. Doesn't seem to matter to her if he's popular, a jock, or on the honor roll."

Blake raised his brows. "You know all that about her?"

"She came to visit Kevin several times while he was grounded—sort of like visiting hours at the penitentiary. But I usually served something better than bread and water. She was easy to talk to. She brought Kevin some books—which he's actually reading to impress her."

Everything Cassie said amazed him. It took a moment to sort through all the questions forming and decide which he should ask first. "He's reading?"

"Not with great joy yet, but I think it might be growing on him. Katherine Ann talks with him about the books he's reading, helps him understand them. Then he can talk about them with Jenny."

"How did you get Katherine Ann to agree to that?"

"I didn't. I only found out by accident, when I heard them talking. Katherine Ann told me later that it was important to Kevin."

"So she just volunteered to help him?"

"Why not?"

Why not, indeed? It was the sort of thing families did for one another—but there was one distinction. Katherine Ann and Kevin weren't really family, even though the blending was blurring a lot of lines. "But you know what's important to Kevin?"

"It would be hard to help guide him if I didn't."

Blake was finding all this difficult to process. Kevin hadn't opened up to him in…well, since Elizabeth's death. "How did you get Kevin to tell you all this?"

Cassie shrugged. "He opened up a little since I didn't embarrass him when Jenny came to visit. I guess he was expecting me to attach a ball and chain and frisk his visitors. But I could tell how important this girl was to him. Don't worry—nothing serious, just a major case of puppy love."

How could she know so much about his son, when Blake didn't have an inkling of these adolescent feelings, certainly not of what was important to Kevin? He admired how well she had grown to know his children. In fact, it impressed the hell out of him. Yet suddenly he wondered if he'd given too much control to Cassie. Was she becoming more their parent than he was? "I wish I'd known how he felt."

Her smile was soft. "You will. You're taking the right steps, spending more time with him." She waved her hands, gesturing around the gym. "Volunteering tonight, for example. He says he's embarrassed, but deep down he's pleased that you're getting involved. Besides, it's easier for me. I'm with them more while you're at the office. Sort of an age-old problem. The wife's at home while—" Her hands flew up suddenly to block her mouth. Flustered, she could only stammer. "Not that I meant you and I… I mean, I know we're not…"

His voice was flat. "I know what you meant. You're doing what I hired you to do—raise my children."

His tone sent a trace of panic through her. Was he regretting that decision? And her growing attachment to his sons? "I'm helping you to raise them," she corrected hastily. "Unless you give up your business, you can't be with them as much as you want. I'm a temporary figure in their lives, you'll be there forever." Realization and sadness swept through her as the truth of her words sunk in. It was a painful truth. She was growing to care too much for his boys, and one day her job would be done. She'd be expected to walk away, like any contractor whose project was completed. She wondered whether engineers and architects left a little bit of their hearts behind when a building was constructed. Could she drive by the Mitchell home to see how time and the elements had affected it? To see whether it was filled with sunshine or storminess?

Blake recaptured her attention. "Right now you know my children better than I do."

"I know what interests them, what they're involved in, but you know their hearts." She was beginning to, as well, but she couldn't tell him that. Any more than she could tell him that he was encroaching on her heart, as well.

His eyes cleared with her last words. "You want to step outside, get some fresh air?"

She reached for humor, needing to chase away the feelings he was causing. "Ready to join Mr. Eldon in the parking lot?"

Blake gestured toward the big double doors at the front of the gym. The principal stood in front of the entrance, talking to a wallflowerish group of teenagers who weren't dancing. "Actually, he just came back inside. He can probably handle the crowd for a few minutes."

"You don't think he'll notice us slipping out?"

Blake grinned devilishly. "There's a back door. Besides, I doubt he can give chaperons detention."

"Now, *that's* a good example," she muttered, pretending to be annoyed, while she allowed him to tug her toward the rear of the gym. They bypassed the punch bowl and a line of giggling girls obviously hoping to attract male attention.

Outside, despite L.A.'s notorious hazy skies, the air was fresh. Blake felt a sudden urge to escape the confines of their roles, to forget that they were chaperons...parents. Purposely he walked toward the perimeter of the parking lot, where it sloped downward to a grassy, tree-covered bank.

"It would be pretty embarrassing if Mr. Eldon had to bust us for hanging out in the parking lot," Cassie joked, a nervous laugh punctuating her words.

"I'm good for the bail," he replied as he tugged her down the slope, not willing to let her escape the mood with humor.

"Blake, um...perhaps we shouldn't get so far away from the dance—"

"Perhaps you can shut up and dance with me."

"Dance?" she echoed.

Blake cocked his head. "You can hear the music.... It's even something recognizable." He held out his hand.

Gingerly she put her hand in his and lifted her eyes to his. This time there were no prying eyes, no children, to be concerned about. And Blake let the more liberated beat move their bodies. Instead of stiff, they were loose-limbed. Closeness replaced propriety, and as it did, banked desire jumped to life.

Blake bent his head, placing his lips on the tender flesh of her neck. Her answering sigh was almost a shudder. He felt the firm yet soft press of her breasts, then moved his hands downward, pulling her hips close to his.

Now barely moving, they swayed to the distant music. Lifting his head, Blake met her eyes, saw caution mixed with desire and a lick of fear. He chose to ignore all but the desire. His mouth, a whisper away from hers, teased her beguiling lips, and he watched her eyes darken in response.

Knowing he was crossing an irretrievable barrier, Blake paused for a fleeting fraction of time, then moved forward, knowing only that he wanted to taste, to explore. He wanted to push her boundaries, peel back the layers of disguise she hid behind. Gone was the knowledge that she was his children's nanny, his employee. In its place, there was simply hunger.

Her lips were soft, yet not yielding, pressed into a firm line of defense. He traced their outline softly, persuasively, then ran one finger down the seductive line from her fragile collarbones to the dip of her provocative neckline. Her mouth opened in a gasp, and he took swift advantage, touching his lips to hers, then gently exploring the tender recesses. She stiffened immediately, pulling back for an instant before limply joining his embrace. He felt her fingers reach around his neck, then thread through his hair, before moving down to his shoulders. Rewarded by her response, no longer reluctant, but eager, Blake emboldened his advances.

Unable to resist, he drew his hands down her sides, then cupped her full breasts, eliciting a gasp as her fingers tightened convulsively on his shoulders. Even as she leaned toward him, he sensed a change, a sudden resistance that had her pulling away in the next instant.

Her face was flushed, her lips were still ripe and full from their kisses, and the gray of her eyes had deepened to dusky pewter, yet she was shaking her head. "That shouldn't have happened."

Blake didn't expect the quick stab of pain that her words caused.

"But it did," he reminded her, refusing to relinquish her gaze.

"It can't happen again," she insisted.

His brows rose, doubting he'd heard her right. "It *can't?*"

"No, it can't." She stepped away shakily, and he watched her struggling to regain control. "And we have to forget it ever happened at all."

Blake didn't plan to make it easy for her. "You might pretend that you don't want it to happen again. But do you really think you can forget?"

The quick darkening in her eyes told him she couldn't. No more than he.

Chapter Thirteen

Cassie pounded the flour-dusted breadboard, taking out her frustrations on the defenseless mound of dough. Since the moment it ended, she'd resolutely told herself to forget the kiss she'd shared with Blake. And she'd done nothing but think of it ever since. If she allowed herself, she could even feel the brush of his lips, his deepening kiss, his oh-so-clever hands, the way she'd swayed into his arms as though someone had softened all her bones.

And that someone was Blake…her employer, her children's chance for a bright future. She'd risked that future by indulging herself, by learning that she hadn't been wrong about his appeal, about the strength of his embrace, or about the powerful pull of the man himself.

And he'd been right, damn him. She couldn't forget what had passed between them. Couldn't stop wishing it could have continued. Couldn't prevent herself regretting that she would never be able to turn back the hands of time, for the outcome to be so very different. For her choices to be ones that might include him. She'd fallen too fast once before. Look what that had gotten her.

"Mama, isn't that about ready?" Katherine Ann asked, watching as her mother nearly destroyed the dough.

Cassie released her death grip on the bread and pushed back a stray lock of hair. "You're right. I don't know what I was thinking.'' She passed the dough over to Katherine Ann, who shaped it carefully into a loaf.

They both started when Blake's study door slammed suddenly. They glanced at each other and then Blake as he stormed into the kitchen.

''Problem?'' Cassie asked, hoping none of her earlier thoughts were transparent.

''You could say that.'' He held up two fingers scarcely an inch apart. ''With the McCutchen deal this close, the whole thing could go out the window.''

''Why?''

''Because McCutchen is a family man, and he wants a nice respectable dinner, complete with wives, before he leaves town. The way he's dithered on this deal, I wouldn't be surprised if he pulls out.''

Cassie hesitated. ''Doesn't he know—''

''That I'm widowed? Yes, he told me to bring the nice young woman he's sure I'm seeing.''

''A date?''

''Yes. And the dates I've had lately wouldn't exactly fit McCutchen's standards.''

Cassie felt a fist of jealousy stab her as she imagined the beautiful women Blake had dated.

''One could, Mr. Matthews,'' Katherine Ann put in shyly.

Both Cassie and Blake stared at her blankly.

''You could take Mama. She's respectable.''

Cassie decided she should have a hole drilled in the floor of the kitchen for just such occasions. Then she *could* disappear at will. But Blake was looking anything but dismayed.

Katherine Ann abandoned the bread and turned to her mother excitedly. ''And you've got that new dress you bought at the sale to wear to my school program.''

''I hardly think Mr. Matthews—''

''Tell me more about this dress.''

Since Cassie was staring at him, openmouthed, Katherine Ann complied. ''It's navy blue velvet, and she looks beautiful in it. She almost wore it to the school dance, but she said it was too fancy.''

Remind me to begin drilling that hole tomorrow morning.

"Well, Cassie, are you going to bail me out, be my 'respectable' date for the evening?"

"I'm sure you had someone else in mind," she said evasively.

His eyes met hers, telegraphing the heat they'd shared, which neither of them had forgotten. "I think you know what I had in mind."

Blushing, Cassie buried her face behind the huge sack of bread flour. *Oh, do I ever.*

"Does this mean you're going, Mama?" Katherine Ann asked, her adolescent enthusiasm filling the kitchen.

"You wouldn't desert me in my hour of need, would you?" Blake glanced pointedly at his watch. "And before you remind me about the bread you're baking and the million other excuses you're going to dream up, it's several hours till we have to be there. And I imagine Kevin wouldn't mind being in charge for a change."

Cassie met twin pairs of inquiring eyes and knew she was defeated. Thank God she was supposed to be respectable tonight.

BUT AS SHE STUDIED HERSELF in the mirror, the dress didn't seem as respectable as she'd remembered. True, it was cut simply, but had it always clung so? And while the high neckline was certainly modest, the dress dipped to a vee at her back, exposing a considerable expanse of skin. And with her hair swept up, there was no hiding the revealing back.

A little desperately, she reached into her closet, flipping through the sparse selection. Other than her one "good" church dress, which was over ten years old and covered everything from her chin to her toes, nothing was even passable. Now, even her "funeral" dress was inappropriate. She reached for the dowdy but respectable church dress just as someone knocked on her door.

"Come in," she muttered from inside the closet.

The door opened a fraction. "Cassie? Are you ready?"

She stepped out of the closet. "Not quite. I need to change. I don't think I'd better wear this."

The door opened a bit wider, and Blake stuck his head inside. Realizing she was dressed, he pulled the door open and strode inside. "Why not? You look great."

She spun around self-consciously, showing him the back of the dress. "I doubt your Mr. McCutchen would approve."

"*I* approve."

She reached up to unfasten the hair clip. "Maybe with my hair down—"

His hand stopped hers. "Leave it."

"But—"

"Leave it."

She met his eyes and felt her throat go dry. Remembering his hands touching her, her nipples hardened in response, and a weakness flooded her.

"Mama? Are you ready? I want to see before you leave."

Blake stepped discreetly away, so that he stood at the edge of the doorway, while Cassie remained in front of her mirror.

"Oh, hi, Mr. Matthews."

"Blake," he corrected.

As he spoke, Katherine Ann glanced across the room. "Mama! You look beautiful!" She all but clapped her hands as she walked toward her mother. "Doesn't she, Mr. Ma—Blake?"

He cleared his throat. "Yes, she does."

Cassie glanced downward. "Thank you. Well, I guess we should be going."

"Katherine Ann..." Blake said, nudging her.

The young girl could hardly contain her excitement as she pulled a package from behind her back. "This is for you, Mama."

Surprised, Cassie stared at the box, which was embossed with the distinctive emblem from an impressive and equally expensive store. "What's this?"

"Mr.—Blake and I went shopping," she announced importantly.

"Katherine Ann was kind enough to be my shopping consultant," he added.

Carefully Cassie peeled away the layers of tissue paper, revealing an exquisite shell-shaped evening bag of navy velvet with a jeweled clasp. "The color's perfect," she exclaimed. "You two are wonderful shoppers."

"There's more," Katherine Ann interjected excitedly. "Keep looking."

Cassie peeled away more tissue paper. Her hands stilled before reaching out to stroke delicate lace crochet. Lifting out the garment, she couldn't prevent a gasp of appreciation as a navy evening shawl shot with silver threads was revealed. She'd never owned anything so frivolous, yet so delightful. "I can't possibly accept this. It must have cost—"

"You needed the right accessories. Since I pressed you into going tonight, it's only fair that I provide them," Blake interrupted.

"Oh, and there's one more," Katherine Ann blurted out, dashing to the hallway and returning just as quickly.

It was easy to recognize the next box. Guessing it contained matching shoes, she wasn't disappointed. Especially when she opened the box and found that they were strappy, sexy slingbacks. Unlike all the practical shoes she owned, these could never double for anything other than evening wear.

Feeling much like a fairy princess, she wondered whether this would all disappear in a puff of smoke. Having spent years hustling simply to make sure the children had school clothes, she hadn't even allowed herself to dream of such luxuries. Ridiculously, she felt a lump in her throat.

Blake gently grasped her elbow. "I think it's time for us to go. We don't want to be late."

Cassie gave him a tremulous smile. "Do I look okay?"

"No, Cassie, you don't." Before clouds could scuttle the happiness in her eyes, he smiled. "You look beautiful."

CASSIE GRASPED HER PURSE with nervous hands, hoping she could pull off the evening and not embarrass Blake. Daphne's earlier words still echoed in her mind, despite Blake's assurances to the contrary. *He has an image to maintain. What will his business associates think if he's seen with his children's nanny?*

Yet he acted as though he was proud to be with her. She'd never seen in his eyes a fraction of the disdain that dominated Daphne's. Who should she believe?

Blake leaned toward her. "McCutchen is already here. Ready to face the firing squad?"

Gulping, she nodded. With his hand on her elbow, she felt more grounded. McCutchen, a stern-looking, hefty man, rose as they approached. On closer examination, Cassie could see that his heft was all muscle. A former football player, she guessed. East Texas was filled with men like him—conservative, ofttimes religious jocks. It was a type she was familiar with. If his first two names were Billy Joe, he could hail from Twin Corners.

She also knew instinctively this was not the time to trot out any of her newly learned sophistication, what little of it there was. Nor would he be a man to appreciate assertiveness. When introduced to him, instead of extending her hand, she smiled instead. "I'm pleased to meet you, Mr. McCutchen." She chose her words with caution, careful not to address him by his first name.

He introduced his wife, and Cassie again did not use a first name, sensing that these were people steeped so deeply in stiff, conservative tradition they were practically in body casts.

And the evening was off to a smashing start. Although the McCutchens hailed from the Midwest, their small hometown might have been a replica of Twin Corners. After talking community, family and high school sports—he'd been the captain of his high school football team—McCutchen had mellowed at least one hundred and eighty degrees. No longer quite so stern, he acted as though he'd finally encountered some of his own type of people.

"I don't know why you were hiding this little lady," McCutchen admonished Blake. "She's a deal *maker*."

Although Cassie smiled demurely, she felt her lips twitch. If only McCutchen knew.

But he was leaning toward her. "You know, Cassie, I was about ready to ditch all these L.A. types. Don't know who to trust in this glitter pit. Nice to meet some real people in old Tinseltown."

Cassie saw that Blake was gritting his teeth. "I don't really think you can judge people by the places they live in," she said tactfully, "While I love my hometown, I can't honestly vouch for every person who lives there."

McCutchen's initial frown eased. "I suppose so, but I'd weigh the population of Springfield against L.A. any day."

Cassie smiled diplomatically. "I don't believe you finished that story about your team taking state in your senior year."

As McCutchen launched into the boring tale, Blake shot her a grateful, if exasperated, glance. And Cassie let out a sigh of relief.

"I CAN'T BELIEVE he actually told that story four times," Blake moaned as they left the dining room and the McCutchens. "I don't know about you, but I could use a sinful shot of something stronger than coffee." He guided them into the nearly empty bar. It was late and only two other people sat in the quiet, semidark room. "You deserve something extra for tonight. You name it—a bonus, an Oscar, diamonds. No matter what you pick, you'll come out shortchanged."

Cassie smiled. "It wasn't that bad."

Blake rolled his eyes. "Deliver me from sanctimonious, pompous..." He stopped himself before completing the description, censoring the remainder. "You amaze me. How did you know just the way to play him? I'm guessing he was ready to pull out and you saved the deal."

She waved aside the compliment. "He's no different than half the men in Twin Corners. True, he lucked on to something that made money." She shrugged. "Other than that, he's stuck in that same small-town mentality, endlessly reliving high school, settling into a safe, self-righteous attitude, shutting himself away from the rest of the world, convinced there's nothing there to explore."

Blake reached out a hand. "Unlike you. There's a whole world waiting for you."

Regretfully she shook her head. "We all make our choices."

"And what were yours, Cassie?" He hesitated, but he had to know. "The ones that still haunt you?"

While a familiar shadow crossed her face, this time she didn't pull away. "The past is just that, Blake. There's no point resurrecting it. And nothing will change by reliving it. I believe wise people just let it die."

"Or let it out, so that it doesn't prey on them."

Cassie smiled—that sad smile that tore at him. Whatever it was that was bothering her, he wanted to fix it, to protect her, to release her from its hold so that she could soar. No matter what secret she was hiding, instinctively Blake knew he wouldn't hold it against her. He'd seen glimpses of her potential, and now he wanted her completely free, unburdened by the past. He wasn't certain when that had become so important to him.

When *she* had become so important, he realized with a start.

He gestured toward the small band playing a soft song at the head of the bar, then held out his hand. "How about a reprieve?"

Nodding, she accepted his hand, easily slipping into his arms as he led them around the dance floor. Protectiveness battled with desire as he circled her body and pulled it close.

He hadn't wanted to rattle her earlier by telling her just how provocative her "simple" dress was. But then, most women couldn't have made it look the way Cassie did.

The music hadn't slowed, yet their movements had. A seductive swaying that had nothing to do with the song that was playing, only with the heat that built between them. Disregarding the other lone couple in the room, Blake cupped her head in his hands, pulled her mouth toward his.

Cassie made a token protest, but the sound turned quickly into a murmur of pleasure.

This time, she was all soft and yielding, encouraging him to deepen the kiss, clutching him with what seemed strangely like desperation. And her need drew him, sending off signals that made him want to protect and cherish her. Even as he acknowledged that she had become far too important to him, he wanted more.

Each taste, each nuance of flavor, intoxicated him. Despite the fire raging between them, he knew this wasn't a hunger that a simple coupling could ease. He sensed that, if anything, their union would forge even stronger bonds between them.

He'd been running from those bonds since he lost Elizabeth, and now he was willingly stepping into their hold. Because Cassie had laid claim to his heart.

Knowing that, he allowed those frozen regions to thaw, accepting the rightness of her claim. Deepening the kiss, he tried to wordlessly convey his feelings to Cassie.

And she translated a portion of his message. She expected the heat, the passion, but she'd never expected the gentleness, the restrained power that did so much more than simply entice. When had her feelings for Blake vaulted into so much more than she'd expected?

As she responded to his kiss, Cassie realized that she loved him. Not in any simple sense, yet in a way that was completely basic, completely right. And knowing it was so, she felt a terrible sadness. Because she couldn't sacrifice her children's future, even if it meant giving up the one thing that could make her happy.

Chapter Fourteen

"Mama!" Katherine Ann hollered as she skidded into the kitchen from a dead run. "Oh, Mama. You'll never guess, not in a million years.... I just can't believe it!"

"Whoa. What can't you believe?"

"Mr. Matthews—"

"Blake," he corrected her, coming into the room at a slower pace.

"Blake," Katherine Ann inserted, without missing a beat. "He said he'd pay for my trip to Russia. Isn't that wonderful? I can hardly believe it."

"Me either," Cassie muttered, turning a questioning gaze on him.

"You forgot to tell your mother that the offer only stands if she approves," Blake reminded Katherine Ann.

"Oh, yeah," she belatedly added. "But you approve, don't you, Mama?" Katherine Ann turned shining, hopeful eyes in her direction.

Cassie took a deep breath, feeling the conflict tear at her. "It's not a matter of approval, Katherine Ann. We can't possibly accept such a generous offer."

Dismay flooded Katherine Ann's young face. She was clearly ready to crumple with unexpected disappointment. "But, Mama—"

Blake cut in. "Katherine Ann didn't ask, I offered. I heard you talking the other night and I ran across the brochure."

In the kitchen drawer, Cassie mused skeptically, *he just happened across the brochure. Right.* She doubted he'd even know there *was* a kitchen if the back door wasn't attached to it. "Still, we can't—"

"Mama, you said yourself it was a wonderful opportunity and that we'd discuss it."

"Taking money from Mr. Matthews isn't a discussion," Cassie reminded her gently, hating to crush her daughter's young dreams.

"Your mother's right," Blake added. "So, let's have a discussion. As far as I can tell, the objection seems to be strictly financial." Blake turned his gaze on Cassie, and she felt herself squirm. "Since I'm willing to advance the funds, what part of that arrangement do you object to?"

Katherine Ann turned her inquisitive gaze on her mother, too.

Cassie swallowed. "We don't take charity."

"I provided a computer for Jim. Why can't you accept this trip for Katherine Ann?"

Cassie had been deeply moved by that very gesture, one that had shown her the depth of his generosity and sensitivity. Blake had known how important the computer was to her son, how much it meant for him to be given such a gift. It was the kind of gesture she would have wanted from the children's father, something they'd never been shown, something she'd been very grateful to Blake for. But the computer had been in place, something she didn't have to approve or disapprove of. The decision had been taken out of her hands. But now, especially since Cassie realized that she loved Blake—how muddled those feelings and their roles had become—it didn't seem right.

"Why not, Mama? What's the difference between the money for my trip and Jim's computer?"

Cassie tried to gather her scattered thoughts. "For one thing, the trip must cost far more than the computer."

Blake discreetly cleared his throat. "Actually, the computer setup was considerably more."

"Wasn't it an extra? One your boys or your business no longer used?" Cassie attempted, knowing she was desperately scrabbling for an excuse, for a reason to not be indebted to him.

"Computers are outdated within six months. It would hardly have been worth it to start Jim on an obsolete system, with an intense interest like his."

So, he'd spent a considerable sum on Jim's computer setup. She hadn't dreamed the equipment was so expensive, but she'd had no experience with computers. "I guess it would be unfair to deny Katherine Ann the same advantages...."

Katherine Ann released an indrawn breath, jumping up and down.

Cassie held up a hand in warning. "Wait just a minute. We'll accept the offer, provided we pay the entire amount back."

"That's okay, Mama. I told you I'd work all the jobs I can, and—"

Blake broke in. "That's not necessary."

"Yes, it is," Cassie replied firmly, shoving back her panic at the thought of more indebtedness. "We appreciate your advancing the money, but we insist on paying it back. We don't want to be in your debt."

Blake shrugged. "Whatever you think is best."

"Oh, Mama, thank you! I can't believe I'm really going!" Then Katherine Ann turned to Blake, her enthusiasm spilling over, brushing away the residue of her shyness as she gave him an equally enthusiastic hug. "Mr. Matthews—Blake—this is the best thing anybody ever did for me! Thanks for being so good to us."

Cassie watched as Blake blinked, obviously surprised and apparently moved by the words. "You're welcome, Katherine Ann. You work hard—at school and here, helping your mother and everybody else in this house. You deserve the trip."

Katherine Ann beamed under the praise, and it struck Cassie that her daughter was as hungry for a father's approval as the boys were. Somehow, her capable, intelligent girl hadn't seemed to be missing that connection, but apparently she had hidden that need deep inside.

Katherine Ann grinned. "I can't wait to tell the guys."

"Don't rub it in," Cassie reminded her gently.

"I won't, Mama. Jim might wish he could go, but he'd much rather have his computer than a trip. Russia! I'm going to Russia!" Between a lilt and a song, Katherine Ann's voice bounced behind her as she sprinted up the stairs.

Left alone with Blake, Cassie rubbed a few aimless circles on the counter with the sponge, even though Maria had already immaculately cleaned the kitchen.

"You did want her to go, didn't you?" he asked, his deep voice rumbling over her, the sound alone evoking too many reactions.

"Actually, I did…if it was possible. But I'm serious. We can't possibly accept such huge gifts. I really didn't have any idea that Jimmy Ray's computer was so expensive." Upset, she forgot to refer to her eldest as Jim.

"I know that." Blake held her eyes. "It's much more gratifying to buy gifts for someone who appreciates the thought far more than the price tag."

"I guess that's something I never thought about. I always wanted to give the kids wonderful gifts, but they were grateful for the little things I could afford. I can't remember them ever thinking about how much they cost. If they had gotten expensive presents, the kids would have thought there'd been a mistake."

"And it felt good just knowing what you'd provided was appreciated?" Blake asked.

"Of course…" She'd stepped right into that one. He'd made his point. But something inside her refused to let her give in that quickly. "I'm glad it makes you feel good, but I meant what I said." Cassie stepped over to the built-in desk in the corner and picked up a notepad and pen, resolutely filling in the lines with quickly dashed writing.

Then she handed him the pad. "It's rough, but it's an agreement that I'll pay you back in full for Katherine Ann's trip."

At first it looked as though he would refuse to accept the paper. His arms tensed as though to push the pad back at her. Then he relaxed suddenly, solemnly accepting the paper. He scanned the few lines, finally meeting her eyes as he reached out with one hand. "Can I use the pen?"

Nodding, she handed him the pen, both curious and inexplicably cautious. Both feelings intensified as she watched him write intently on the paper. When he finally glanced up and held out the paper, she was reluctant to accept it. Deciding that she was being foolish, she grasped the paper and read his additions. With a growing sense of disbelief, her eyes widened as she took in his words.

"Should I explain the additional terms?" Blake asked, a wicked smile curving his lips. Before she could reply, he moved closer to read the paper. Too close. Their bodies were nearly touching. "I'll outline the terms. First…" He pointed to the top sentence. "This is the payoff clause—as you can see, a kiss will pay the debt in full." Cassie's face tightened, but he was just getting warmed up. "And this is the prepayment penalty—it doubles if no kisses are exchanged before it's fully paid."

"So you're making fun of my homemade agreement?" Cassie asked tightly, suddenly feeling very much like a small-town hick.

"No, Cassie." Surprising her, he reached out and tipped up her chin. "I'm dead serious. And since I know what a strict financier you are, I figure I can't lose either way."

Realizing they were no longer speaking about the agreement, Cassie felt suddenly uncertain. "It was just a kiss," she finally whispered, referring to the previous evening.

"Are you sure?" he asked, his mouth dangerously close, the heat from his body reaching out to envelop hers.

She opened her mouth, but no sound emerged. Blake took the opportunity to draw even closer. As he bent his head toward hers, the back door burst open.

Cassie and Blake jumped apart, both trying to look normal—neither sure what that was anymore. They looked away from each other, to the parade of kids bounding inside. D.J. and the twins, returning from Scouts, apparently didn't notice anything amiss. It had been another special evening outing to earn badges.

Cassie hoped her voice didn't shake as she spoke. "I hope you thanked your den mother for taking everyone in the van."

D.J. dug into the cupcakes. "Sure, Mama. She said it was easier to keep track of everyone that way."

Cassie searched for enthusiasm and a smile. "So, does this mean you'll earn another badge?"

Todd pulled his Scout book from his backpack and opened it. "Look, Cassie."

Trying to tame the flush in her cheeks, she read the page he pointed to. "This is great, Todd." The enthusiasm came naturally now, along with a dose of pride. "Hey, you've finished the service badge, and that one takes a lot of work."

Blake watched them, the easy interaction between Cassie and his sons. Somehow the lines between being the nanny and being something more had blurred.

"You'll have a grundle of badges for the awards ceremony," she continued, the smile coming easily now, as well.

"What's a grundle?" Mark asked.

Cassie glanced at them proudly. "Judging by your books, probably more than any of the other boys."

"Nope." D.J. shook his head as the twins chimed in. "We gotta have one more."

"That shouldn't be too hard," Blake commented, taking one of the cupcakes D.J. offered.

"Yeah it is, Dad. It's gotta be a badge in this group." Todd pointed to his still-open book. "And we've done all of them except the overnight camp-out."

"It's been a long time since I've been on an overnight camp-out, but surely they're not that difficult." Blake glanced between his sons, seeing that they didn't look any more cheerful. "Are they?"

"It's not that, Dad. There's not an overnight camp-out scheduled till after the ceremony." Mark bit into a cupcake with a resigned expression.

"Yeah, and we worked our tails off trying to get the most badges," D.J. mumbled around a mouthful of cupcake.

"Are there any rules about where the camp-out has to be?" Cassie asked, a new gleam in her eyes.

"Not that I know about, Mama."

"How come, Cassie?" Todd asked.

"I have an idea. Your den mother may not approve it, but it can't hurt to ask."

"What, Mama?"

"How about a camp-out in the backyard? You could set up camp, pitch your tent, plan your own sup—dinner."

"Can we do it tonight?" Mark asked, abandoning his cupcake in excitement.

"No. First I have to make sure your den mother will sign off on your badges if we do the overnight here, and second, *if* she says yes, it has to be on the weekend."

"Why, Mama? We won't have to drive anywhere."

She smiled. "No, but I don't imagine any of you will get much sleep." Reaching out, she ruffled a trio of heads, each in turn. "Right?"

Grinning, they grabbed cupcakes as they tried to talk her into calling the den mother that very moment. As she laughed and joked with them, Blake watched. And wondered. She had openly given the full measure of her affection to his children. Why was it so difficult for her to share more of that affection with him?

BY THE WEEKEND, D.J. and the twins were nearly rabid with excitement over the impending camp-out. Per regulations, they'd insisted on shopping for all the supplies themselves. They'd made countless trips from the house to the backyard, setting up the tent, then hauling out their food for the cookout, along with the mountain of snacks Cassie had allowed them to buy for this special event.

The kids really wanted this badge, and were working without complaint to make sure they performed each task to specifications. She was proud of all her boys. Shaking her head, Cassie smiled ironically. It was hard to remember that the twins weren't hers, especially when she was filled with pride.

Blake had agreed to be home early enough to spend some of the evening with them, and she knew he would share her pride. At that thought, Cassie paused, no longer seeing the list in her hand. It was important that Blake establish this link with his sons. But even as the thought came, another wove in, insistently demanding to be heard. What about her? What was *her* link to Blake?

No matter how she tried, she couldn't forget their growing closeness. It was as though Blake's challenge had imprinted the sensations permanently in the forefront of her thoughts. She could be swimming, cooking or shopping, and the feelings would suddenly swamp her, returning her to the intimate moments they'd shared, away from children, away from their usual roles.

Deliberately she tried to block those feelings, but then others just as treacherous would intrude—like how touched she was by Blake's unending generosity to her children. Katherine Ann had been in a constant glow since Blake financed her trip. And Jim was fulfilling the promise she'd always known he had, blossoming in his advanced classes, excelling scholastically, and finding his own group of friends. He was a world away from the small town he'd left behind. While part of her was saddened by the ease with which he'd left behind his roots, the other part of her knew Blake had been right. Jim had needed the challenges and opportunities they'd found in L.A. She was torn, having to admit to herself that Blake had seen her children's needs better than she.

"Daydreaming?"

Startled, she twirled around, unable to believe she was actually hearing Blake's voice. "What are you doing here?"

Mild amusement flavored his words. "I live here, remember?"

As though she could forget. "Sure. I meant what are you doing home now?"

He picked up an apple and polished it against his trousers. "Tonight's the big night, right? I figured I'd give the boys a hand."

"They've got everything pretty much under control," Cassie replied, then saw a flash of disappointment cross his face. "But I'm sure they could use your help." Crossing two fingers behind her back to offset the coming fib, she made herself look thoughtful. "In fact, I was wondering how we were going to manage the campfire."

"Something I'm pretty good at," Blake replied, just managing not to brag. "I'll change into some jeans and go help them."

Cassie smiled as he left, whistling. All boys, no matter what their age, wanted to be in the thick of things. As soon as Blake was gone, she raced out the back door. She had about three minutes to tear down the perfectly constructed campfire base. Good thing the boys hadn't planned on lighting it until dark.

BLAKE AND CASSIE both raved over the beanie wienies. The boys swaggered a bit, accepting the compliments as though they'd cooked a full-course French dinner. The first round of s'mores was now melting and congealing in the base of the fire. But D.J. and the twins, undaunted, were putting another batch together. The foil-wrapped vegetables had gone from well-done to charcoal before Todd dug them out.

Todd held out a charred pack of foil-wrapped vegetables. "You want some, Dad? Cassie?"

"If I do, I won't have room for those wonderful-looking s'mores," Cassie explained, putting some regret into her tone. As she watched another s'more bite the dust, she realized the regret might be very real.

"I could eat a potato," Blake offered.

Todd grinned as he passed his father the blackened potato. "You can have more than one, Dad."

Blake patted his stomach. "I'd better not. I ate two big servings of beanie wienies."

Cassie slanted him a sidelong glance as Todd moved away. "Brave soul."

Blake gestured at the new round of melted goo that D.J. was trying to scrape off a charred stick. Most of it landed in the fire. "You'll eat those words…if you can get a s'more down first."

"I'm tough," she replied airily.

"Not so that it shows," he responded.

Seeing the warmth in his glance, Cassie self-consciously straightened her posture.

"Let's tell stories," D.J. suggested, losing the battle with his s'more and reaching for another.

"Yeah! *Scary* ones," Mark agreed.

"*Real* scary ones," Todd added. "None of those baby kind."

Blake quirked his eyebrows, and Cassie groaned inwardly. She hated to think what story he'd dream up to rise to his sons' challenge.

"It's good and dark," D.J. added. "Time for the spooks to come out."

"And there's a full moon...." Mark said, in a deliberately shaky voice.

Unconsciously Cassie drew her jacket a little closer. Something about frightening stories told in the dark still gave her a few shivers. "So, who's got a story to tell?" she asked, forcing enthusiasm into her voice.

"Dad!" The twins said in unison.

"Yeah!" D.J. agreed immediately.

Blake shrugged. "You don't want one of my stale old stories."

"Sure we do," Todd replied tactlessly.

Philosophically, Blake sent Cassie a wry grin. "Okay, boys. Which one will it be? 'The Headless Horseman of Riddle Ridge'?" The eyes surrounding him widened. "Or 'The Blood-Filled Crypt'?" Already widened eyes blinked before widening even further. "Happened in a place a lot like this one." Blake lowered his voice. "It could even be this place...." He continued the story, deliberately adding drama to his inflection. The boys and Cassie drew a shade closer.

"...the lights stopped flickering and it was suddenly pitch-black. As the boy tried to see in the darkness, he heard screams, then he felt the blinding pain in his head and grabbed—"

Pitching forward, Blake grabbed Cassie, who promptly screamed and then launched herself into his arms. Her screams set off a chain reaction, as the boys all echoed her cries.

Taking full advantage of the situation, Blake held Cassie's trembling body close in his arms. Feeling the whisper-silk of her hair feather past his chin, he luxuriated in her feel, her quick vulnerability, her utter femininity. Gently he tucked her hair behind one ear and whispered, "Boo."

She clutched at his arm for a moment. "I'm not scared."

He kept his grin contained. "Of course not." He pointed to the boys, who were hiding in their sleeping bags. "Neither are they."

She released him only long enough to glance at the boys, and then a reluctant smile tugged at her lips. "Bunch of sissies, aren't we?"

He shrugged modestly. "Not everyone can be a big, brave, tough guy like me."

That did it. She swatted him as she eased out of his arms. "You're incorrigible."

"I hope so, ma'am. It's not an easy act to follow, but I work hard on my material."

"I'll just bet you do." Disengaging his arms, she moved forward enough to tug on the sleeping bags. "It's okay, guys. Just a story."

D.J. was the first to emerge. After glancing at the surrounding trees to make sure none of them hid an ax-wielding murderer, he sat up. "Of course it is, Mama. You didn't believe it, did you?"

"Guess I'm just not as perceptive as you are."

Todd and Mark were both peeping out of the cover of their sleeping bags, looking for all the world like a pair of reluctantly emerging groundhogs.

They stared between their dad and Cassie as Todd spoke up. "So who's telling the next one?"

Cassie groaned. "That's all for me, folks. I'm going inside to my nice warm bed."

Squawking protests filled the air. "Stay, Cassie!"

"Yeah, Mom. Stay!"

"Sorry, guys, there's no room at the inn." She pointed to the larger of two small tents. "Your tent only holds three."

"But Dad's tent will hold another sleeping bag," Todd protested.

"You dope," Mark said, addressing his twin.

"She can't sleep in the same tent with your dad," D.J. informed them, rolling his slightly older eyes in disgust.

"Sure she can," Todd insisted.

"They aren't married," Mark informed his brother.

"Yeah, but she's family," Todd retorted.

Blake watched Cassie, saw her expression mist suddenly, and then met her unguarded eyes as they watched the twins. Gratitude, hope and something that looked strangely like love flooded her expression, crowding out any evasiveness. His son was right. Cassie had come to mean more to them than any of them had dreamed possible. She *was* more than just the nanny, and in that moment he decided to find out just how much more. Not with three children a few feet away. But…soon.

Chapter Fifteen

Cassie knew she was crazy. She'd decided the night before, after a long, sleepless night imagining herself in Blake's tent, that it was time to stick to her resolution. She had to refuse any more extracurricular activities with Blake, to ensure that she wasn't endangering her children's future. And here she was at Venice Beach with him.

True, Blake had said he needed her help. And, true, she was in his employ. But how much help could he need scouting a location for one of the restaurants in his new chain? The words *trumped-up excuse* flew into her mind, then nagged at her. If it was just an excuse, why?

Having parked in one of the tightly packed lots at the beachfront, now they walked past stalls of T-shirts, purses, jewelry, electronics and more. Hawkers competed with street musicians, artists, and performers. Performers who ranged from the captivating to the bizarre. One daring man juggled a chain saw while roller-skating, and another limboed beneath a cane pole. Between them all, in-line skaters whooshed along the sidewalks. Shoppers and strollers were torn between all the choices. And Cassie was no exception. Especially when they stopped at Muscle Beach.

"Even though I haven't been many places and I don't have much of a point of reference, I've really never seen anything like this," she said finally, her eyes riveted on the hulking young men performing on Muscle Beach.

"It's an eyeful," he agreed ironically, watching the younger men pumping iron.

Dragging her gaze away from the lineup of blond Mr. Universe candidates, Cassie reached out to teasingly tug at Blake's dark hair. "You're not comparing yourself to them! Although I *did* think *everyone* in California was supposed to be blond."

He waggled his brow at the young men in front of them. "And muscle-bound?"

Cassie felt her throat dry suddenly. Blake was both muscular and far more appealing than the obvious hulks strutting on the beach. But it wouldn't do to let him know just how appealing. She cocked her head instead. "California's just full of surprises."

He laughed then. "You're too smart to get tripped up in semantics, aren't you?"

She pretended to consider his words. "I'll leave the tricky stuff to you."

"Uh-huh."

But Cassie was scarcely listening, her attention caught by the psychic she'd just spotted. That was something that had always fascinated her. Imagine knowing the future…the possibilities…

Blake caught the yearning look on her face and gently touched her shoulder. "Why not have your cards read?"

"It's an expensive bit of foolishness," she replied, not sounding very convincing.

"I guess it's not very practical," Blake agreed.

"No." Still, she didn't move away, watching as the psychic carefully laid out a circle of exotic-looking cards, far more unusual than tarot cards.

"But then, everything doesn't have to be practical. Besides I can write it off as a business expense."

"Oh, in that case…"

Blake hid a smile. Normally, she would have protested, or at least been suspicious of such a feeble excuse. So, he'd found one of practical Cassie's weak spots. He wondered how much luck he'd have discovering others. Although one particularly vulnerable spot on her neck jumped to mind.

After Cassie slid into the folding chair, the psychic picked up her hand. "Hmm."

"Oh, I thought you were going to read my cards," Cassie said, her eyes following the woman's fingers as they traced the lines in her palm.

"I am," the woman answered briefly. "But first I must acquaint myself with you. Hmm…with you I should have a sand tray reading, but the cards will do." Black, inscrutable eyes stared at Cassie for a long moment before the woman dropped her hand and reached for the haphazard stack of cards. With meticulous precision, the psychic dealt the cards, then studied them.

As the woman interpreted the cards, Blake studied Cassie's reactions, seeing that she was almost childlike in her enthusiasm. He couldn't resist being captivated. It was such a far cry from her normal practicality. And today he wanted to move them past the norm, past the barriers she usually kept firmly in place. The psychic zeroed in on Cassie's love of children, although initially guessing that she had more than three children. From that she moved on to Cassie's love of sports, her own special abilities. And through it all, Cassie was spellbound.

"You have many thoughts that are not shared." The woman met Cassie's eyes. "Many things, past and present, are still in the shadows. But that will change. Because the future depends on it."

The psychic's face softened unexpectedly as Cassie began to rise from the chair. "But you are a strong, wise woman. The future will be kind to you."

A sudden smile transformed Cassie's face into a burst of sunshine, and Blake was reminded of the day he'd taken her to Little Tokyo, how she'd embraced all the foreign sights and sounds, enthusiastically tried the sushi and loved each new and different experience. If he could bottle her enthusiasm, he would be the wizard of Wall Street.

Blake picked up Cassie's hand as they walked away from the psychic's table. "I couldn't help noticing your rather unusual shade of nail polish. What do you call that—'fabulous fuchsia'?"

She grinned. "Actually it's called asphyxia—I think fuchsia is a little outdated for this *cool* color." Cassie held her hand up as though examining her polish. "You think *this* is wild?" Her grin grew as she pointed downward and wiggled her toes.

His eyes widened. She wore at least ten outrageous colors, one on each toe, ranging from blue to green to crimson to gold to black.

Her grin grew. "Katherine Ann talked me into it. It's what the kids are all wearing. But I insisted on having just one color on my fingernails. But it's tamer than 'acid rain' or 'oil slick,' which are Katherine Ann's favorites."

Blake shook his head. *Practical Cassie?* "You have anything else on that's wild?"

A slight flush tinged her cheeks as she averted her face, making him wonder, and also making him itch to discover her other wild secret.

"You're going to think this is silly," Cassie began, scrabbling to fill the silence. "But this isn't what I thought Venice Beach would be like at all. I mean, I loved the psychic—that was great—but I always thought that Venice would be like the one in Italy, and it's nothing like the pictures I've seen." She stared pointedly at a street performer who was riding a unicycle while strumming a banjo.

"Ah, but you haven't seen all of Venice Beach." Blake took her arm, feeling a ripple of pleasure in the contact. Then he turned her toward the streets of houses. "I want to show you something."

It didn't take long to reach the charming neighborhood filled with palm trees, oleander and bougainvillea. The streets arched upward, curving in a bridgelike fashion. "See, it's a canal. Venice was originally designed like its namesake city in Italy, with vacation bungalows built along the canals."

Cassie swung her head upward, immediately looking for the bungalows.

"Only nine of the original cottages are still standing," Blake explained.

"You could imagine you were about to take a ride in a gondola," she breathed, obviously caught up in the fantasy.

"You don't have to pretend. There are gondola rides not far from here. Would you like to go on one?"

Temptation tripped across her face, then faded. He wondered what had suddenly bothered her. "I don't think so. We're supposed to be scouting a restaurant location. I don't imagine you're planning to put one in the canal."

"Why the sudden change, Cassie?"

She met his gaze evenly. "I don't think it's wise for us to spend any more time as anything but employer and employee."

Blake purposely stepped closer, eliminating her safe distance. "You don't?"

She nervously waved her hands, tried to back up, and found herself out of road, with Blake blocking her escape. "No, I don't. After all, we live in the same house—"

"And the proximity is driving me crazy."

"I can't help that," she replied, as primly as possible with him breathing literally down her neck.

"What am I supposed to do? *Live* in a cold shower?"

The sound of water rushing beneath the street jolted them both.

"Cassie Hawkins!" A voice rang out behind them.

While Blake turned in surprise, he didn't expect the shock he saw on Cassie's face.

"It *is* you. I told Ray Don it was you, and he didn't believe me," the large, gaudily dressed woman shouted as she held on to her floppy brimmed hat. "We saw you on the beach and I tried to catch up to you, but those dancers got between us. I thought we'd missed you for sure."

"Madeline, Ray Don," Cassie answered weakly. "I didn't expect to run into you here."

"It's a long way from Twin Corners, that's for sure," Ray Don answered, his florid face further reddened by the sun.

"We didn't know where you'd gone to—your mother hasn't said a word." Madeline's gaze took in Blake's good looks and expensive clothing. A more thorough gaze settled on Cassie, noting her upgraded clothing, as well. "Looks like you're doing real good, Cassie." Her gaze flicked over Blake's Rolex. "Real good."

"It's nice seeing you, Madeline, Ray Don. But we were just headed home."

Madeline's eyebrows rose a fraction. "Aren't you going to introduce your *friend,* Cassie?"

Blake held out his hand. "Blake Matthews."

Ray Don accepted the handshake, vigorously pumping his hand. "Ray Don Gardner. Nice to meet you."

"We'd like to see more of you, Cassie," Madeline hinted.

Seeing Cassie's distress, Blake stepped in. "Unfortunately, Cassie's leaving the country tonight."

"She *is!*" Madeline exclaimed.

"Yes, she has a date on a gondola."

"In *Venice?*" Madeline choked out the words.

"That's where they keep the gondolas," Blake replied, taking Cassie's arm and guiding her in the opposite direction. "You'll have to forgive us for rushing away."

"Nice to meet ya," Ray Don hollered after them.

"You too, Ray Don," Blake muttered, resenting that the couple had interrupted what could have finally been a moment of truth. "You too."

CASSIE HEARD the distinct slamming of the phone from Blake's study. Although grateful to him for rescuing her from Madeline and Ray Don, she'd kept her distance, not wanting to continue their own aborted conversation. She was still reeling from his revelation. Cold showers? While she knew she'd been fighting a losing battle with her hormones, she hadn't realized she'd pushed Blake right to the edge. That didn't bode well for an extended contract as his children's nanny.

Hearing his footsteps coming closer, she stiffened. Knowing she could lose everything if they crossed that invisible line, fearing she'd lose even more if they didn't.

Disgruntled, Blake threw a notepad on the kitchen counter as he came in. "That's where you can reach me for the next week."

"Oh?" She hadn't meant to sound so disappointed.

"I have to fly out in the morning."

Cassie knew she should be relieved, but it wasn't relief she felt. "Problem?"

"More than one." He pushed his hands through already disheveled hair, knowing he could discuss his work problems with Cassie. Also knowing that, with her keen intelligence and insight, she'd proved to be a valuable sounding board in the past. But he also knew she was uncomfortable tonight. Still, he couldn't resist pushing one more button. "I'll count on you to keep the home fires burning."

Unable to reply, Cassie met the message in his eyes, along with the burning frustration he didn't bother to hide. When he turned away, she couldn't resist trailing down the hall to the stairway, pausing near the top step. From the direction of Blake's suite, she heard the bathroom door slam and the distinct sound of water running. Cold water?

CASSIE KEPT HERSELF BUSY, certain that the time would pass quickly and that she would barely notice Blake's absence. It amazed her that she could be so wrong. She looked forward to his daily phone calls with little more patience than a kid waiting for school to end and summer to begin. When one week turned into two, she had more time than she needed or wanted to examine her feelings. It had been far too long since a man stirred her so. It was deeper than the passion he'd resurrected, more complex than the gratitude she felt for his generosity to her children. No, it was the man himself, the man she knew she could never have.

Checking her watch for the hundredth time, she realized it was still too early for his call, yet she couldn't concentrate on anything else. When the phone finally shrilled, she leaped toward it, yanking it up before it could ring twice.

"Cassie?"

She tried to still the rapid beating of her heart. "It's me."

"What color are your toenails today?"

Warmed, she laughed, wiggling those same toes in pleasure. "Guess."

"Do they match anything else you're wearing?"

She glanced down at her abbreviated gown, knowing she'd had his call in mind when she chose it. "Not especially."

"Then they're not blue to match your jeans...or maybe you're not wearing jeans."

She sucked in a nervous breath. "No jeans."

"Should I ask what else you're not wearing?"

Nerves jangled loudly in the silence.

"Maybe not," he continued after a moment. "Since we're thousands of miles away."

"At least," she finally managed, as far-too-vivid images danced in her thoughts. "Have you about worked out the problem in your Paris office?"

"Afraid not."

Silent disappointment flared over the transcontinental phone lines.

"Can you see the Eiffel Tower?" Cassie asked, repeating her standard question when he was in Paris, rather than voicing her disappointment.

"No. But I did see the Champs Élysées."

Cassie's eyelids fluttered shut. Missing him desperately, she wished she was there with him. How would it be to walk with him down the Champs Élysées? Hand in hand with the handsome man who was no longer a stranger?

"Cassie? Are you there?"

"Yes...yes. I was just thinking about you...about Paris."

"That sounds like a good combination to me. You, me, Paris."

Cassie tightened her grip on the phone. "Uh, the boys really miss you."

"Just the boys?"

She gulped. "We all do. Katherine Ann asked about you again today."

"She already packing for Russia?"

"Several times so far. Then she decides it's all wrong and starts over again."

"Maybe she needs a new wardrobe for the trip."

"Blake—"

"Put that one on hold. I didn't call to argue."

Cassie clutched the receiver. "You didn't?"

"You know—"

Crackling static drowned out the rest of his words. He repeated her name several times, and then the line went dead. Cassie caressed the receiver, unconsciously trying to reestablish the contact, then reluctantly dropped the phone back in place. He would be home in a few days, and she suspected she would know then what he did intend. And despite the herd of butterflies in her stomach, she wanted to know...needed to know.

BLAKE CURSED LONG AND LOW at the phone, knowing the weather was playing havoc with the phone lines. But a logical explanation didn't relieve his frustration.

Although he hadn't wanted to leave L.A. while he felt so unsettled about Cassie, he'd had no choice. And once in Paris, he'd found himself reaching for the phone as often as his briefcase. It was difficult to devote the single-minded attention to his work that had always been second nature to him. Instead, he found himself thinking of Cassie, wondering at the secrets she still kept hidden...and wondering why she didn't trust him enough to confide those secrets. And whether she felt even a fraction of the unsettling emotions he did.

He'd tried to tell himself that it was nothing more than a physical attraction. But he knew better. He'd also tried to tell himself that with distance he could put things into perspective. But the distance just made him long to see her more.

The only thing he didn't tell himself was that he could shut off the feelings. He didn't even try.

But there *was* an alternative. For the first time since Elizabeth's death, Blake called on an assistant to handle the crisis in the Paris office. For the first time since he'd been single again, he felt there was something...someone...besides his children, more important than his work.

Chapter Sixteen

Disappointment filled her, yet Cassie resolutely flicked off the light switch in the living room. She'd been so sure Blake would make it home that night. It wasn't like him—at least it wasn't anymore—not to show up without a call.

She left the hall light on, knowing the three oldest kids were still out. Katherine Ann and Jim had gone to Kevin's soccer game to support him, since Cassie had taken D.J. and the twins to the Scout spaghetti dinner. She suspected the three older kids had stopped for something to eat afterward. Kevin still acted tough, but she knew he appreciated having someone root for him at the games.

Heading upstairs, she turned on one lamp in her bedroom, dousing the bright overhead light. Trailing into the bathroom, she filled the tub for a warm bath. As she reentered the sitting room that opened into the bedroom, her gaze skipped to the fireplace, and she saw that Pedro had laid fresh kindling.

Turning on the gas jet, she quickly lit the fire, then extinguished the gas. Impulsively she also lit a row of candles, soothed by their gentle glow and the scents of gardenia and magnolia. It was as though she'd opened a window to a night-blooming garden. With that thought, she opened one of the French windows just a bit to let in some breeze.

After soaking for a long time in luxury, Cassie climbed into an oversized robe, still searching for patience, finding only emptiness in its place. It was one thing to tell herself that she must keep a distance…and keep their roles strictly business. It was another to fall asleep each night dreaming about Blake, then wake to find herself missing him desperately. She could no longer deny her feelings.

A quiet knock on the door surprised her. But then, Jim and Katherine Ann often liked to talk to her at the end of the evening. "Come in."

Blake eased inside. "You sure?"

She blinked her eyes, unsure whether she'd conjured him up out of her thoughts. "Is that you?"

"Last time I checked my passport."

Although she wanted to rush across the room, she hesitated. "I thought you weren't coming home tonight."

"I got in earlier, but Kevin had a game."

She blinked again. "You remembered?"

"Don't sound so surprised. It's a bad habit, I know, but you're the one who got me hooked."

Her smile slipped out on its own. "That's great. Did you see Katherine Ann and Jim?"

"Sure, we all had pizza after the game."

Cassie thought of the gourmet dinner she'd prepared, and pushed away the brief regret. It was far more rewarding to think of Blake with his son…and her children. "I bet they loved it."

He patted his stomach ruefully. "Yeah. They weren't on the edge of jet lag."

"Oh, you haven't slept. You must be tired and ready for…" Her words trailed away as she met Blake's gaze.

"The kids went to bed about half an hour ago. I had to make a few calls."

"Oh?" Despite her best efforts, she still sounded weak and breathy.

"It's all quiet on the home front now."

And their suites were in another wing, an entire hallway away from the kids. Private…isolated.

Cassie lifted her hands in a nervous gesture, then lowered them, unable to reply.

Blake shifted in the doorway. "Why don't I just say goodnight?"

Her feet moved awkwardly of their own accord, taking her closer to him. "If that's what you want."

Cassie knew she wasn't imagining his low groan. "You're killing me, you know."

"I am?"

"It's like your fried chicken and buttermilk biscuits. I know the cholesterol will kill me, but I'll die one happy man."

"You think I'm like fried chicken?"

"Well...now that you mention it...all crispy and hard to get through on the outside, tender and juicy inside. I don't think it's an unfair comparison."

"Tender?"

He groaned louder this time. "I'm going to be waterlogged, I know it."

"Maybe you should stay out of those cold showers."

His eyes narrowed. "I should?"

Cassie thought of their tentative future, then the need, the want, the spiraling feelings, the risk she was taking. It was a choice she had to make, not one she could place on Blake. She closed her eyes briefly, then met his. "You should."

Blake's briefcase thudded on the floor, unnoticed, as he kicked the door shut. But he didn't grab her and kiss her sense-less, as she expected. Instead, he grasped her shoulders, giving them a gentle shake. "Maybe you're not thinking straight."

"Yes, I am."

"Maybe I'm misinterpreting what you're saying."

"You're not."

Blake stared at her. "You wanted to forget everything that passed between us."

She reached out a hesitant hand to his chest, fingering the fine merino wool of his European-tailored suit. "Do *you* want to forget?"

He answered her with a kiss, the one she'd expected when he walked into her room. The one she'd dreamed of since he left the country. Then she met his unguarded eyes, seeing the love that neither of them had yet voiced.

Even as she told herself it couldn't happen, Cassie had imag-ined this moment countless times while he was gone, but she'd seen herself gowned in a beautiful peignoir, rather than the shapeless terry robe she now wore. She made an ineffectual gesture toward the worn, oversize robe, but Blake stilled her hands. "Do you know how beautiful you are, Cassie?"

Her heart melted a bit more. "I wanted to look pretty for you. Instead, I'm wearing this…this…"

He sucked in his breath. "Ah, Cassie." One hand slipped beneath the weight of her hair, caressing her neck, then twining through the length of her tresses. Gently he massaged the tense knot between her shoulder blades, knowing he was creating as much tension as he was relieving.

She swayed toward him, and every nuance of her body that he'd imagined now tantalized him. Breathing in her alluring scent, he had to remind himself that this moment was one to savor, since he wanted nothing more than to rip away their clothes, to end the frustration they'd been living with. The want was hot, feverish, barely controlled. And the need equaled the want.

When her hands tugged impatiently at his jacket, both feelings escalated. It took only a moment to snap off the lamp, leaving only candleglow, moonlight and the growing flames from the fire to illuminate the room.

Then Blake's hands joined hers, pulling off his clothing. When only one garment, Cassie's robe, stood between them, he reached for her belt, untying it. But, to his surprise, Cassie grasped the lapels, pushing the robe back to slide down her shoulders, over her back, to land in a pool at her feet.

Blake sucked in his breath. She was magnificent. While he'd expected her to be, the reality outshone his most vivid imaginings. Every trite expression of male approval, from *babe* to *goddess,* tripped through his brain, but they still fell short of expressing the awe he felt.

Emboldened by her move, Cassie reached out to stroke his muscular chest, warm velvet over steel. Not certain where her courage was coming from, she knew only that she wanted it to continue. She'd dreamed of this moment, feared it might happen, despaired that it might not.

And now nothing stood between them. Absolutely nothing.

Savoring the sensation of bare flesh that hungered for his touch, she knew Blake read her mind, as he picked her up and carried her to the bed. Somewhere she registered the press of the mattress against her back, but it was overpowered by the meeting of flesh against flesh. Every fantasy she'd played out about him paled in comparison.

Then his hands began a masterful pursuit, blotting out any rational thought process. Each touch, each stroke, assaulted her overloaded senses. He was taking heat to an edge she hadn't known existed, creating a flame she feared would sear her soul. When his thumbs skimmed over her breasts, traced a line over her rib cage, then danced across her hips, she could only quiver in response, feeling the temperature unbelievably, impossibly, continue to rise.

Then, just as unexpectedly, he turned the heat into tenderness.

Tenderness that was her complete undoing.

Whisper strokes caressed fragile collarbones, teased the valley of her waist, traced a line up her inner thigh until she was pliant as wax. And the tenderness melted her bones to a degree that eclipsed the heat.

Meeting his eyes, she found their dark sapphire depths held the tenderness he was playing out over her body. There was so much emotion there, she wished she could reach out and capture it, freezing the moment to savor always.

Blake marveled at her silky, sun-kissed skin, the sheen of each long limb, already anticipating the feel of her legs wrapped around his back. Each perfect breast filled a hand, and their dusky tips lured him to taste, but first he wanted his fill of looking, touching, absorbing the unbelievable delicacy that defined her lean, limber arms and legs.

In response to his exquisite tenderness, she trailed her lips down his throat, over the curvature of his chest, lingering at his nipples. The taste of him seeped inside her, jolting her, searing itself in her memory.

His hand glided down, cupping her, finding her moist and hot. When she arched against his palm, Blake reached out to taste in return, taking one perfect breast to suckle, rewarded by her sudden bowing, her whimper of pure pleasure. With his lips, he followed the path his fingers had just taken. At each curve, she trembled more. Pausing at the golden juncture of her thighs, he pleasured her until her trembling turned into a helpless quiver.

She could scarcely breathe as his tongue laved over her, eliciting a response from each tender spot. She felt herself drifting, floating, on the waves he created. The sensations were so intense, she wavered between uncertain borders of exquisite pain and pleasure. Then the boundaries were destroyed as Blake took away his mouth, fitting their bodies together, plunging inside with strokes that made her cling to his shoulders, then dig into his back in ferocious response. Embraced by strength, she could only grip him more tautly, reveling in his fullness.

Blake couldn't believe she was so snug and delicious...so responsive. Her hips rose to meet each stroke, pushing them both faster, more furiously, her long legs wrapped tightly around his back as he'd imagined they would. She was a fulfillment of fantasies he had yet to dream. It took all his will to not rush, to hold back until he was certain she'd reached another ultimate peak.

The window, propped slightly ajar, allowed the tang of orange blossoms to spice the air, while woodsmoke drifted from the fire, surrounding and blending with their unique scent of love. Forgotten, the nearly gutted candles flickered, casting minuscule shadows.

Then her orgasm rippled around them both, sharp and ecstatic, fluid and joyous. Caught in the exquisite fist of her pleasure, Blake took them over the edge. And into the star-kissed sky, their hearts caged together for the ride.

Chapter Seventeen

Blake still rested inside her, and Cassie wished she could keep him there forever. Their bond seemed to strengthen in the tender aftermath. A bond she also wanted to keep forever.

Cautiously she kissed the ridge of muscle on his shoulder, rewarded when she elicited yet another shudder. When she moved ever so slightly, tightening her internal grip on him, he groaned.

"You're going to kill me one way or the other, aren't you?" He nuzzled the tender curve of her neck, lingering at the delicate shadows of her collarbones.

He started to ease himself away, but she reached for him in the same moment. "Stay." Her silver eyes gleamed. "Please."

As if he could deny her anything. As if he wanted to.

Staring into her eyes, he found them unguarded, shining with a promise he could only hope was real. When her eyelids fluttered shut in an unexpectedly shy motion, he kissed each one. When they opened again, he traced the contours of her face, his thumb lingering over the imprint of her lips, then reaching up to follow the line of her high cheekbones and the gentle curve of her neck.

Simply looking at her melted any bit of reserve he had left. She had completely and incredibly snared him. Not through design. No, her arsenal was far stronger than that. Far more lethal. Because she'd killed his doubt, freed his soul, letting him glimpse a glorious future. Dusting off his buried emotions, he felt a resurgence of hope.

Her hands were weaving whisper-soft caresses over his body, searching for sensitive spots and, when finding them, lingering, anointing each area. When she began nibbling a similar path, he felt himself harden. And saw the satisfied look of feminine power cross her face.

"I think you're trapped," he warned.

"I hope so," she managed to answer, swamped by his slow, insidious movements.

He'd expected a protest about propriety, a reminder about the children in the other wing, the need to return to their own rooms. "There's no reprieve in sight."

She wound her arms around his neck, pulling his head down so that their lips grazed. "I hope that's a promise."

Unexpectedly, he rolled her over, deftly placing her on top. "I never break my promises."

Throwing her long neck back, she reveled in the newfound sense of control, her face a mask of pure passion.

Moonlight spilled through the parted curtains, bathing her in an otherworldly glow as she sat atop him, her long, glorious hair streaming over her shoulders, tempting him with occasional glimpses of her breasts through the golden tangle. When he thought he couldn't take more of her sweet torture, she threw her head back triumphantly, swinging her hair to glide over her back, allowing him full access.

Greedily he reached for those dusky peaks, then skimmed his hands over her rib cage to her sloping hips, reveling in each purely feminine curve. As his magnificent goddess sprinkled him with moondust, the stars swayed with the impact, seeming to topple in the midnight sky.

CASSIE TESTED her new capacity for hope and trust and found that they both held. It had been a week of new heights, new hope, new belief. It was as though the past that dogged her had finally let go its death grip. Relaxation penetrated a newer, deeper layer, one that had never before completely lost its wariness.

Cassie allowed herself to look at Kevin and the twins as more than just her charges, allowing them an even larger place in her heart. Although she'd secretly thought of them as her own for some time, now it was as though she'd been given permission to let that attachment show. She was tempted to pinch herself black and blue, yet it was still real, better than any dream.

The phone rang, interrupting her reverie. When she heard Blake's voice, warmth infused her voice. "It's the middle of the day. I'm surprised you found time to call."

"I have to catch a plane tonight—to Paris."

She fought the disappointment, trying to sound supportive. "Business beckons."

"Come with me, Cassie."

Excitement leaped for a brief moment, then faded. "D.J. and the twins have their play—the one they've been rehearsing for weeks. And Kevin's big game is this Thursday."

A muffled curse crackled through the lines. "Those *would* be this week. I had it all planned out—the Eiffel Tower, of course. The Left Bank, and the…"

"Champs Élysées,". she chimed in with him, wishing the timing wasn't so bad. "I guess there'll be other trips."

"Since I have an office in Paris, you can guarantee it, but I wanted us to get away, just the two of us. You realize that between us we have six full-time interruptions? One of them's always going to have something going on."

"We could plan ahead, plan to go when nothing major is scheduled."

He sighed, and she immediately caught the translation. *And when would that be?*

She longed to shed her responsibilities, pack a bag and jump on the plane with him. But she'd been a mother too long for that to happen. "Oh, Blake, I *want* to go."

"At least I can be sure you'll keep those home fires burning. You've got quite a way with welcome-home greetings."

She blushed, remembering her abandon, grateful she'd found the courage to shed her reserve.

Blake swiveled around in his desk chair, ignoring the crackle of aged leather as he stared at the open jewelry box in his hand. A round diamond solitaire winked back at him. It was a traditional engagement ring—one he thought suited Cassie, especially since he'd chosen to custom-design her wedding band with six matching stones, one for each child. Blake listened to Cassie as he eyed the ring ruefully. Paris *was* going to be the ideal place to propose. "Can't talk you into the Champs Élysées?"

"Oh, Blake…"

Hearing the longing in her voice, Blake decided to let up on the pressure. She couldn't prevent the bad timing. When he returned, he'd bring some frivolous bit of Paris back with him—along with the ring, of course. "I'll make the trip as short as possible. You won't even know I'm gone."

He heard a quick, breathy sigh. "Don't count on it."

"And those home fires?"

She laughed—a deep throaty, sexy chuckle that had him rethinking the trip. "Might burn down the whole city."

"I could cancel the trip.…"

She laughed again. "And jeopardize a deal you've been working on for months? No. Besides, by the time you get back, those fires will have time to really heat up."

Blake withheld a groan. He'd never dreamed how much Cassie would come to mean to him in such a short time. If they'd both been single, without entanglements, he'd have considered taking a longer time before making such a big step. But with their six dependents, all of whom needed a stable family situation, they needed to affirm their commitment.

"Cassie?"

"Yes?"

"If I talk to you any longer, I'll combust before I board the plane."

"Have a safe trip," she replied and he could envision her tongue-in-cheek expression.

"Don't scorch yourself," he shot back, chuckling as he replaced the receiver. Thank God he could count on Cassie. She was steady as a rock.

CASSIE STRETCHED OUT on the chaise longue beside the pool, relaxing in the growing twilight. Blake had been gone less than twenty-four hours, and already she missed him desperately. She'd just finished twice the distance she usually swam, hoping to tire herself into oblivion, but it wasn't working. Instead, she was remembering the night before he left, the time they'd spent together in the pool, hours after everyone else was asleep. Hours that defied any other time she'd spent in a pool. And she'd thought diving competition was exciting. How little she'd known.

Hearing footsteps approaching, she turned with a smile, wondering which of the kids was seeking her out. But her smile faded. It couldn't be…it simply couldn't…

"Cassie, my girl, in the lap of luxury." The man whistled, low and long. "And it suits you, but then, I always thought it would."

Cassie snatched a towel from the nearby table and started to rise.

"No, no. Don't get up. I didn't mean to disturb you."

Anything Tommy Brewster did was meant to disturb. "What are you doing here?"

He placed one hand dramatically over his heart. "You wound me. Is that any way to greet an old friend?" He reached forward to touch her cheek, but she shifted away before he could. Shrugging philosophically, he took some grapes from the bowl at the table. "Nice digs, Cassie."

"How did you know where to find me?"

Tommy laughed. "That's a puzzler, isn't it? You know your mother wouldn't tell me, and you managed to escape Dullsville without even a hint of where you were going. No one had any idea where you moved. If Madeline and Ray Don hadn't run into you, you might have stayed a mystery forever."

The Gardners. Of course.

Tommy smiled again. "And Madeline couldn't say enough about your new lifestyle." His eyes lifted to take in the rich surroundings. "Can't say she exaggerated, either. Looks like your time with me was just training for the big-time." His gaze settled back on her. "She had a lot to say about your new boyfriend, too."

Panic clutched at her, and every shred of faith that things would be all right dissolved. "Madeline didn't know what she was talking about. Bla—Mr. Matthews is my employer. I'm the nanny."

"Yeah."

"No, really." She spoke frantically, hoping to convince him. "He was one of my boarders in Twin Corners."

"Then he knew all about your *hospitality?*"

Cassie recognized the anger as it fought with the panic she was feeling. "You've got it all wrong, but then, you always did."

"When you were sixteen, you didn't think so."

"I was an idiot," she replied flatly.

He glanced around again. "You've definitely moved up in the world, sweetheart."

Cassie felt a slow burn at his casual assessment. "What do you want, Tommy?"

"You could work on that hospitality. Makes a guy think you're not glad to see him."

"Then a *guy* would be right," she retorted.

"Maybe your new boyfriend will be more friendly."

"He's not here," she blurted out. "And he'll be out of the country at least another week."

"Is that so?" His eyes roved over her bare legs, and she jumped up from the chaise, dropping the towel to grab a modest cover-up. "Don't get all bent out of shape, sweetheart. Maybe we could renew our...friendship."

"Why don't you crawl back into the hole you escaped from? Our *friendship* then didn't extend to what you have in mind, and it certainly won't now!"

His easy grin dimmed. "And I thought we could handle this business real friendly."

Long-nailed fingers of panic clawed her again. "What business?"

"The way I see it, you've set yourself up real pretty. And it looks like there's plenty to share with your old partner."

"I told you, I don't have any money," Cassie protested.

"Oh, sweetheart, the way I see it, you've got more than enough."

Cassie fought the desperation bubbling inside her. "I told you. I'm the nanny here. I get a monthly salary, that's all."

"And there's nothing between you and your rich boss?"

Although she tried to hide the truth, some of it must have flashed across her face.

"You never could play poker, Cassie. Just tell the boyfriend you need a...bonus."

"I can't."

"I'm afraid you'll have to, Cassie. With your past, it'd be easy enough for him to believe you've just latched on to him for the money."

"No, Tommy! Please!"

He studied her face. "Then get the money. I'll call you tomorrow and tell you how much."

New belief turned into hopelessness. Even without hearing the figure, she knew she didn't have enough money to satisfy Tommy.

Casually he reached into the bowl of fruit, pulling out an exotic ruby creme banana, careless of its value. "Don't they have apples in California?" Not waiting for a reply, he peeled the banana and took a bite of the rare, exquisite fruit, as though it were a common orange plucked from a nearby tree. "I'll be in touch, sweetheart."

With a sickening lurch of her stomach, Cassie knew it was a certainty.

AFTER A SLEEPLESS NIGHT and a morning that had had her practically snapping the children's heads off, Cassie watched and waited beside a silent telephone.

When it finally rang, she yanked it up. "Yes?"

The line crackled—a bad connection. "That didn't sound good," Blake said.

Cassie squeezed her eyes shut, willing the tears not to fall. "I wasn't expecting you."

"Glad to hear it. I'd hate to think that greeting was for

me..." The phone crackled again, drowning out the rest of his words.

"There's something I need to talk to you about," she began, hating to, but knowing she couldn't hide the truth from him.

The phone crackled again, blurring both sides of the conversation. "This is a terrible connection—but I'm on a mobile. I'll call you later, but whatever it is, it is you decide. I trust you, Cassie." The crackling intensified, and reluctantly she replaced the receiver, knowing the conversation had ended, knowing she couldn't hold on to him through only a phone connection.

I trust you. The words echoed and repeated, assaulting her.

Dropping her face into her hands, she allowed herself to remember a time that had brought only pain.

She'd been in high school when she met Tommy Brewster, a slick twenty-year-old who swept her away, and also swept the truth under the rug.

At that time, because she and her mother needed the money, Cassie had been employed cleaning the houses of the many rich people in Twin Corners who were enjoying the profits of the oil business before boom turned to bust. She'd confided impressive details of the magnificent homes and their contents to Tommy, never dreaming that he would make copies of her keys, so that he could burglarize those same homes.

When Tommy was suspected of the robberies, he'd sworn he was innocent and convinced her to run away with him. After they were on the run, and by then both labeled suspects, she'd discovered the truth. Embarrassed by her naiveté, the fact that she was clueless about Tommy's actions, she couldn't bear to return and face her mother's disappointment.

When the police caught up with them, Tommy had told the officers that Cassie was the mastermind, the one who had purposely obtained work from the rich so that she could set them up for the robberies. She'd protested, telling the police she knew nothing about the robberies until after she ran away with Tommy. However, she'd admitted to staying with him after she discovered the truth.

With a previous record, Tommy had been sent up for hard time. Because of her age, her spotless record and a somewhat understanding judge, Cassie had been given a lesser sentence to be served in a correctional institute. Still, she'd served eighteen months—time that she could never erase.

While other kids were enjoying their senior proms, she'd been mopping gray tile floors. Her beloved dream of swimming and diving had died, as well. The closest thing to sports at the correctional facility had been hoeing beets and digging for potatoes. The band trip she'd worked so hard for had been forfeited, along with her graduation, and what was left of her innocence.

Lifting her face from her hands, Cassie imagined Blake's expression, should he ever discover the truth. *I trust you, Cassie.* Her eyes squeezed shut. The truth would kill every shred of that trust.

The phone rang, startling her, even though she'd expected the call. Forcing her voice to be steady, she answered and then listened to Tommy's exorbitant demands, her own voice turning dull.

"I told you, Tommy, I don't have the money."

"I wonder how you'll feel after I have a chat with your boyfriend."

Cassie clutched the phone, willing herself to sound convincing. "There's no need to speak to him—he already knows all about my past."

"Then you won't mind if I drop in and pay him a visit."

"No—"

"You wouldn't want him to think you're a money-grubber, would you, sweetheart?" The vision ran through her, chilling every cell of her body. But Tommy was still speaking. "That when times got tough, you turned to what you knew best? A man who could provide the money, no matter what you had to do to get it."

Could Blake believe that their sweet love had been engineered on her part?

"Forget it, Tommy." She tried to bluff once more, knowing her heart wasn't in it, now that hope had been snatched away. "I'm not interested in your threats, and Blake won't be, either."

"Don't count on it, sweetheart. And as long as I'm breathing, I'll be in your face. Starting with your boyfriend."

She heard a click in her ear, but she still held the phone, frozen in place. The horror of everything she'd kept hidden for years was now a nightmare from which she couldn't awaken. She could never expose Blake to this pain...to the truth about her. Before he returned, she had to be gone, taking her love and the power to hurt him with her.

CASSIE STARED at the three shocked faces of Blake's children and felt her own heart splinter. "I know this is unexpected," she said, trying again. "It has nothing to do with you, but I have to leave."

"You can't go!" Mark wailed, forgetting to be cool.

"It's not what I want—"

"Grown-ups always say that," Todd protested. "Then they do things that hurt."

"Like going away," Mark added.

Kevin was quiet, but his facade had disappeared, too. In its place was a confused, betrayed boy. "I thought you cared about us. *Really* cared."

"I do, Kevin. I..." She stopped short of telling them how much she loved them, how each of them had seized portions of her heart, pieces that no one else could replace. She feared knowing that would make the fact that she was leaving forever even worse.

"If you cared, you wouldn't leave us," Mark protested.

"Please don't go," Todd pleaded.

Hopelessly she stared between them. "I can't explain...but always know how very much I care for you." Her throat worked and she could barely speak. "I will *never* forget you. Ever."

"Then don't leave," Kevin replied.

Closing her eyes against the betrayal on their faces, Cassie knew she had no other choice.

JIM AND KATHERINE ANN pushed their suitcases into the darkened front hall, fruitlessly flicking the light switch.

"I don't think the electricity's on," Cassie told them wearily. Anticipating complaints, she sagged for a moment against the column on the porch, wilting in the warm, humid night.

"I know where some candles are," Jim offered, to her surprise. He had been the quietest since she hustled them into packing, the one most outwardly affected by their departure.

But he'd been his stalwart self, except during their goodbyes to the Matthews boys. All three of her children had been shaken by having to leave behind the boys, who had become like family.

Cassie could still see the Matthews sons, the betrayal painted on their faces. Although Maria had agreed to watch over them until Blake's return, Cassie still felt as though she'd abandoned them. Now there was another rip in her heart, to accompany the one she'd made by tearing herself from Blake's life.

"Thank you, Jim. I'll have the lights turned on tomorrow."

"The house looks sad," D.J. added in a small voice.

And lonely and neglected, Cassie added to herself. Instead of being a welcoming safe haven, the house seemed to commiserate with them in their sorrow.

Katherine Ann slipped her hand into Cassie's. "It'll be okay, Mama. Things will look better tomorrow with the electricity on."

Cassie swallowed a lump in her throat. Despite the confusion she knew they must be feeling, her children were being troupers. Of course, they were no doubt still in a state of shock. It all still seemed unreal to her. If it could only have been a dream, instead of her old nightmare.

DAPHNE IGNORED Maria's not-too-subtle suggestions that it would be best to visit when the *señor* was home. Unable to believe her good fortune, Daphne strolled through the halls of her late sister's home, pleased by the renewed feeling of control. She didn't know what had sent Cassie packing, but she was celebrating. It had looked as though the little hick were making irreversible inroads, but now....

Daphne hummed as she ascended the stairs, determined to see that Cassie's room was indeed empty. One glance told her that, despite her hasty departure, Cassie had left the room neat, tidy and most definitely empty.

Daphne's smile grew. Feeling delightfully possessive, she pushed open the door of Blake's suite. She swept the room with a proprietary gaze, then started to withdraw when a bit of paper on his dresser drew her eye. Insatiably curious, she moved closer. Seeing Blake's name written in a clearly feminine scrawl across an envelope, Daphne picked it up. Feeling no guilt, she slipped the letter from the envelope. She read for a few lines, her giddy happiness disappearing. Daphne knew that Cassie's explanation and avowal of love would send Blake scurrying to Backwater, Texas, without hesitation.

Needing no further convincing, Daphne crumpled the letter. Careful not to leave it in the trash can, she stuffed it in her purse as soon as she was downstairs again. Leaving an upset Maria and her sad-looking nephews without a further word, Daphne departed, new plans already brewing.

Chapter Eighteen

Baffled, Blake stared at Maria, watching her wring her hands in an agitated fashion. When her words still didn't sink in, he turned to his boys, seeing matching expressions in their eyes. From sadness and disappointment to hurt and betrayal, their gazes echoed what Maria had just told him.

Cassie was gone.

Maria seemed equally upset as she answered his most obvious question. "I don't know where, Señor Matthews, only that it must be something very serious to take the *señora* away so suddenly, not even waiting until the morning light to leave."

"She left in the middle of the night?"

Maria shook her head. "In the evening. Still…"

Still, it was bizarre, and totally out of character for Cassie. "Did she leave a note?"

Maria shrugged. "I did not look, *señor*. The boys—"

"Took your time," he interjected, still entrenched in disbelief. "It's all right, Maria. I'll look." He started to turn away, then brought himself back to face his faithful housekeeper. "And thank you for taking care of the boys."

"*De nada, señor.*" She hesitated. "This is not like Cassie."

"No." He sighed heavily. "It's not." Turning to his sons, he draped one arm around Kevin, and with the other pulled first Todd, then Mark, toward him. "I don't know what's going on, guys, but I'll find out."

Mark shuffled his Reebok-clad feet. "Dad, make her come home, okay?"

"Yeah," Todd echoed his twin. "We need her."

Kevin dipped his head. "They're right. Can you fix things?"

Blake fought the knot in his throat and the pain in his heart. "I'll do my best." Gravelly emotion resonated in his voice. "We all need her."

CASSIE OPENED THE DOOR for the dozenth time, plastering a smile on her face, accepting the tuna noodle casserole from another neighbor who'd heard they were home. It hadn't taken the Twin Corners grapevine long to get the word out. The doorbell hadn't stopped ringing. It had been a blessing to learn that the phone couldn't be connected for a while. That, too, would no doubt have been ringing, as well. It seemed her neighbors' curiosity couldn't be satisfied without their seeing or hearing for themselves that the Hawkinses were back.

And there wasn't anyone Cassie wanted to call...at least not in Twin Corners. Her mother spent every spare moment with them, but that wasn't exactly a comfort, since she thought Cassie had been crazy to leave without talking to Blake. But Cassie knew she'd done the right thing, that she couldn't drag him down because of her past. He was too decent. He deserved someone who could soar with him, instead.

But that didn't stop her heart from breaking.

Leaning against the door, Cassie heard another update on what had gone on in Twin Corners during their absence, forcing herself to smile and pretend interest. She finally escaped more questions, closing the door and turning to her children with the casserole in hand. "Tuna noodle—I guess this is lunch."

The irony struck them all simultaneously. How Cassie had cooked the disastrous tuna noodle casserole the first night they were in L.A., and all the changes they'd been through since then. She glanced around at the dusty furniture. The air of neglect was so much stronger in the daylight. What should have seemed familiar no longer did.

"I wish we had some fruit." D.J. spoke up as he accepted one of the plates she handed him.

"Or grilled chicken," Katherine Ann added.

"We'll have to get used to fewer choices," Cassie answered, trying to keep her voice even, refusing to let her despair leak through.

"It's okay, Mama," Jim told her, not mentioning the more important things they'd left behind, the opportunities that had been snatched away. "It's just lunch."

As Cassie stared between her children, she knew it was far more than lunch. She'd assumed they could come back here and resume their former lives. But none of them were the same. The children were tiptoeing around that truth, one they'd already recognized. Despite her blindness, the kids all knew what she should have. They'd all changed, grown, and none of them fit back in the neat little molds they'd left behind. Those shells had been outgrown, discarded. Their hearts and lives were in Los Angeles. And because of her past, she had to leave them there.

BLAKE STOPPED SHORT of pitching the phone across the room. Cassie's phone in Twin Corners had not been reconnected, and the phone company refused to tell him whether there was a reconnection order in the works. All attempts to reach her mother had been fruitless. The phone rang endlessly, but no one answered. Was it possible Cassie had gone somewhere other than Twin Corners? What could have happened to make her take such drastic action?

"Hey there, handsome!" Daphne's voice washed over him like glass shards as she entered the room without knocking. "What are you doing hiding out in here?" She waved toward his nearly darkened study. "It looks positively bleak."

"Matches my mood," he responded shortly, out of the patience needed to deal with his sister-in-law.

"What you need is some cheering up," she responded with a seductive smile. "And I'm just the one to do it."

"Forget it."

"But—"

He passed a weary hand over his forehead. "I'm sorry, Daphne. But the truth is, I really want to be alone."

"If this has something to do with that Cassie creature—"

"Daphne!" His voice was as stern and effective as a whiplash. "I won't have her spoken of like that."

"I haven't heard you so defensive of anyone since my sister...." Daphne's voice trailed off as she stared at him. "You're in *love* with her...with that little country girl."

"Ten points for you."

"But she left," Daphne protested.

"Without a word," Blake agreed, unable to disguise his pain.

"You're going after her, aren't you?"

He nodded. "As soon as I find out where. I've booked a morning flight to Texas. I haven't left yet, because I'm not sure she's there and I didn't want to charge headlong in the wrong direction. But I've got to start somewhere."

Sighing, Daphne opened her purse, pulling out the crumpled letter and shoving it across the desk. "This should give you a clue."

He read a few lines, then jerked his eyes back toward Daphne. "I don't know whether to thank or strangle you."

Daphne's smile was sad but wise. "You two deserve each other."

"I think Elizabeth would approve," Blake said finally, in a gentle voice.

"Yeah, I know. But you don't have to rub it in."

A hesitant knock on the door interrupted them. Maria's face wore its now perpetually anxious expression. "I'm sorry to bother you, *señor,* but you have another visitor."

"It's okay, Maria. I have one minute." He glanced at Daphne. "Then I've got a flight to pack for."

Chapter Nineteen

Late-afternoon sun was pushing past the drapes when the doorbell rang. Cassie could have groaned in annoyance.

"Do you want me to get it, Mama?" D.J. called out.

It would be another neighbor, requiring another explanation. Much as she wanted to run and hide, it wasn't a job to foist on her children. "No, I'll get it."

Pulling open the door, she prepared herself by breathing deeply. But then she forgot to exhale.

Blake and his sons were lined up solemnly across the width of her porch. Unable to do anything other than stare, she felt her heart shattering into a thousand bits at the longing in Blake's eyes. His voice was like music in a deep silence, and it took her a moment to understand the words.

"We've come calling, ma'am." Blake pointed to his boys. "To ask your hand in marriage. We're a package deal, you see. If you take one, you take all of us."

"But..." she stumbled over her words—along with her heart, which had become irretrievably lodged in her throat. "I don't..."

"You can't say no," Mark announced.

"*Please* don't say no," Todd amended.

"Say yes," Kevin said encouragingly, for once looking like the young teenager he was. "We...we need you."

"Please come home," the twins begged.

Turning uncertain eyes on Blake, she fought for courage and

the truth. "You don't understand. I have something to tell your dad…that…"

"If it's about the good old days, I've already heard enough. Spent some time discussing it with one of your friends from high school days. He didn't have anything to say worth listening to. Nothing that makes any difference to me." There was a fierce light in his eyes, and she was suddenly reminded of a warrior protecting his lady. "By the way, Tommy Brewster won't *ever* be bothering you again."

Cassie's lips trembled, and she knew that tears sparked her lashes.

"I love you, Cassie Hawkins, and I won't take no for an answer."

Somewhere Cassie registered that her children had crowded behind her to hear Blake's proposal. As he pulled her into his arms, whoops and hoots of glee filled the quiet Texas sky. Cassie glanced down once more at Blake's boys, sons of her heart, and knew her life wouldn't have been complete without them, either.

While their children celebrated, Cassie felt the noise recede as Blake slid an engagement ring over her finger. "I'd planned to do this on the Champs Élysées, but somehow it's even more fitting here, where I met you." His grip on her hand increased. "I love you, Cassie. I didn't know it then. But I know it now, and I'm never letting you go."

"I'll hold you to that." Tears of joy escaped, to slide down her cheeks. "I don't deserve you, Blake."

"You deserve the world, Cassie and I'm going to give it to you, one city at a time."

"What about all our little dependents?" she managed, past the knot of emotion choking her.

"They'll be the best-traveled kids in the world—starting with London."

"Not Paris?"

He smiled then, tucking her against his side, now and forever. "Afraid not. Paris is reserved for honeymoons. And I love 'em all, but they're not going on our honeymoon."

"Our honeymoon?" she echoed.

"Where else but Paris? The Eiffel Tower, the Left Bank..."

"And the Champs Élysées," she filled in softly.

"After Paris, we can meet the kids in London for more traveling." He gestured at the tree-shaded porch around them. "And we'll want to keep this house to escape to in the summers when we don't feel like trotting around the world. Especially if your mother won't move out to L.A." His voice gentled, thickened. "You need to hang on to this part of your roots. It's where we started our memories, too."

"It sounds like a dream," she breathed, unable to believe it was real, unable to believe he'd dispelled her nightmare forever.

"But I need you to make it come true. I want us to soar together." He spread his arms out to include the children. "All of us. Don't ever run away again, Cassie. Together, we have the world."

"Having you is all I need," she confessed. "And all I want. Are you sure this isn't a dream?"

He laughed then, holding her at arm's length as he pulled them into a spin. "We have plenty of volunteers to pinch you and see if it's a dream."

She fell into his impromptu dance, knowing he would always carry her to unknown heights. "I love you, Blake Matthews."

He answered with a grin, whirling her in the circle of their happy children. Leaning forward, he sealed the words with a kiss, their embrace as enduring as the love they shared, their future as bright as the sun-drenched skies above.

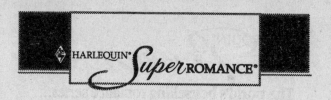

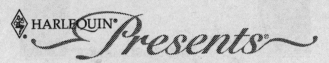

HARLEQUIN Presents

The world's bestselling romance series...
The series that brings you your favorite authors,
month after month:

Helen Bianchin...Emma Darcy
Lynne Graham...Penny Jordan
Miranda Lee...Sandra Marton
Anne Mather...Carole Mortimer
Susan Napier...Michelle Reid

and many more uniquely talented authors!

Wealthy, powerful, gorgeous men...
Women who have feelings just like your own...
The stories you love, set in exotic, glamorous locations...

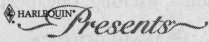

Seduction and passion guaranteed!

HARLEQUIN®
INTRIGUE

WE'LL LEAVE YOU BREATHLESS!

If you've been looking for thrilling tales of
contemporary passion and sensuous love stories
with taut, edge-of-the-seat suspense—then
you'll love Harlequin Intrigue!

Every month, you'll meet four new heroes
who are guaranteed to make your spine tingle
and your pulse pound. With them you'll enter
into the exciting world of Harlequin Intrigue—
where your life is on the line
and so is your heart!

THAT'S INTRIGUE—
ROMANTIC SUSPENSE
AT ITS BEST!

HARLEQUIN®
Makes any time special ®

INTDIR1

Harlequin® Historical

From rugged lawmen and valiant knights to defiant heiresses and spirited frontierswomen, Harlequin Historicals will capture your imagination with their dramatic scope, passion and adventure.

Harlequin Historicals . . . they're too good to miss!

Visit us at www.eHarlequin.com   HHDIR1

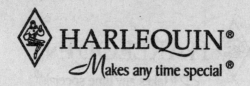

HARLEQUIN®
Makes any time special ®

AMERICAN *Romance*

Upbeat, All-American Romances

HARLEQUIN®
Duets™

Romantic Comedy

Harlequin®
Historical

Historical, Romantic Adventure

HARLEQUIN®
INTRIGUE

Romantic Suspense

Harlequin Romance®

Capturing the World You Dream Of

HARLEQUIN® *Presents*

Seduction and passion guaranteed

HARLEQUIN® *Super*ROMANCE®

Emotional, Exciting, Unexpected

HARLEQUIN®
Temptation.

Sassy, Sexy, Seductive!

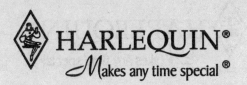